The Other Dress

Also by Emmy Engberts

Her Elysium
The Other Dress

As E. Engberts
BASE Status: Online

As Skylar Heart
Shattered
Unraveled

As Rosa Swann
Mated to the Alpha Serial
The Baby Pact Trilogy
Second Chance Mates Serial
Making a Family Serial
Omegas' Destined Alpha Serial
The Vampire's Past Trilogy

The Other Dress

Flowers and Keyboards 2

Emmy Engberts

© 5 Times Chaos / Easily Distracted Media
ISBN 978-90-825832-9-8
NUR 285

20190221

This lovely story takes place in the Netherlands. Groningen and Utrecht are real cities. Groningen is the city I was born in and have returned to after my studies. The things that happen within this story are fictional, though.

I have chosen to write this story in British English, although there are some elements of American in it as Dutch people grow up with a lot of American TV and we do use some American loan words. Some of these have been kept in place.

Before *Izzy*

These days, I live my life according to the motto 'What if I didn't…'

- *What if I didn't wear that beautiful dress?*
- *What if I didn't go to that party?*
- *What if I didn't study for that test?*

Some of the answers are quite simple.

If I didn't go to the party, I'd probably miss out on having a great time with my friends, but maybe whatever else I was doing would make up for it.

If I didn't study for the test, I'd probably fail it. This can mean that I'll have to retake it, or I'd have to make up for it with my other grades on that subject.

I tend to ask the 'what if I didn't…' question a lot when it comes to the books I have to read for my literature class. I love books, but I never seem to be able to focus on what I need to read for class, I much prefer reading fanfic. So, I'd put off reading the book, or writing the essay, until it was far too late. Which is why even though everyone knows me as a bookworm,

I only barely have a passing grade on the subject. Oops.

'What if I didn't…' usually doesn't have very fun answers, which means that I will be doing the thing, just because I want to.

But my life never used to be like that. I'd never ask myself "What if I didn't…"

Instead, I worried about what other people would think of me if I *did* do things.

> - *What would they think of me if I did wear that beautiful dress?*
> - *What would people think about me if I did go to that party?*
> - *What would they think of me if I did study for that test?*

The answers to these questions never really satisfied me, they scared me. They never made me feel good, they made me feel like I should just stay in line, not move too much and definitely not stand out from others.

The answers made me scared that people would think badly of me. That if I wore a beautiful dress, that people would think I was showing off or trying too hard to be girly. That if I showed up to a party, that people would think I was trying to get all the attention and that people wouldn't even want me there. That if my grades were too high, that they'd think I was a study and only doing it to show off to the teachers.

So, I never wore the dresses, I didn't go to the parties and I only had grades high enough to pass a class, never more than that. Staying as invisible as possible, because my life was complicated enough without being scrutinised by my classmates or other people.

My life existed in greys and muted colours. My grades never surpassed those of my most average classmates and I never ever stood out, it was what I thought was best for me.

I believed that I wasn't someone who stood out. I believed

that I was average, plain, boring. I tried to blend into the background, I tried for people not to notice me, because if they did, I'd have to face their judgement, their mocking. Because I shouldn't be standing out, I was strange enough without bringing attention to myself in other ways.

And if it wasn't for one person, one person I didn't even know, one person who had no idea how much she would influence me. If it wasn't for her, I would have never been here now. I would never have stood here, I would have never stepped forward and I would never have demanded my place in the spotlights. I would have never demanded to be accepted for myself.

It's sad that she'll never know. Because she's no longer here. She'll never know how her final words have inspired me to not let anyone take my light away from me.

Her final words, because her tragic death is the only reason why I know about her.

The beautiful girl, she was my age, still in secondary school, and she killed herself. I don't know what her motto, or her question in life was, but her life ended with the words 'I can no longer do this'.

That's what her final letter said, 'I can no longer do this, I can't keep hiding myself from the world just because they won't accept me.'

I learned about her when my own life had lost all of its colour, I learned about her when my life was a dark charcoal colour with a few spots of black. I had little to lose at that point and couldn't see anything that would keep me going anymore.

I remember it so clearly, that final moment of the old me. That final moment of the old and innocent me. When my mum looked at me, sitting next to my dad, holding hands, holding each other so tightly that their knuckles were white, that I could see the white outline of their tendons against the red on the sides.

I don't know why I remember it so well, maybe because this was the first time that they told me that I had to *do* something. The first time that, instead of letting me take the lead, they sat down and *told* me that I needed help, that I needed to live my life being me, not hiding in the shadows.

Or maybe it was because I was immediately aware that this was the final moment of what my life used to be like, that everything would be different from there on out.

I didn't know who she was before that fateful day, but I know her name now, Vicky. I know that she was in many ways like me, and that what happened to her, what she ended up doing, could have happened to me too. Though, I think my parents understood that better than I did at the time.

That day, as I came home from school, my parents were both already at home, waiting for me. Which was odd because normally I'd be alone for a couple of hours before either of them even came home. I immediately knew something was wrong.

One moment, I knew nothing, I was still unaware. I walked through the door, unsuspecting of anything ever changing, having in a way accepted the fate of never-ending grey days.

But in only a couple of minutes time, I knew about Vicky, I knew that she was also living in this dark place in her mind, and I knew that she'd killed herself.

Vicky, like me, had been born a boy, and in many ways we grew up the same way. But she had resigned herself to the shadows, only living half a life, struggling to keep her head above the water. She could no longer live hiding her true self, hiding who she really was inside, and even after she started living her life as a girl, she couldn't get out of that depression. It had gotten too deep, and wouldn't let her go. Depression took her because people didn't realise that that darkness in her head didn't have anything to do with her being trans, but everything to do with bad brain chemistry. They were so focused on treating her gender, that they never thought to look elsewhere for her darkness.

My parents didn't ask me if I wanted to talk to them, they didn't ask me anything that day. They told me that they didn't want the same thing to happen to me, they didn't want to lose me to depression too, and that they'd made an appointment with a psychologist for me.

They didn't want to lose their daughter, they understood that this constant grey I was living in had a name, depression, and that unless I got help, I'd never get out.

That day I realised three things:

1. I didn't want to die.

2. What is the whole purpose of life, if I didn't live it to the fullest?

And I no longer cared about other people's responses to the most important question of all:

3. What if I did wear that beautiful dress?

What could go wrong?

1

Izzy

Anime = Short for *animation* = Used in Japan to refer to animated media, but in most of the rest of the world, it's specifically used to refer to animated works from Japan. These animations are often characterised by their colourful style, the characters' big eyes and the (overly) dramatic storylines. At least, those are the ones I like the most. I especially love the ones that are really over-the-top in their character proportions, with big eyes, really big hair and poofy dresses that stand out more than gravity should allow.

Two years ago

I roll my suitcase into the hotel room. My parents finally allowed me to attend the AmAnime convention in Amsterdam with my best friend Jason.

His parents are in the next room over and will be at the event too, but I already know that we're probably not going to be seeing them much, luckily. They're just here to 'supervise' us. We're sixteen, so we don't need that much 'supervision'. Though my parents, and the people organising the con, really want people under eighteen to always have adultier adults around. *Sigh.*

I put the suitcase at the end of my bed and sprawl all over it, letting out a long breath. "Fiiiinally."

Jason sits down on his own bed, grinning as he looks my way. "What? You don't like being all folded up in a tiny car for hours on end?" He also stretches out, but it doesn't take long before he's sitting up again. "The event starts in an hour, we should get dressed." He's, of course, talking about the opening ceremony, which is supposed to be this big event with lots of cosplayers and music and everything. I've seen a few of them online, but I've never been to one, so I don't know what to expect from it.

"Already?" I groan, but then I sit up too.

"People are already messaging me, they have been for an hour, asking where we are. They're waiting out in the front halls for us." He opens his suitcase and starts pulling out clothes, spreading them over his bed, sorting through them. "You don't have to meet with them if you don't want to, you can stay here and just play games or something."

"No, I'm good." I also open my suitcase and pull out the outfit I've got planned for today. It's a Japanese Lolita style black dress with bright green elements and I'm wearing really high heeled shoes with it. I've worked on this outfit for months, I'm not letting this opportunity pass. I know I can, and will, pull this off. I take the dress and everything I'll need with it in my arms. "I'm changing in there." I point to the bathroom.

Jason nods. "Of course, just as long as you remember that I need help zipping this thing up later." He grins, pointing at his back.

He's used to me disappearing into bathrooms to get changed. I always do that, he doesn't know any different from me. That, and I don't really have to watch him change either. We may have been born with generally the same body parts, but he's a lot more comfortable with them than I am.

Understatement of the century.

I close the bathroom door behind me and hang the clothes on the bath's edge, keeping them off the floor. Then I check myself in the mirror. My eyes are wide and intense, and I can feel a little anxiety chipping away at my sanity.

I know I'll be fine. Rationally, I know that I'll be fine and that there won't be any problems. Jason has said so himself, there is nothing to worry about when we're here, no matter what happens. Still, it's one thing to dress up all cute when everyone around you just identifies you in a binary way: boy, girl. But AmAnime is known for having a lot of cosplayers and crossplayers around, so people may not identify me the way I want to...

And even after years of living as a girl, that still scares me more than it maybe has to. I don't know. I've not been misgendered in months, if not for more than a year. But this isn't a situation I've encountered before, a place where people's genders and gender expressions are a little fluid to begin with.

I sigh. I've been so looking forward to today, I've been waiting all year to attend, but now I'm actually here, I'm starting to freak out a little.

What if people... What if people are going to make an issue with how I dress? Or the way I act? Or the way I am?

Jason knocks on the door. "Izzy." His voice is calm, but I know he's checking up on me.

"Yeah?" I look up, breaking the staring contest I'm having

with myself.

"I'm not hearing you move. Come on, get changed." He's so excited, even though he tries to be calm for me, and I can't help that his cheer lifts my own mood too.

"Yeah, yeah." I quickly strip off the leggings and comfy dress I wore during the car ride here. Then I look at the outfit I'm about to put on and sigh. "Moving now, you can stop standing there."

"I know, I can hear you." Jason laughs. "Going to put on some music, get in the mood and everything." He walks away from the door, and I can hear him stream some J-pop from this phone to his portable speakers.

I sit down on the side of the bath, taking off my socks and sliding on the fishnet stockings, trying not to get stuck in them. Today I'm not going as some anime character, cosplaying is for tomorrow when the real convention starts, instead, I'm wearing a cute gothic lolita style dress. When my stockings are on, I quickly put on the pristine white socks with the frilly edge, to go with my shoes, and then I stand up and pull on the dress. While the sleeves and skirt are all pretty and fiddly, the body of it is plain, but that's because I've got a corset to go over it. That was the one thing of this outfit that took me months to finish, the corset, but the end result is definitely worth it.

I look around, realising I've left something in my bag. "Jason!"

"Yeah?"

"Can you get me the black petticoat from my bag?" I open the door a little.

Jason moves around the room and is back with the petticoat in no time. "Here."

I take it, pulling it into the bathroom. Then I close the door again. I'm not going to flash him while putting this on, no way. I smile a little as I think about it. Yeah, flashing Jason wouldn't even surprise him, he'd probably find it funny. Strange guy.

I pull the petticoat on and then pull the dress over it, smoothing them both down. I check myself in the mirror again, plucking at the top of my dress. I wish I had more to fill out the bust, but that's the advantage of making clothes yourself, you can just design the fit to hide the things you don't want people to see, like my lack of cleavage.

Which will be different soon, hopefully. I'm definitely old enough now. As I think back to the conversation I had with my parents last night, I'm fairly sure that I'll be taking the next steps in my transition in not too long.

Then I grab my old clothes and get out of the bathroom, making sure I enter with flair and a quick spin to show off the skirt, of course, which suits a dress like this.

Jason stares at me. "That, with heels and a corset?" His eyebrows go up.

"Yes." I grin.

"Wow." He grins too. "I should have gotten myself a bodyguard outfit instead."

"Hey..." My cheeks flare up, and I quickly drop my clothes on the bed. "You know I can kick anyone's butt any day." My parents insisted I take some classes in self-defence when I was younger, just so I would be less of a target.

"I know." Jason turns his back to me. "Can you zip me up? I'm not as flexible as you are."

"Sure." I pull the back of his dress tighter and then zip him up. We're somewhat of a matching pair. I'm all black and green, and he's all black and white, both wearing similar styles of dresses, though mine is a little more extravagant. "I'm going to need you to do my makeup, though."

"Of course." He grabs his makeup bag, pulling a chair between the beds and puts the bag on it, going through it. "I actually got you some fake lashes for today, if you want them."

"Which ones?" I normally wear my own, but for this look I've just got plain black fluttery ones, nothing too extravagant.

"Green." Jason grins. "Should match your dress." He picks up a small box from the bag. "Check them out."

I open the little box, and he's right, they're bright green, a close match to the details on my dress, and they're really soft and long. "Wow. Thanks. How much do I owe you?"

"Nothing." Jason winks. "Got them in a two-for-one sale at a new place I was trying out. They had the perfect lashes for the cosplay I'm doing tomorrow."

"You have to stop doing that. Just giving me stuff when you feel like it." I pick up the green lashes. They do look really nice, if a little strange, but that's not a bad thing in this case.

"You make me things that would have otherwise cost me a lot of money, or repair some of my clothes when I ruin them. This is the least I can do." He sits down on his bed. "What are you looking for? Anything specific you want with the makeup?"

I shake my head. "Nah, with these lashes... Just something simple would be good."

"Okay." Jason leans in. "I hope you're ready to have a lot of pictures taken."

I shrug. "Isn't that what this weekend is all about?"

I'm not sure what I expected of the opening ceremony, but I don't think this was it exactly... There are a lot of people waiting around in the hallway, and I'm a little overwhelmed as I look around. Most of the people here are dressed up, though many are just in regular clothes too, probably half-half. *Wow.*

Jason keeps hold of the sleeve of my dress as he looks over the crowd. The guy is tall, but today he's wearing heels, which makes him easier taller than almost anyone here. "Ah." He waves and then turns to his parents. "The people I'm meeting are at the other end of the hall. The guy with the pink hair and the white princess dress is one of them." He points.

His mum looks over and nods. "Just be careful, please?"

"Yeah, yeah." Jason grins.

Careful? Him? Us? Yeah, not likely.

"Are you going with him?" Jason's mum looks at me. "You can always find us or just call us. We'll probably be at the cafe upstairs."

"I'm going with him." I've gotten a little used to all the excitement now and am calm enough to be curious again.

"Good. Have fun." She grins and then takes her husband's arm, and they walk off.

"Come on." Jason tugs on my arm a little. "You really need to meet Ruby, he's awesome. And I think you'll get along well with him, he makes his own dresses too." Jason starts dragging me through the hallway, through the crowd.

I do my best not to get stabbed by weapons or hit in the face with bags and hair. But, we make it to the other end without getting hurt, too much. *Yay.*

As we get out of the crowd, I'm faced with a sight I should have expected, though I'm still not prepared. We're standing in front of a group of people who're wearing some of the most extravagant outfits I've seen yet. If I thought that I'd stand out in my black and green dress with the green fake lashes, I shouldn't have worried. These people... they definitely stand out

18

more than I do.

"Jay!" A guy with a pink wig and in a big white dress comes over, taking Jason into a hug.

"Ruby." Jason laughs, wrapping his arms around the other man. "You look extra princess-y today."

"I did my best." Ruby laughs, then he looks at me, smiling. "Do you hug?"

I nod.

Ruby steps closer and lets me initiate the hug. When I wrap my arms around him for a hug, he takes me in his arms and whirls me around, spinning us a couple of times. "You're adorable. I love that dress." He lets me go again, and I have to take a moment to get my breath back.

"Thank you. Made it myself." I feel my cheeks heat up a little.

"Cool. I'm Ruby, as you've probably heard. And you are?"

"I'm Izzy."

"Izzy? So you're the one Jay is always bragging about." Ruby eyes Jason. "I don't think your description did her justice." He grins. "Okay, let's get you introduced to the rest of the group." He turns around. "So, everyone, this is Izzy. Izzy, this is the strange group of people who Jason hangs out with when he goes to conventions."

A guy with black hair and also a black and green outfit comes over, looking at me closely before he smiles. "I'm Kevin, and I believe I've met my match for the evening. And those lashes rock."

I'm pretty sure that these people aren't as scary as I made them out to be in my head. Just like Jason, they seem to just accept that I dress this way and am who I say I am.

This could turn into a very cool weekend. And this definitely could be the first time I get to share my passion of geeky and creative things with a lot of people instead of just one or two friends.

This convention thing rocks!

2
Elliot

Cosplay = Costume play = Dressing up as a character from an anime, manga, film or even a band. Cosplayers, people who cosplay, often try to get as close to the original character's looks as they can, but will also play the personality, accents and things like that to get the whole package. Many of the costumes take months or even longer than that to make, as trying to find the right materials to recreate an outfit or weapon can be a real adventure. But that is what I enjoy about doing it most, the adventure, the challenge.

Now

I never really thought much about how people look at girls who cosplay as female characters. To be fair, I've had my share of times that I stared at a girl in a sexy outfit as she passed me by, but that was always because, you know, that was what I thought was normal. I enjoy looking at girls who dress nicely because I enjoy looking at girls, in my mind, it was that simple.

I also know how some people look at guys who cosplay as

female characters, especially the ones who play a very over-the-top kind of female character and how they combine their masculinity with the female character's outfit and personality.

But for me, neither of these things were things that I would think about very much. Usually… That was, until I found myself cosplaying a female character at an anime convention and had to consider both of these views at the same time.

The thing is, I'm not broad, I'm not bulky, I'm not even very tall. So, while I can easily cosplay the lankier male characters from most anime, the really masculine characters were never something that I thought I could pull off. But on the other side of things, there's been something I've been hoping to cosplay as one day, even though I'd never shared that idea with anyone until a few months back.

I've always wanted to cosplay a female character, a magical girl character specifically. There's just something about them, their strength and their cheeriness, that has always attracted me to them. Well, that and the dresses... I don't know. Cosplaying a magical girl character has always been one of those things I wished I could do, that I wished I could pull off and that I wished I had the courage for. Only, I've always been too scared, too anxious, too nervous, never daring to really step out of my comfort zone.

But not this year, this year I'm going to crossplay Aoi from the Magical Princess Club! Anime, and it's made me really, really nervous.

Most anime and gaming conventions I tend to go with a group of friends, but this year they're too busy working during summer break to come along. They're trying to save up money for a gaming convention later this year, so they don't want to spend it all on this convention first. Well, most of them anyway, one of my friends is still here with me, Mya. Though, I'm pretty sure that she wouldn't skip any anime or gaming convention that she could attend, within reason, because she loves them.

Even though it's going to be just the two of us, I appreciate that I won't be on my own this weekend, that I won't be on my own when I'm going out in public in a dress for the first time. Not that she'll be at my side the whole time, she'll probably be off doing her own thing this weekend most of the time anyway, but it's nice to have her here.

Mya is not as much into cosplaying as the rest of us are, she's here for the swag, the collectables and the fan-items. The most she's ever done for cosplaying is putting on a pair of dark jeans, a white t-shirt, some smudged eyeliner and putting her hair up so that it looks all short and fuzzy. I don't really think that can even be considered 'cosplay' to be honest. But I don't mind that she's not into it so much, it means that when we travel together, she can drag some of my props and bags for me, since she won't have as many. I've gotta make use of our situation somehow, right? It's not like she doesn't do the same thing with me either, especially when we go to game releases, and she makes me stand in line, keeping her spot, as she walks off to talk to people she knows. What else are friends for?

Of course, when I'm nervous, I start thinking in weird ways and rambling inside my head. This AmAnime is even worse than usual because I'm doing something scary, for me anyway, I'm stepping outside of my comfort zone big time. Luckily, most people here don't really know me or recognise me that well, so I don't feel as scared of their judgements as I would of my friends. And Mya already knows about all of it, so it's not really a surprise to her.

This year is the first year I'm not just cosplaying, I'm

crossplaying all weekend, and even my non-cosplay outfits for this weekend are a bit more on the feminine side.

What most of my friends I normally attend cons with don't know is that I regularly crossdress. I wear women's clothes, dresses, skirts, frilly shirts, things like that. I also finish the look off with a long-haired wig, since my hair is way too short to do anything interesting with. Mya has helped me out a lot with clothes and makeup in the last months, and she's been great about it all. It's always nice to have someone at your side who at least understands you somewhat. Or, well, someone who doesn't mind answering silly questions, mostly.

I take a deep breath as I walk into the large hall of the convention building, a little nervous as I keep glancing around me. Today, I'm wearing a black unisex cotton skirt with chains running across it and a fishnet shirt. It's not exactly crossdressing, but it's still on the more androgynous side of things. My other option for his outfit was a tight black shirt with floral lace patterns, but I'm not brave enough to put that on today, not for the opening show of the event. I may feel braver later in the evening, but for right now, I'm not doing it, going like this took me long enough. I just spent twenty minutes in front of a mirror doing my makeup while Mya was on the bed reading a manga. It took her not even two minutes to put on some eyeliner and be done with it.

"Elliot!" Mya waves, motioning for me to come over.

"You were suddenly gone." I glare at her. We stepped out of the elevators and she'd suddenly disappeared from my side.

"Yeah, sorry. Saw someone. Don't worry, I'm not running off. You want to wait here until the opening show or go outside for a moment?" Mya keeps moving, all energetic.

"Let's go outside." It's seriously hot this weekend, and I'm not so sure anymore if the cosplays I've got planned for the event will be a good idea. They may be too hot and stuffy. Though, once you're through the front hall into the main part, those are usually pretty okay in temperature. But right now, it may be a little less overly hot outside.

We walk to the front doors, showing our festival bracelets to the guy at the doors as we step outside. Outside it's just as hot as inside, but at least there is a little breeze here.

We go over to some picnic tables at the side of the building and sit down. Mya immediately pulls out her phone, scrolling through something and then shows me the screen.

"We really need to find this stand tomorrow." She grins. Mya is showing me a picture of a stand with what appears to be fan art of some popular manga and anime, including some fan-made mangas. "Their description lists it as having some Destruction of Elysium anime fan art, which, you know, I always need more of."

"Really?" I take her phone, trying to find something in the picture that could tell me more, but it's too small, and there is too much going on. "Do you think they'll have some Deimos and Athena art? That would be awesome." Destruction of Elysium started out as a video game but they also made some anime seasons because of how popular it was. This season, they're not running a new season of the anime but the last one was last winter. There is some really interesting fan art of two of the main characters going around, which I would love to get my hands on. I cosplayed Deimos, one of the main characters in the anime, last year at this convention. "Maybe I should have gone as Deimos this year too... They could have given me a discount at the stand, maybe." I grin.

Mya smiles, shaking her head. "I don't know. I don't think

that they would really do things like that though... Plus, hey, you finally get to cosplay the character of your dreams, a magical girl."

I nod, though my smile falters a little. "Still, I wish you'd also cosplayed as someone from the anime, even just a side character. I'll feel so obvious when I'm playing Aoi on my own tomorrow."

Mya keeps smiling. "I know that you'll be fine. There's nothing to worry about. The cosplay looks great, and I'll already be carrying your things, remember?" She grins now. "I won't be your distraction but I'll be your mule all weekend. Seems like a fair tradeoff, right?"

I reach out to her, and she takes my hand, squeezing it a little.

"You know that I'm right." Mya winks.

"Yeah, I know." I sigh. "Just nerves."

"I know." Her gaze softens. "They'll be gone tomorrow. Like always, you'll get into character, and all the nerves will be gone like they were never there, that always happens with you."

"Yeah." I squeeze her hand too. They may be gone tomorrow, but they aren't yet today.

From behind us, someone raises their voice. "The opening ceremony is about to start. Anyone who wants to watch, you better get inside."

I grin, standing up. AmAnime always has really cool opening ceremonies, with acts and cosplayers and some actors and things like that on stage, introducing the panels and the signings and everything. It's an experience.

I take a deep breath as I tug Mya along with me. Time to start the weekend!

I check myself in the mirror again. This morning I woke up and I immediately knew that something was wrong... I don't know what it was, but it seems I had a reaction to some makeup or cleaner or whatever and now I have a patch of red skin on my jaw. Not fun. I was able to hide it with make-up, but it's not perfect. I'm just hoping it doesn't get too much worse. You can't really see anything right now, it's just itchy, but that doesn't mean that it won't be visible again in another hour or two, I'll have to keep an eye on it.

"Elliot." Mya sighs, standing in the doorway. "You can't cover it more than you already have, unless you pull a bag over your head, but that would ruin your hair."

I glare her way. There is no way I'm letting anything near my hair, the twin ponytails with ribbons were hard enough to put in the first time, I'm not redoing them.

"Well then." She shrugs. "It's covered up. I'll tell you if something starts sneaking out again or something." She's just a little too relaxed for my taste.

"Yeah, yeah..." I take a deep breath. "Can I just be nervous for a bit?" I fluff at the hem of the dress, making the ruffles more even, trying to not think about leaving the room just yet.

"You've been nervous all morning, and last night, and the whole of last week." Mya rolls her eyes. "I kind of want to get to one or two stands before they run out of prints, you know?"

"I know, I know." I push away from the sink. "I guess it's time to get moving then."

"Yay." Mya grins. "Finally." She almost jumps up and down, but then glances my way.

"Hey." I glare her way again, but can't help my own smile. She's right. I've been trying to hide in here long enough.

I leave the bathroom and give Mya my wallet before I slide my phone into the top of my dress. If you don't have anything to fill the top of a dress with yourself, it makes an excellent spot for phone storage. Although, I know that some people who do have enough to fill the bodice of a dress do it too, but you know, still handy.

"You'll be fine, you know that." Mya puts her hand on my arm. "You look great. The cosplay is spot on. Not many people are going to take a second look at you being you, they're going to see Aoi."

"I just." I sigh. "I don't want to look strange. I don't want people to like... stare at me and stuff."

"Everyone is going to stare, but that's because your cosplays are always so good. You know that. This time the only difference is that *you* feel different about being dressed like this. You felt like that when you started crossdressing too, remember? And now you're actually crossplaying one of your favourite characters of all time at an event that you know is going to be a safe place to do so. I'm pretty sure that's brave and cool, no matter how you look at it." She smiles. Mya is always my biggest supporter, even when I don't always deserve it. Like when I complain way too much to her.

"Thanks."

"No problem." She shrugs a little.

I nod. "Let's go."

Time to face the world, time to do this. Time to be someone I really want to be for a day.

Time to not stumble and fall flat on my face the first time someone looks my way, or trip over my own shoes.

My stomach is all in knots and I feel a little sick from nerves... Why did I think this was a good idea again?

3

Izzy

Genderswap = When a female character is portrayed as a male character or a male character as a female character. This also includes genderneutral characters, though genderswapping from or to a genderneutral character is less common. Genderswapping is common in fan art and other fan projects of anime or game characters, it gives the creators of the fan project a certain freedom to try out things with a character in a different context than they would usually be able to do. Genderswapping can be done poorly, in ways that alienate or harm transgender, crossdressing or other gender non-conforming people, but that's not always the case. I've seen it being done both ways, it happens. I've not done any genderswaps of characters myself, I've got enough on my gender plate as it is, but I've got a lot of friends who do it. Including last year, when Jason genderswapped Athena, the main female character from the Destruction of Elysium anime.

Jason lifts my hair up as I clip in another extension, so many of them, way too many. Sometimes it would be so much easier if

I'd just wear wigs, but they're really uncomfortable when it's hot, especially when you have long hair that you have to hide under it. I don't like it. So, instead, I get to do a lot of work with extensions and clips and other things to make my hair look longer and bigger and poofier, and to get it to stay in the shape that it has to be in. Luckily, cosplaying Sakura from Magical Princess Club! means that I can mostly let my hair flow and do its thing. It just needs to have a lot more volume and poofiness.

Most of the time, this is the better solution for me, but when you have to do this with pigtails and things like that... Sometimes my head really hurts at the end of the day and I curse myself. I do it all to make the best cosplay that I can, including the hair.

Sighing, I move my shoulders and neck. We've been getting dressed for the last hour and I'm ready to be done with it. Luckily, we're on the final steps, just the hair and then touching up on the makeup.

"Already regretting your choice?" Jason laughs, then he sits down on his bed. "You could have gone for something a little less... extravagant, you know?"

I shake my head, grinning. "You know that at the next convention, there are going to be fifty Sakuras. I just have to make sure I'm the first, or, you know, one of the first."

Jason lets out a short laugh. "Right. Remind me again why I let you do this to me each year? You make the clothes, and you'll wear them, but I have to do all the makeup and hair and stuff for you."

"Because you know that it will be awesome?" I raise an eyebrow at him. A very well designed eyebrow, thank you very much.

"True. And you'll win the cosplay contest, easily." He stands up again, grabbing his makeup box. "Okay. Let me just touch up

30

the makeup and we can go, right?"

I check the time. "Yeah. The doors opened like... twenty minutes ago."

Jason shrugs. "That's called fashionably late."

"No, that's called late because of fashion." I laugh. We had a small costume issue this morning, and I had to fix the hem of Jason's skirt over breakfast. Which meant that we started getting ready a little later than planned. It seems that Jason's skirt had been ripped when he packed or something. I don't know. I never understand how he tears and breaks things so easily.

"Fine." He opens the box. "Sit still, this won't take long."

I close my eyes, taking slow breaths. This is the perfect moment to try and relax a little. To try to not be as overwhelmed as I really feel. This is my third year attending AmAnime, and every year has been more crazy and more amazing in equal amounts. A few weeks ago I was at a friend's birthday party and the way they looked at some of my cosplays, even the ones that I don't think are very good, reminded me that what I see here at the con is special, I just see the really good outfits, not the mundane ones. What we do isn't just some boring task, it's magic, at least, it is for the people who only see the end results.

I sometimes forget that. I get so wrapped up in everything, in the competitiveness, in the comparing, that I forget that this isn't about that, this is about getting dressed up, about portraying our favourite characters. About having fun.

It was a good reminder, one which I really needed at the time.

And today, I get to do exactly that, I get to be here, play Sakura, have a good time, and all the things that come with that.

It's going to be awesome, like always.

The first person staring at me started when we were still walking down the hallway from our room to the elevators. The girl got a huge smile on her face and she grinned as she waved at us. I waved back, always happy to greet people who get excited seeing me like this.

We had to wait for a second elevator, as the first one was already full and I wouldn't have fit in with my dress. One of our friends, Kevin, was in it though, and greeted us, giving me a big thumbs up. The second one wasn't as full, luckily.

Jason keeps his hand on my arm, trying to make sure I don't fall over when the elevator starts or stops. It feels good, safe, steady. I know that he won't drop me, at least not if he can prevent it.

When the doors open, Kevin and Ruby are already waiting for us.

Ruby gasps like he's in a theatre play and has to convince the people in the back of the audience of his surprise. Although, I'm not entirely sure that that isn't what he's trying to do anyway, reach the people at the back of the hallway with his performance. You never know with him. "I saw the pics you shared. But this…" He shakes his head. Then he makes a twirling motion with his hand. "Show us."

I turn slowly, showing the dress off. Getting all the lace in the right locations and making sure that the dress wouldn't sag or hurt my hips like crazy wasn't easy, but I'm really proud of the results.

"Best one you've done yet?" Ruby comes closer. "Do you think?"

"Probably." I nod. "And not too common yet. I hope." I

grin, glancing around.

"You never know." He smiles. "I haven't seen a Sakura yet, not from Magical Princess Club! anyway, I did see one or two from Cardcaptor Sakura, of course."

"You decided to match with Kevin for the day?" I look between them both.

"That was a total accident." Kevin shrugs. They're both cosplaying the same character, Violet from Violet Evergarden, but Ruby is wearing a cosplay of the original design, and Kevin is wearing a genderswapped version, all tightly pressed pants and well-tailored jacket. "It wasn't planned, but I guess it works out anyway." He looks out over the group of people waiting to get into the event hall. "I guess we should start getting in line."

I take his arm. "I think I can do that, with a handsome soldier at my arm."

"What about me?" Ruby play-pouts.

"Of course." I grin. "Wouldn't leave you alone." I hook my arm through his too.

"Okay." Jason grins. "Just... stay like that for a moment. This deserves a picture." He takes a couple of steps back and digs his phone out of the top of his dress, then he makes a couple of pictures of us.

The next moment, five more people have joined him, taking pictures of us and I keep smiling. This is normal, this is what you get when you cosplay, especially when you stand out like we do. Pictures, loads of pictures.

Kevin lets my arm go, instead sliding his arm around my waist and I lean back against him. There are more people taking pictures now, and a couple of girls are grinning like crazy as they see us, I'm also pretty sure I heard a squeal from somewhere. It has to look cute, the both of us together, my dress is mostly pinks and whites, and Kevin's outfit is mostly dark green. He looks very handsome, and I do feel a little like a princess in his arms.

When this has gone on long enough, I stand back up straight and Kevin lets me go. "I can do more pictures later, but I'd really like to get in line now." I smile at the people around us, and we make our way to the line. Sure enough, on our way to the line, and while we're standing in line, more people start taking pictures of us. I'm used to it, I keep smiling and waving at people, showing my best smile. If I didn't want this, I wouldn't have cosplayed...

As we're waiting to get in, more of our friends start joining us, and when we reach the entrance of the halls, we've grown to quite a sizable group of people. Most of us are in cosplay, though, a few are simply dressed up in pretty clothes and we have one photographer with us, Justin, who is in plain black clothes.

This group has been together for years, though I only joined them about two years ago. When it comes to people I trust, people I really care about, they're top of the list. I don't know what I'd be like, what these last years would have been like, if it wasn't for them. Them, and Jason of course.

I smile, my heart light. I can't help this happy feeling inside as I look around the convention hall. "I think I need to be at the back of the hall, near the stage, to sign up for the cosplay competition." Practical things first, then fun.

"Well, let's go there, then." Kevin starts walking, pulling me along. "I think a few more of us need to be there." He grins, his eyes sparkling. "Let's crush this competition. Again. It's our tradition." He looks back. "We can't break the streak."

"No. We can't." I grin too. Our group has won most of the spots in the competition four years in a row now, and the last

34

two years we've even taken the number one spot, twice.

Well, I took the number one spot for individual cosplay two years in a row, Ruby, Kevin and Evelyn took them for group cosplays. And now I want another win. I want to win this year too. I'm not going to lose. I worked as hard as I could on this cosplay so I could win, and win I shall.

I quicken my steps, trying to walk next to Kevin, whose longer legs make him walk much faster than me in my heels.

There is no way I'm letting him walk in front of me. I'm not going to be dragged around like a princess, I'm going to rule like one instead.

Magical Princess Club go!

The line for the sign-up table is long, again, of course. I check out the competition as we wait. There are some really cool cosplays in here. I can see someone cosplaying Elias from The Ancient Magus' Bride, very impressive and tall, and also 2B from NieR: Automata. They look really good.

I recognise most of the cosplays, which means I watch way too much anime, and then there is just the general culture around everything, so even if I haven't seen an anime, I'd probably recognise the most common characters from that anime if I'd see them.

Then my eyes fall on someone in a light blue dress at the other side of the stage, and I stop moving, my heart beating faster.

No way. You've got to be kidding me. *No way.*

"Jason?" I pull on his arm. "Please tell me I'm not seeing things."

"What did you see?" He turns in the direction I'm staring in, but when I look again, the person in the dress is gone.

"I think I just saw someone in Aoi cosplay." I try to focus on what I saw, try to figure out if I really was seeing what I thought I was seeing.

I was just too surprised to find someone cosplaying the same anime, that I sort of zoned out a little. Aoi is the best friend of Sakura in Magical Princess Club!, so finding someone cosplaying her too would be really cool. I can already imagine a couple of cool things we could to together today.

"Really?" He looks around again, but then shrugs. "Not seeing her anywhere right now. Are you sure?"

"Pretty sure. It was just a flash though. But what I saw. Yeah. She looked like Aoi. Though I only saw her back, so it could be another magical girl cosplay, but, you know, it wouldn't be that surprising." I keep looking around, trying to find the girl again.

It would be so cool if there was an Aoi cosplayer walking around. We could take pictures together, especially if her cosplay is as good as it looked from the back.

Great. Now I'm really excited about meeting a random girl, just because she also cosplays a character from the same anime I'm cosplaying.

Well, it *is* one of those awesome ways to make friends at conventions like this, find the people who have the same interests as you have, and cosplay is as good a way to do that as any...

But now the waiting in line is even more annoying.

I want to find Aoi.

4
Elliot

Crossplay = Crossdressing cosplay = When the gender of the cosplayed character doesn't match the gender of the cosplayer. This is a sub-type within cosplaying. Sometimes people try to match the gender and look of the character being cosplayed as closely as possible, but other times it's done within the confinements of what the cosplayers themselves are comfortable with and what they feel best matches their body type. For example, not all men crossplaying female characters will put on fake breasts, and not all women will bind their breasts when they crossplay a male character. For my first time, I'm not doing anything complicated, I just want to be as comfortable as possible while trying something new.

As I looked at the row of people standing in line to sign up for the cosplay competition, I decided against joining them in the line for the moment. It's too early in the day to wait that long, and Mya is way too impatient to stand still for too long at a time. She wants to visit the stand she's been talking about since yesterday. I get it, the excitement and not wanting to wait part, I've been like that before. But I don't know if I was every this annoying about it, to be honest. Maybe I'm just a little grumpy right now because I'm still not that comfortable being dressed up like Aoi, and Mya is way too comfortable being her fangirl self right now, enabling all the other people to fawn on me too. It would have been fun, if I'd had more confidence in myself, I guess.

"Aoi! O-M-G!" A girl wearing a Sailor costume from a Sailor Moon character I don't immediately recognise comes rushing over to me. "Ah! Can I take a picture? You look so cute!"

I open my mouth to answer, but then decide against it. Instead, I nod. I grab my staff with two hands and pull one of Aoi's signature poses. At least, one of her signature poses that doesn't take too much space to pull off, since it's kinda busy around here and I don't want to hit anyone accidentally.

The girl takes a few pictures, grinning constantly. "Thank you so much! You look great!" She steps closer. "Can I hug you?" Her eyes shine from seeing someone cosplaying a character that she probably likes, or at least recognizes. But apparently, my answer doesn't come fast enough. I froze up a little, not sure what to do, not sure how to act. So she shrugs her shoulders, still smiling, her grin not faltering one moment. "That's okay, don't want to invade. Have fun today! I bet I'll see you at the cosplay competition, right?"

I nod again, smiling now. That was easy enough.

"Cool! See you there!" And she's off again, waving at me for a moment.

Mya bumps her shoulder into mine. "You've got fans." She winks. "It really doesn't matter who you cosplay as, you always have fans in like no-time flat." She keeps grinning, shaking her

38

head a little.

"Should I..." I look around, now even more self-aware about my voice. "Like... speak or not speak? Doesn't speaking, my low voice, break the illusion?"

Mya shrugs, thinking. "I don't know if it matters, really. And you do get very far with just that smile of yours." She turns around. "We should be close to the stand now." She checks her map, her fingers moving over the aisles and stands, counting them.

"Let's go, before I get photo-bushed again." I tug on her arm.

"Photo-bushed?" She raises an eyebrow at me.

"Ambushed for more photos?" I grin.

Mya now rolls her eyes at me, shaking her head. "Yeah, let's find the stand first. Maybe I can buy some manga or something to entertain myself as you get fawned over by fangirls and fanboys." She grins, looking decidedly... evil.

I follow Mya through the crowd until we get to a stand filled with fan items. Art, key chains, doujinshi, cards, t-shirts, plushies, basically anything you can imagine being made as fan art seems to be here. Some of it is official swag, but a lot of it is fan made.

I let out a squeal as I find the one item I've been trying to get my hands on for months. "Deimos plushie!" I can't believe they have one here. I've been trying to find one online for months without luck, after I saw one on Twitter.

Mya rubs her hand over her ear, moving away from me. "You've got the fangirl squealing down. Now, next time, please make sure you're at least three steps away from me before you do it again." She grumbles a little, but still smiles.

"Do you like Deimos?" The girl behind the stand leans over. "He's pretty popular. That's the last one I've got, I already sold five today."

"Already?" My mouth falls open. The con opened not even an hour ago.

"Yeah." The girl grins. "He goes pretty quickly, but takes a while to make, so I don't usually have many of him with me at cons."

'Takes a while to make.' I need a moment to let that sink in. "You make these yourself?" Now I'm really surprised.

"Yeah."

"Wow." I look at the little guy in my hands. "I'm buying him now, then. I don't want to miss out. I cosplayed him last year, so I kind of *need* to have him."

"Last year?" The girl thinks. "I may have seen you last year."

"I was with a Phobos, Athena and this girl." I point at Mya. "I don't think I've got pics of the cosplay with me right now, though."

"That's okay. I think I remember you, yeah." She smiles. "You looked very cool. And this Aoi cosplay is super cute too. It must have taken a long time to make." She looks me up and down, and I totally forgot about being Aoi for a few moments. But it doesn't seem to phase the girl.

"Thanks. I'm Elliot, you are?"

"I'm Emma. Nice meeting you." She looks over to the side, there are other people looking at her stand, she probably needs to keep an eye on them, and I need to not distract her too long.

"I'll just pay for this little guy, and then I'll stop distracting you." I hold out Deimos.

"Thanks. Good plan." Emma lets out a laugh. "Cash or card?"

"Card." I turn to Mya for my wallet.

Mya sighs as she takes my wallet from her bag. "I'm going

40

to have to carry Deimos around all day, won't I?"

"You love him too, I know you do." I grin, then take my card out of my wallet and pay for Deimos. "And we can always dump him in the hotel room if it gets too annoying." I shrug as I take the plastic bag with Deimos in it from Emma. "Thanks."

"Have fun! And have a great time at the con." She smiles, then she turns to another customer.

Mya moves a little down the aisle to a stand with all sorts of magazines and books. She steps to the side of the stand, digging through a box full of magazines, fanzines and other paper things. She's really focused, and I'm pretty sure that I know what she's looking for.

There is this sports anime, an ice skating one, and she really wants some slash doujinshi of the two main characters. I keep forgetting the name of the anime, but she's been obsessed with it, especially since they announced that there would be a movie made of it too. I'm not into sports anime, so apart from seeing memes and screenshots of it on Twitter, I don't really know anything about it. Which, according to Mya is a shame, but I watch too many anime anyway, I don't have time for more.

I step to the side, letting other people get to the stand and just scroll through my social media, watching the pictures of the event being uploaded. So many people. The event organisers are calling it their biggest edition of AmAnime yet, which is pretty cool because we don't get many anime conventions around here. So as long as the event keeps growing, I'm happy, because it also means that they'll probably keep running it.

Then I stop scrolling. I stare at the picture, and then again. That's... Someone is here as Sakura from the Magical Princess Club! anime!

I enlargen the picture, looking at the details of her dress, of her hair. She looks... *Wow.* Sakura doesn't really fit my personality, and her outfit is way more complicated to make than Aoi's outfit was, so I never really considered cosplaying Sakura. But this girl. *Wow.* She really looks like a real-life copy of her!

"What are you gaping at?" Mya tries to look at my phone screen from the top. "Show me."

"Sakura." I turn my phone to Mya. "Someone's here as Sakura."

Mya's eyes grow, and she starts to smile. "That's impressive." She looks up at me. "And now you want to go find her?"

I hadn't even thought about that part yet. Meeting someone who is cosplaying the character who is Aoi's best friend in the anime? While, as a fan of the anime, I totally want to meet the girl, as someone who isn't really sure if he can really show up in his own cosplay... I'm too scared. "Maybe? I don't know." I shrug. Any other day, I would have immediately tried to find Sakura and hoped to take a picture with her as soon as I'd seen the photo. But next to this girl, my crossplaying will be so obvious, and what about just... I don't know.

"Come on." Mya grabs my hand.

"Where are we going?" I stumble after her, trying to not fall flat on my face or lose my staff or the Deimos plushie.

"The cosplay competition sign-up table."

"Why?" I don't think the lines are gone yet.

"Because that's where the picture was taken?" Mya looks at me for a moment, like I'm being dense and stupid.

I was too busy looking at the cosplay that I hadn't even realised where the picture was taken. I slow Mya down as we reach the area near the stage and the table. "I don't know if I should do this."

"Why not? At least go and take a picture with her? You always do that with cosplayers who cosplay the characters you like. Why should this be different?"

"But... I'm in a dress." Why isn't that obvious? Next to her, I'll look… silly.

"Yes." Mya nods. "Has someone crossplaying ever stopped you from taking a picture with them?"

"No."

"Has them crossplaying ever stopped you from taking a picture with someone who liked your cosplay?"

"No..." I sigh. "Just... I'm scared."

"I know." Mya smiles a little, her eyes softer. "But the best way to get over that is by doing the things that scare you. Plus, I'd really like a picture of you two, just to have the first picture of the Magical Princess Club together at AmAnime." She grins now.

"Fine." I take a deep breath. She's right, the only way I can stop being so self-aware is to do things that I always would do, like taking pictures with people. "I'll try to find her."

Mya looks over my shoulder, her eyes growing. "That won't be hard." She takes a step back, carefully distancing herself from me a little.

"Aoi!" A girl calls my name, well, my character's name, but there is an accent to her voice, like she's trying to copy the voice from an anime.

I turn around to the sound, not sure what to expect. Then I spot Sakura, in all her pink and poofy glory. She's eyeing me, her eyes shining, then she opens her arms, tilting her head a little, raising an eyebrow.

She's beautiful.

I open my arms too, well aware of what that means.

Sakura jumps up a little, then sprints towards me and jumps into a hug. I spin her around, catching her weight, and keep my arms around her a moment longer.

I'm holding Sakura. I'm really holding an almost perfect copy of Sakura in my arms.

Then the girl steps back a little, grinning. "I knew I was right. I knew I saw you before."

"What?" I blink.

"While I was waiting to sign up for the cosplay competition. I was waiting in line, and I was sure that I saw you, Aoi, just walking off."

"Ah." I lift my arm up, wanting to rub it over my other arm, nerves running through me, but put it down again, awkward. "Yeah. The line was just too long, and my friend wanted to see one of the stands first, before they sold out of all of the cool stuff."

Mya steps next to us. "Hi, I'm the friend in question." She grins, way too satisfied.

"Hey. Do you hug?" Sakura looks at her, her eyes still shining.

"With a princess? Are you kidding me? Always." Mya opens her arms and Sakura takes her in a hug too. Then Mya looks at us side by side. "I thought that E... the Aoi cosplay was good, but yours is super pretty! It has to be really hot in there, though."

Sakura shrugs. "A little. But... It's worth it if it gets me the third number one spot in a row at the yearly competition." She grins, and I totally get why she would play Sakura, she has the same competitiveness as Sakura in the anime has.

Also, potential third win in a row? "Really?"

"Yep. Champion two years running." She puts two fingers up, her eyes shimmering and I start to wonder if it's her

44

personality or the makeup that make it seem like that.

Wow. That means I've totally met her before, because I've participated in the competition for the last couple of years too. *Oh.* That means that she would also know that I'm crossplaying right now, she would know me as boy-looking me.

"Izzy!" Another voice behind me, a guy this time, at least, it's a pretty low voice. "There you are." Footsteps, and then a guy stands next to her, but his eyes are on me. "Wow. You were right."

All I can do is stare back at him. He's crossdressing, or crossplaying, I don't know, the style of his clothes is too generic to really figure it out in two seconds, especially since I don't know how to react and my brain is now running in a constant loop. I'm crossplaying and talking to a really cute girl, and this guy is crossdressing or crossplaying and he seems to be her friend?

Sakura, no, the guy called her Izzy, totally didn't react when she hugged me and must have realised that I wasn't a girl, at least, I'm missing the whole 'filling at the top of the front of my dress' thing that most girls have. But I guess that makes more sense when you're used to guys crossdressing...

It makes me a little nervous, but at the same time, something relaxes in me, at least she won't push me away just for crossdressing. At least she's used to that.

Right?

5

Izzy

Con = Convention = An event ranging from a single day to a whole weekend or even longer where people with similar interests come together to talk about their favourite things. You have conventions for anime, videogames, movies, but also other hobbies or even for specific professions. I've been to a few anime and gaming conventions, as long as they were sort-of local. It's one of the coolest ways to meet new people.

Jason wouldn't let me get out of the long line for the signups for the competition for even a couple of moments so that I could find Aoi, which was very frustrating, but as soon as I'd signed up for the cosplay contest, I went looking for her. I just *had* to find her. I just had to find the only other person I've seen at this convention to cosplay someone from same anime as I'm cosplaying. I just had to check her out.

Though, I didn't have to search for very long. As soon as I'd stepped out of the crowd, she was standing there, talking to a friend. They seemed to have some discussion, but I just had to make sure. When I called out for Aoi, she looked up and didn't seem particularly surprised to see me, though the look on her face was still priceless.

Aoi seemed to be stunned, even though she appeared to sort of expect me or something. I don't know. Lots of pictures have been taken already at the event, so she may have just seen me on social media already and kind of expected me to show up at some point.

And then she totally accepted the hug attack, which is one of Sakura's main shows of affection when it comes to her friendship with Aoi. Which was really sweet, as not everyone would have let a total stranger just jump on them like that.

Up close, Aoi's cosplay is really, really good. I may actually have competition in the cosplay contest this year. And I don't know if I care or not, since we're from the same anime and everything.

Of course, then Jason found me again.

Aoi seems a little uncomfortable under Jason's gaze, but at the same time, she's looking at him pretty curiously too. I don't know. They can figure that stuff out themselves.

"Hey, can I get a picture of you two together?" The girl with Aoi motions for us to step closer together.

"Sure." I grin, then I look at Aoi. "If you're okay with it?"

Aoi nods. Is she starting to blush? That's cute.

"What do you want us to do?" I look at the girl.

"First a normal pic." She waves her hand. "You can do whatever weird poses later."

"Sure." I step closer to Aoi, standing next to her, my arms at my side, not really sure. Aoi seemed pretty comfortable to do a hug earlier, but she doesn't seem as comfortable anymore.

The friend pulls a face. "Okay, can I get like, a hug or

something? Don't be so awkward." Though she mostly seems to be talking to Aoi.

Aoi lets out a sound, but then she slides her arm around my shoulder, and I slip my arm around her waist. We fit together pretty well like this.

The friend takes a couple of pictures as we keep moving just slightly, creating a few different poses. Then she stops. A group of people have gathered around us and are also taking pictures. "Okay, now you can do those magical girl moves. I know you want to."

I turn to Aoi, who's grinning, and I can't help but grin too. We definitely want to do that. And in the way Aoi's eyes twinkle, I suspect that I've found my match when it comes to how far we like portraying our cosplays.

I hold up my staff, and Aoi taps hers against it, then we slowly start doing the sequence for one of the finishing moves that our characters always perform together in the anime. And even though the first moments are a little awkward, that soon disappears, and we finish the sequence fluidly and synchronised. *Wow.* That was totally unexpected and fun.

A laugh bubbles up in me as I'm trying to regain my breath. It's fun, but with this heat, even doing a simple sequence can get a little tiring and hot.

"No way." Jason is now standing next to the other girl, then he looks at her. "You also have one of *those* friends?"

They share a look, enjoying teasing us apparently.

"Hey." Aoi steps to them. "I'm not that bad."

The girl levels a look at her now. "You know every one of Aoi's sequences. You know every move Deimos makes in the anime. And you know the history of every character you've cosplayed, ever, including important events in their friends' lives that are somehow related to their friendship…"

"That's normal. Right?" Aoi now looks at me, almost pleading me with her eyes to agree with her.

I shrug a little. "It is for me." And I see the look between Jason and the girl. "You two are just being mean. It's not that strange."

"No, we're just confirming something." Jason looks around. "Okay. I'm in desperate need of fluids or something else cool. That line was way too long and too hot."

"There's a stand where you can buy bubble tea and iced coffee near the entrance." Aoi looks at him.

"Iced coffee sounds good." Jason grins.

"Bubble tea?" Now, *that's* something I like to hear.

"Yes." Aoi grins too. "I checked it when we walked past them as we came in. They have a lot of flavours, but I think I'd like to try their strawberry first."

"It wasn't there last year, was it?" I can't remember there being something like a bubble tea stand at the event, and I'm pretty sure I would have found it if it had been there.

"Nope. New this year." Aoi's friend smiles.

"We have to try it!" I grin at Jason. "Have to. Seriously."

"Fine. Let's go." Jason lets out an exaggerated sigh before he smiles, then he turns to Aoi's friend. "I'm Jason. And you are?"

"Mya." The girl grins.

Jason looks my way. Oh, we're doing introductions now? "I'm Izzy." I do a small wave to everyone.

Aoi looks at Mya for a bit, who raises her eyebrows before she shrugs, but then Aoi seems to make a decision. "I'm Elliot." Elliot, so a guy, potentially?

"Elliot?" I turn to them. "Do you go by he/him pronouns?"

Hey, gotta make sure I get this right. I don't want to hurt anyone, even by accident.

Elliot seems to think this over for a moment. "Yes. And I'm not that deep into cosplaying that I want to change my pronouns when I cosplay as a girl."

"Okay. That makes sense." I slide my arm through his. It's not an uncommon choice for people.

"I keep using he/him pronouns too, no matter how I'm dressed." Jason shrugs.

"She/her pronouns for me." I get a tenseness in my chest for a moment, but Elliot looks at me like he hadn't even considered anything else. Which, I guess, is good? Why am I getting so aware right now? I've not been this anxious about myself in years…

"Also she/her for me." Mya laughs, hooking her arm through my other arm.

I nod, tugging on Elliot and Mya's arms. "Now, let's go get that bubble tea. And I want you to tell me about that thing about cosplaying Deimos from Destruction of Elysium." I eye Elliot.

Elliot is tense in my arm for a moment, but then he relaxes and smiles much more easily than I've seen him yet. So, that's what he looks like when he's not worrying, he's cute.

Maybe I should have asked about names and pronouns sooner? I never know when to ask it. I know that I personally don't mind if people guess for a while, especially when I still didn't look as feminine as I do now, because it tended to stop them from saying stupid things. But I think that Elliot is much more of a worrier. He's apparently not as confident crossdressing or crossplaying yet, and that's okay.

But I don't want to make him uncomfortable. I think he's pretty cute, no matter how he dresses. He just has that kind of androgynous face that allows him to do whatever.

He's cute. I admit it to myself. He really is.

And while I like it, I also know that this thing between us probably won't go any further than just hanging out and doing some photoshoots together. Because if there's one thing that I know for sure it's that I'm going to try to get Elliot to agree to a photoshoot with Justin this weekend. If anything to remember this by, just a photoshoot.

Finding someone to cosplay a magical girl with and get some cool shots, I don't get that opportunity often. So I've got to make use of this moment.

If anything, it will be a nice reminder of this weekend…

W A S D

Outside the convention building, it's a little bit quieter and there is a light breeze, cooling the air down some. We all sit down at one of the few empty picnic tables.

I drape my dress under and around me, because the metal benches are kind of too hot to sit on directly, and then I slide my feet out of the heels, pulling them up. *Freedom!* I don't mind wearing heels, I wear shoes with heels basically all the time, but if I don't have to wear anything on my feet for a while, I like that even better.

Elliot and I both got strawberry flavoured bubble tea, and Mya and Jasper got iced coffee. They made the drinks fresh at the stall while we were waiting.

I take a sip from my drink, enjoying the taste. This is like… so different from the premade bubble tea you can buy at the store, or the instant versions.

I collect a couple of the orbs from the bubble tea into my straw at the same time and then suck them up, popping each one in my mouth individually. These bubbles are quite different from the instant ones, not as squishy, but they're still really nice, and really fun too. And they're cold, so that's an extra bonus.

I realise Jason and Mya are staring at Elliot and me. I look at Elliot too, and just watch him pop a few bubbles in his mouth. Then Jason looks at me and grins, winking.

Okay, so maybe I've found someone who drinks their bubble tea the same way I do. "See? It's not that strange."

Jason takes a breath, and then shakes his head a little. "No, still not convinced. Now I just know *two* people who drink their bubble tea the same way. Doesn't mean everyone drinks it like that."

"What?" Elliot looks up, a little distracted. "I was drinking. What is it about drinking bubble tea a certain way?"

"Nothing." Jason grins. "Just drink it."

"Right." Elliot raises his eyebrow at me, and I pull up my shoulders.

"No idea." I smile. "Good stuff though."

"I know. This is *really* nice." Elliot nods. "Do you have any place or panel you want to go see later?"

I think for a moment. "There is a stand with The Ancient Magus' Bride fan stuff, I want to go there. And... I don't know. Usually, I don't get to 'do' a whole lot, with people trying to get my photo taken all the time and everything."

"Yeah. Right." Elliot nods, he probably gets that a lot too, if he cosplays regularly. Then he looks at Mya. "You want to go anywhere?"

"There is a panel on fanfic and fan art in like..." She checks her phone. "Two hours."

"*Oh!* Oh." Jason holds up his hand, grabbing his own phone. "There's a cosplay panel in like... thirty minutes. You wanted to go there, right?" He looks at me.

"Oh. Yes." I always love learning more about making costumes. I study fashion design at higher professional education, but that's mostly fairly normal type of clothing designs, 'regular' clothes. I love learning stuff at cons because they often have to recreate things from anime or games and such that aren't supposed to work in this world, like the skirt I'm wearing right now. "We should probably try to get to the room then, they're going to stop us a lot on our way there." I eye Elliot. "You coming too?"

Before Elliot can answer, there are loud voices behind us. "Izzy! Jay!" Ruby and Kevin come our way, also carrying drinks. They're followed by Evelyn and Mark, two more of our 'gang'. "Look who we—" Ruby's mouth falls open, staring at Elliot. "Whoa! Where did you pick up that cutie?"

I sigh, rolling my eyes at Ruby's antics. "Ruby, everyone, this is Elliot. Elliot, these are friends of ours, Ruby, Kevin, Evelyn and Mark. Don't worry, they're not actually dangerous."

"Hey, talk for yourself." Kevin grins.

"Yeah, yeah." I roll my eyes at him this time. "Oh, and that's Mya." I point at the girl on the other side of the table. Maybe I can distract them for a bit with her?

"Hi!" Ruby waves at Mya, then he sits down on my other side. "So, anyone have you done anything fun yet? Bought something cool?" He takes a sip from his green bubble tea. "It's so busy inside that it's hard to see if I actually want something."

"I bought a plushie of Deimos." Elliot's voice is a quiet.

"Really?" Kevin steps a little closer. "Can I see? You should know that Izzy is addicted to that game, though I don't know about the anime." His eyes shine.

"Addicted?" Elliot eyes me as he pulls a really cute version of Deimos out of a bag. "I got the last one from the stand. Emma didn't have any more."

"Ah, you got it from Emma. That makes sense." Kevin sits down on Elliot's other side. "She makes awesome things."

Elliot looks from Kevin to the plushie and then to me. "Yeah. I'd seen it online once, but I never knew where I could get one."

I shrug. "Emma isn't that active online. She likes to keep a low profile. But you said something about cosplaying Deimos before?"

Elliot nods. "Last year at the con."

Last year... I try to think back. "Both days or just one day?"

"Both days, but I was in the competition too. We went as a group, me and two friends. We went as Deimos, Athena and Phobos."

"Oh. *Yes.*" I now remember him. "You got second place for the group cosplay. You looked really cool. I wished I'd gotten a picture with you, but it was just too busy." I shake my head.

"You got a pic this time." Elliot's eyes sparkle a little, and I laugh.

"That, I did. We should totally get more, though. But maybe later." I shrug, not wanting to overwhelm the guy by being too excited, which I know I can be.

"Sounds good." He seems fine with the idea?

"Hey, you two would probably look totally cool in Destruction of Elysium cosplay. Elliot in Deimos cosplay, and you as FrIzzyBang." Evelyn leans over.

"FrIzzyBang?" Elliot frowns at me.

"My Destruction of Elysium character in the game. I cosplayed her a while back. Though, I'd have to create a totally new cosplay. My gear has been upgraded, and I don't look like

54

that anymore." That, and... Ehhh... Yeah... My body has changed some, so I'm not even sure if all the parts of the cosplay would still fit comfortably. But I don't have to share that with the others, that's just... my body.

That's just one of those things that happen when your body is starting to shape more like the body you want and wished you were born with. Things like needing bigger bra sizes when you've not gained any significant weight on other parts of your body. And if you have to wear tight clothes for a cosplay, just one bra size up means that you'll have to remake it or deal with the extra squish from the fit... Remaking is usually a better idea.

But none of those specific details are important in the first fifteen minutes of getting to know someone, especially since I can get graphic when nobody stops me...

6
Elliot

Doujinshi = Self-published works in Japan. When it comes to mangas, this usually refers to either fan-made mangas (fanfiction) or original work made by amateur or professional mangaka (manga artists) that isn't published through a mainstream publisher. Doujinshi aren't as easy to get your hands on around here, though with the internet and scanlation groups these days, it's a lot easier, at least in digital form. I like doujinshi because it allows me to read stories that aren't just mainstream, and they can go a little weird sometimes. I tend to look them up for fanfiction about my favourite characters. Usually, doujinshi features things that wouldn't show up in the original manga or anime but that a lot of us fans would enjoy reading about, like more explicit scenes or just wish fulfilment type of love stories of certain characters in the story that aren't actually together.

I'm surrounded by people who really don't seem to care what I wear or look like. It's strange but also makes me feel more at ease with my choice of costume. They're friendly, if sometimes a little too touchy-feely and coming too close to me, and that still makes me nervous, I just don't really know why. Maybe because I'm not used to it, the being close or the way I'm dressed.

We nearly didn't make it to the cosplay panel on time, as Izzy and I kept getting asked to pose for pictures and hugs and stuff like that. It was fun but also kind of made getting here a little more complicated, which we knew, and we still left too late…

After being with the others for a while, I seem to get used to them more, and their general banter and interactions start to feel comforting. Even Mya gets on really well with Evelyn, who seems to watch the same type of anime and read the same type of manga, all ones I don't really enjoy. I'm not into the whole guy on guy and slash and stuff like that. It's just not for me, though… that doesn't mean that I've not enjoyed my fair share of doujinshi, it just tends to feature guy on girl or girl on girl couples.

Izzy is paying very close attention to the people giving the panel, listening to everything that they're saying, the serious look in her eyes making me smile.

I carefully bump my shoulder into hers, and she glances at me, blinking a moment. "Don't you already know all this stuff?" I know that she's been the contest winner two years in a row, isn't this old news to her?

Izzy shrugs a little. "I always learn something new. There's always something I don't know yet." Her eyes flit to the front of the room and then she looks at me again. "I'm studying fashion, so I often need to design new outfits. Even if I'm not going to be using something for a cosplay, I often find that I'm using these ideas for other things I design for my classes too."

"Fashion?" I hadn't expected that.

"Yeah." She smiles. "It works together well with designing cosplays, and I get to spend even more time making clothes. I also sell dresses and other things I make. It's really fun." Her eyes start to shine as she talks about it.

"Cool. I'm very boring, I study English Literature." I shrug a little.

"Nah." Izzy shakes her head. "You have to do what you're good at or what you like. I'm just good at making dresses and other clothes."

"I agree." I purposefully look her up and down. "You're really good at it." A compliment can't hurt, right?

Izzy blushes a little. "Thanks?" She smiles. "Oh, they're talking about props. Gotta pay attention to this." She flashes me a quick smile again and then focuses on the front of the room. She's definitely interesting, even just to watch.

I listen to the panel, though I don't know how much I find that's useful for me. That may be because last year they had the almost exact same panel or because there is someone much more interesting right next to me.

Either. Or. Both?

W A S D

I find Izzy, Evelyn and Mya sitting at the front of the room during the fanfiction and fan art panel. I'm joining them a little late as I just got back from signing up for the cosplay competition.

Between the line being too long at first and then getting distracted, I still hadn't done signed up and I don't want to miss out. With Izzy to compete against, I don't know if I'll even make a chance, but that doesn't mean I shouldn't at least try.

Jason and the other guy, Ruby, are standing to the side. The room is really full. I don't know why exactly, but it's busier than it was during the cosplay panel earlier.

"Hi." I stand a little awkwardly with the other two. "Anything interesting?"

Jason leans over a little. "The guy on the far side of the table, the furthest away from us, he draws like... boy love stuff, and he also writes fanfics. So there have been a couple of people *very* interested in listening to him." He raises his eyebrows as he looks at Izzy, Evelyn and Mya, and then I also spot Kevin on Mya's other side.

Right. "They want to meet a famous person then?" I grin as I look at them.

"Yeah. Sort of." Ruby laughs quietly. "This always happens. You always lose one or two people to the panels." He checks his phone. "Hey, wanna go sit somewhere else? This is going to take at least another half an hour, and my legs are getting tired."

"Sounds good." Jason nods.

"Yeah." It's not like I can join Izzy and Mya at the front, it's too crowded, and just standing here, in my heels, it's going to be a long panel that way.

Ruby walks back to the door, quietly leaving, and we follow him.

"Any preference for where to go?" He turns around, looking at us.

"Somewhere we can sit, preferably." Jason laughs. "There's a bar thing just around the corner here. We can try there, and it will be easier for the others to find us again later." He eyes us both and then starts walking.

The bar-thing, really just a maid cafe setup, is luckily not as busy as I'd expected it to be and there are a couple of free tables around.

We sit down at one of the tables at the edge of the cafe and as soon as we're seated, both Jason and Ruby take off their shoes under the table.

"Way better." Ruby grins, letting out a satisfied sigh.

I shake my head, smiling, quickly slipping out of my own heels. They're right though. This does feel a lot better, especially since the day is still going to be very long. It's just past two in the afternoon, but while the main event closes at seven, there is a ball tonight, so we've got a long day ahead of us still.

"Hey." Jason looks my way, a little more serious than I've seen him before.

"Yeah?"

He licks his lips a few times. "Izzy is going to kick my butt if she hears about this, but whatever." He takes a deep breath. "Don't hurt her. Don't do something stupid. Yeah?"

Independent Izzy, yeah, I can see her giving him problems for talking about her like this. "Why are you telling me this?"

"Because you haven't kept your eyes off her since you first saw her." Jason raises an eyebrow, like he's challenging me to deny it.

"Maybe. But that doesn't have to mean anything. She's cool, and sweet, and funny." I shrug, he's not wrong. "Lots of people look at her."

"'Lots of people' don't get to hold her hand." Ruby looks around and holds his hand up. One of the maids comes over. "Can we have a green tea, a..." He looks my way.

"Milk tea." I smile at the maid.

"And a..." Ruby looks at Jason.

"Also a green tea, thanks." Jason smiles too.

"Two green tea and a milk tea, coming up." The maid

flashes us a big smile before she bows and walks off again.

"Anyway." Ruby looks at me. "She doesn't let a lot of people close. So, don't hurt her."

They're acting like I'm some stupid prick who would hurt a sweet girl over nothing. I'm not sure if I should be annoyed or seriously offended right now.

"We're not trying to be mean, or trying to keep you away from her." Jason shakes his head. "Like we even could with Izzy. We're just asking you to be careful with her. She's..." He licks his lips again, looking at his hands and then at Ruby before he looks at me. "She's been through a lot."

Ruby also nods, his eyes serious. "Life hasn't always been easy on her. She's been better lately, but it's not always like that. And… Just be careful with her."

I look at them both. Are they going to give me more details about why instead of just this cryptic stuff, or what? "And this is so important for me, why?" Like life is easy for anyone.

"Because once Izzy decides someone is her friend... You'll get dragged into the experience that is Izzy's life." Jason lets out a short laugh. "That comes with ups and downs."

"True. Very true." Ruby nods. "And what an experience that is. Hey." He frowns at Jason now, apparently changing course in our conversation. "Did she fix that skirt for you this morning? Or isn't this your outfit for tomorrow?"

"Oh, no. Izzy fixed it. Hence us being later than planned this morning, but I've got a different outfit for tomorrow. We decided on something else at the last minute." His eyes sparkle with joy.

"Are you going to share what it is?" Ruby raises an eyebrow at him.

Apparently, the whole discussion about being careful

around Izzy is over now. Just as well, I don't know how to respond to it anyway.

"Nope. You'll have to see tomorrow. Izzy and I came up with a cool idea together." Jason leans back a little as the maid comes back with our drinks.

"One green tea, a milk tea and another green tea." She puts the cups down in front of us. "You want to pay now or later?"

I look around at the others, but Ruby grabs his card out of somewhere. "I'll pay for all three of us. I'd like to pay by card."

"You don't have—" I almost stand up, but Ruby holds out his hand to me.

"It's just a drink, don't worry. We're all friends here." He stands up.

The maid looks a little amused at us. "If you'd like to follow me. You can pay by card at the till."

"I'll be right back." Ruby winks at us as he follows the girl. I can just about hear him compliment her on her outfit as they walk off and she giggles.

As I sit back down, I realise something else. I don't even have my wallet with me. Mya has my wallet. I couldn't even have paid, even if they'd let me, unless I'd gone to pick it up first. *Ugh.*

"What is it?" Jason laughs.

"Mya has my wallet. I only have my phone on me, not my wallet." I let out a groan. "I couldn't even have paid for the drink." Why do I always forget these things?

Jason laughs louder now. "Ah, yeah. That complicates things. You don't have pockets in the skirt or otherwise on the dress?"

I shake my head. "Never done them before. This is my first..." I take a deep breath. "This is the first dress I've made." There, I've said it. That's why I'm still a little uncomfortable dressed like this. It's my first time.

"Ah. Yeah. You should talk to Izzy about that. She'll teach you how to hide pockets in a cosplay outfit." Then he looks a little more serious. "Is this your first time crossdressing, or just crossplaying?"

"First time crossplaying. I've crossdressed for a while. Just…"

"Usually not outside with people you know?"

I shake my head. "Not usually. Mya knows, but nobody else really knows."

"Don't worry. Honestly, as long as you like it, what's the harm?" He smiles. "I've been doing it since I was… I don't know, before puberty hit." He grins. "Long time."

"Yeah. I've never had the courage before. I don't know. It's scary." I run my hands over my dress, they're getting sweaty from nerves now.

"It can be. But, don't worry here. Lots of people really don't care. That's the best part."

"I know. It's just in my head." I shrug. Lots of things are in my head. As usual.

Ruby comes back, carrying three cupcakes with him. "I do hope you're not allergic or have an aversion to sweets, do you?" He looks at me.

I shake my head, grinning. "Nope."

"Good." He puts one of the cupcakes in front of me, then one in front of Jason and then he sits down. "They looked too good to pass up."

"They do look really good, yes." I nod, picking it up. It also smells really sweet, and it makes me realise that we haven't actually had lunch or anything yet.

I take a bite, savouring the sweet and sugary goodness. Oh,

this is definitely good.

Time passes quickly as we're talking sweets, food, dresses and other things that come to mind. Jason and Ruby are pretty cool guys, and they're easy to become friends with.

Until there are quick footsteps and Izzy is standing next to me, her hand on my arm.

"Come. Come. We need to get to the competition. They're about to start lining everyone up!" Her eyes sparkle, and she's grinning broadly. "Come on. We don't want to be late!"

7
Izzy

Slash = In fanfiction, the pairing of the fanfic in question is usually written as name/name, the slash between the names is now synonymous with a specific type of fanfiction, the male/male (and as fem-slash, female/female) fanfiction. Using the word slash in this way is not appreciated by everyone, and some people feel that there should be a better way to refer to these types of fanfiction, even though it's an easy shorthand to talk about non-straight fanfiction. Related to this is the term 'slashable', which is a way to refer to official anime or manga which makes it very easy to write fanfiction of certain characters because they're already really close, or because they act in ways that could be interpreted as more than just friendship. I like things that are slashable because I love imagining characters together, and to imagine them having a happy loving ending in the story, even if they may not end up like that in the real story.

After the fanfiction and fan art panel, Evelyn, Mya, Kevin and I just kind of got stuck in the room for a while. It was so fun to talk to people who make fan art of fandoms that I really love, that I kind of lost track of time. So I had to rush to get us all to the cosplay contest on time. But we did make it, luckily, only barely.

One of the cosplay contest staff, Annabelle according to her name tag, looks at Elliot and me. "And you're going together, right? That means you need to talk to—" It seems like she doesn't even question it, just confirming what she's already assuming since she's the one in charge of the individual cosplayer section of the contest.

"No." I shake my head. "We're both on our own."

"Oh." Annabelle looks surprised, blinking. "Right. Sure. Could you point out your name on the list?" She holds the board with the list in front of me.

Then Elliot tugs on the sleeve of my dress and I turn to him, curious. "Yeah?"

"We could do it, you know." He looks a little awkward.

"Do what?" I'm getting lost now, my eyes scanning the list again, trying to find my own scrawls from the signing up.

"Go as a team. We'd make a pretty good chance at winning."

I look his way again. "What?" I've not done that before, I've always gone on my own, I've always preferred to go on my own.

"If we go as a team, we'd probably win, and we wouldn't have to compete against each other." He's got a point, there.

I look at Annabelle. "We're going to need a minute."

"Not much more than a minute." She smiles, but her eyes already scan the other people waiting around. "I've got to finalise the list."

"Sure." I nod, tugging Elliot to the side. "Are you sure?" Because this is kind of a big change so suddenly, especially since we didn't prepare anything.

He shrugs, and I'm not sure how I should read the way he looks. "Unless you think I'd pull down the quality of your cosplay." He keeps looking so insecure. "I guess that *could* be an issue. I'm sorry. Forget I said anything."

"No." I shake my head. Does he really think that? "I've just... I've always been on my own. I hadn't thought about it." I look at Elliot and then at how well we work together, how easy getting to know him has been and how easily we've been able to pull some of the team moves for shots. "You think we can do it? Pull off a signature move together? We still need to have a little 'act' thing, you know?"

He nods, smiling a little. "I know. I don't think that should be an issue. We just have to time it correctly. Just make sure that we don't step in each other's way and stuff."

"I guess." I shrug. I *guess* that could work. And Elliot is right, it would mean that we wouldn't have to compete against each other. Because no matter how insecure he is about his skills, I'm not sure I'd win against him. "We should give Kevin a chance to win too, you know." I wink at Elliot, who grins. Kevin is competing as his genderswapped Violet.

"True. Gotta give the peasants a chance too." Elliot grins even more when he spots someone behind me.

"Who is calling me a peasant?" Kevin steps up right behind me, his arms around my waist.

"Nobody." I laugh, trying to get out of his embrace, away from those tickly fingers that could start at any moment.

"Right." Kevin laughs too, then lets me go. "You need to get ready, they're about to begin."

"Right!" I grab Elliot's hand and pull him along. We've got to change our sign up sheets.

My grin tugs on my cheeks and I try to look normal again.

This is fun, this is so unexpected and fun. Wow.

⌨ W A S D

I'm out of breath, trying to keep the final pose of the sequence long enough as I look at Elliot from the corner of my eyes. He's out of breath too, but also grinning broadly.

Then we stand up and take a little bow.

"For group cosplay number twelve, Sakura and Aoi from Magical Princess Club." The announcer sounds really excited about us, though, he sounds excited after every contestant.

The audience claps loudly, cheering and calling.

I take Elliot's hand, mine is shaking from the adrenaline, and then we take another little bow before we walk off the stage at the back.

That was so awesome, that was just... *Wow.*

Jason shows up with two bottles of water. "Nobody would have figured out that you only decided on that like... ten minutes ago." He grins as he hands us the bottles.

"Shut it." I carefully keep taking breaths, the dress isn't as easy to breathe in as it looks... It's kind of tight around my waist and I'm still out of breath. I thought it was just the adrenaline, but maybe I should have considered more than just walking around when I made the costume…

"Need me to loosen the back a little?" Jason steps closer, but I shake my head. Then I walk to a chair near the wall at the back of the area where the contestants wait during the contest.

I sit down, carefully breathing, long and as deep as possible breaths. It's just too hot. Way too hot in here, that's making it worse. I'm sure of it.

"Take a sip." Elliot holds an opened bottle out to me. When I don't take it immediately, he raises an eyebrow. "I didn't do anything with it, I didn't even take a sip yet. Just take it. You can't accept another win in this contest if you're passed out cold, you know. That would be a shame."

I accept the bottle and take a couple of deep gulps from it. The water is still cold, which is good because it cools me down.

I shouldn't have done that sequence in this dress. The one shortcoming of this dress, and this whole outfit, it's hard to breathe in when it's warm, it sticks to my skin too much.

Annabelle comes over to us, looking at me closely. "Are you okay? Do I need to get someone from the first-aid?"

I shake my head. "I'm good. Just a little hot. I'll be fine in a moment." *Probably.* I smile at her.

"Okay. Just let me know, yeah?" She keeps looking at me.

I smile. "Yeah, will do." I get why they get worried, like… the organisation is responsible for like… not getting people injured and all, but I really am good, just a little too hot.

"Okay." She walks off again, though keeps looking back a couple of times.

I lean back on the chair, my head against the wall. My breathing now easier. "Everybody can stop staring at me. I'm good. I'll be fine." I know that Jason and Elliot are still looking at me.

"Yeah, yeah. Just finish the bottle." I hear Elliot move, and when I open my eyes for a moment, he's standing next to my chair, leaning against the wall, also sipping from a bottle.

I like that they care, but do they have to be this overbearing? It's not like I can't take care of myself, you know. Though, it's not like I've not done the whole 'going against the floor from overheating' thing around Jason before… More than once…

"How long until they announce the winners?" I sit up straight again, looking at the back of the stage.

"Half an hour or something." Jason shrugs. They had the individual contestants first, and now they're doing the 'groups' second. After this is all finished, there will be voting and everything, and only after that will they announce the winners.

I look around, half an hour... That's not enough time to go outside for some fresh air and get back here on time for the ceremony. Bummer.

Because if we move out of this area, we're going to be stopped for pictures every step of the way, as has been happening all day. So it'll probably take half an hour just to go out there, let alone trying to get back here...

I sigh.

Right.

Staying here it is.

W A S D

"Third place goes to group number five, Ren, Pito and M from 'Sword Art Online Alternative: Gun Gale Online'."

The crowd cheers, as three amazing cosplayers step onto the stage, and wave at everyone. They're out on stage a couple of minutes as they get asked a some questions, and then, as people keep cheering, they come back off the stage.

I'm too nervous to really listen to what's going on, just focusing on the names being called out.

We're just waiting with the fifteen 'groups' back here, all waiting to hear the results.

"Second place goes to group number fifteen, Henrietta and Marielle from Log Horizon." Again, not us... Two people step onto the stage, and everything starts all over again.

I grip Elliot's hand, too nervous. I'm just so nervous. I guess that going on my own doesn't give me as much anxiety, but this...

Yeah… This really does make me nervous.

I'm not good with sudden changes, I should have thought of that before I agreed to all of this, I think. Maybe. *Probably.*

When Henrietta and Marielle come back off the stage, I hold my breath.

"And now… We all want to know which group won, right? Who are your favourites?"

The crowd calls out a lot of names, but I'm not sure if I'm imagining things or that Sakura and Aoi are the names called out the loudest.

The announcer waits until everyone is quiet again. "First place, the winners of this year's group cosplay contest, are…"

I gasp, because holding my breath really isn't such a good idea.

"Number twelve, Sakura and Aoi from Magical Princess Club!"

My mouth falls open, and I stare at Elliot. *We won!* We did it! Not that I really believed anything else, but this is awesome. This is *so* cool.

"Come on." Elliot grins as he pulls on my hand.

I nod as we both walk onto the stage.

We won!

The crowd is cheering, yelling, and I keep grinning. Awesome.

We walk to the front of the stage where Annabelle is standing, holding a trophy for us. She hands it to both of us. Then she turns to the crowd. "Let's hear it for our winners!"

The noise is almost deafening now.

"Okay." Annabelle turns to us. "What is it like to cosplay probably *the* most slashable female couple of this anime season?"

I look at Elliot, stunned by the question. Annabelle is not

wrong, Sakura and Aoi kind of are very slashable, I hadn't even thought of that when we decided on this…

"Ehhh…" Elliot looks a little uncomfortable and then looks my way. Oh, yeah. The speaking thing…

I take a deep breath, turning to the crowd. "I guess it's kind of special, but especially unexpected. We hadn't really planned this." I grin. "This working together was kind of a last minute thing."

"Really? You pulled it off really well though." Annabelle smiles.

"It only comes from the power of being such fans of the anime that we can do anything when it comes to Sakura and Aoi, no matter if we practised it ahead or not." I grin, shrugging.

"Kiss! Kiss!" Someone starts chanting, and I glare in the direction of the voice, but others start to take it up too.

Kissing? Oh, no. *Nope.*

"Hey, that's not nice to ask of such cute girls." Annabelle must have seen that we're not really comfortable with it, plus it's just a bad move to demand something like that.

"Boo!" Of course, not everyone agrees with that, and I know the way some guys look at people cosplaying cute female characters... It's like we're just here to make their dirty fanfiction dreams come true.

I take a quick breath, putting on my best smile. Then take the microphone and turn to the public, especially in the direction of the people calling out for us to kiss. "Be nice to kawaii princesses. Or I'll have to defeat you with the power of *chuu.*" I put on my best anime voice and make the most exaggerated movements and faces, ending by blowing a kiss into the public.

There is one way to stop people from being too creepy, and that's to give them just enough to satisfy whatever interest they have, while keeping enough of a distance and putting boundaries in place about what you'll do. You learn to do this quickly, but it's never easy, especially when you don't exactly know if it could have a worse effect down the line.

But I have to stop this before it gets worse. Elliot isn't that comfortable crossplaying, and this would only have added to him being uncomfortable.

And I don't really want to kiss just some guy, just because some guys call out for me to do so. Nope, no way.

Okay, a really cute and sweet guy, who I wouldn't mind kissing in general, I just don't want our first kiss to be in front of all these people on a stage. Just, nope.

I bow to the crowd one last time and then tug on Elliot's hand as we get off the stage.

Time to get away from all the crazy, preferably to some fresh and cool air, and not with stupid people around.

8
Elliot

Trap = A derogatory term used to refer to people who are crossdressing. Usually of the male to female variety, where the man in question looks so much like a woman or girl that they're mistaken for being a woman or girl until the 'big reveal' of the sex of the man, usually by revealing a big ehh... member from under a skirt. This is a horrible way to refer to people or to use in stories, and I don't like it. But that doesn't mean that you don't sometimes run into the term, usually in explicit manga or anime. It's even worse when it's applied to people who are transgender, because it invalidates their whole being and their problems, since trans women aren't 'men in a dress' and trans men aren't 'women with short hair and in jeans'. I hate the word, it feels wrong on many levels.

After we won the cosplay competition, I was so overwhelmed, my head spinning. I just didn't know what to do when I stood on that stage, I didn't want to talk, too scared that my voice would break the illusion, and then they wanted us to kiss... I was mortified. Luckily, Izzy was able to save the day, and in a very cute way too. She probably has more experience in that department than I have, trying to get people to stop being creepy, this is my first time that I had to deal with it.

"Let's go." Izzy grins, still holding my hand. "I really want to go outside now, I need fresh air." Then she looks at me, her eyes going more serious. "Are you okay?"

I nod. "Just a little... overwhelmed." I try to smile, but it falters just a smidgen.

Izzy nods, smiling at me, her gaze warm. "We need cool drinks and probably stock up on some sugar." She tugs on my arm again. "But let's get outside first, we can figure things out from there. Air!" She pretend-gasps, making me snicker.

"True." I walk after her. "It's not like we have to be places now the competition is over."

"Right?" Izzy nods, her eyes shining. "We can relax now. Finally."

I feel that someone is staring at us, a shiver going through me, and not in the good way. "Did you hear that?" A low voice a way off sneers. "*Trap*. Like, real life trap. Broken dream here, you know? Can't the cute girls be actually girls?"

"Oh. God. That's a *guy*?" Another low voice joins in.

Izzy stills, her body going tight, then she turns around slowly, dangerously.

"Yeah. Like... No wonder Sakura didn't want to kiss *that*." The first voice is at it again.

When I look at Izzy, her eyes are flaring. Uh, oh. "Izzy?" I'm not sure that's such a good idea... We're not allowed to fight in here, and she seems ready to draw blood.

"Wait here for a moment." She flashes me a smile, almost only teeth, that I don't really trust.

"Izzy?" I try to keep holding her hand, but she's moving too quickly.

Izzy stands in front of the guys, who are way taller than she is even in her heels, her legs a little apart, steady, her whole body wired for a fight. I'm not sure this is going to end well. I look around, trying to find any of her friends, but I don't spot anyone.

"*What* did you say about Aoi?" She puts her hands on her hips, glaring at them.

"Nothing. Just... You know... He's *that.*" The first guy doesn't look so sure anymore, and people are stopping around us, looking on. Nothing draws a crowd like a fight, and I'm getting really nervous now.

"He's what? Dressed up as Aoi and the winner of the cosplay contest?" She cocks her head to the side, and I feel how others are stepping in closer.

"He's got a... *thing.*" The second guy now frowns. "And he's dressed in a skirt."

"So?" Izzy looks back at me, her eyes going over me, almost like she's looking at me from their perspective, making shivers go down my spine, but when I meet her eyes, there is no joking or fun in them, just anger. Then she looks back at the guys. "He looks good in a skirt, and him just winning the contest means that a lot of people think that he looks good as Aoi too."

"But..." There is something in Izzy that makes the guys back away a little.

"If you're so small minded... Maybe you shouldn't be coming here. If you're so superficial, this place isn't for you." Izzy stares them down. "People here are openminded and accepting, this is a safe place. We do not accept bigotry and hatred at AmAnime."

"No, we don't." Two girls step next to Izzy, hooking their

arms through Izzy's, standing between the guys and me. "Small-minded thinking is not welcome here."

I didn't know what to expect. But definitely not this. I take a deep breath, suddenly feeling a lot safer and protected.

And maybe I'm feeling even a little *more* for Izzy right now, my heart beating faster.

I step behind Izzy, putting my hand on her shoulder. "Yeah. If you can't accept people for who they are, or what they do, this is not your convention." Being surrounded by people who get that gives me courage, let me speak up again.

"I'd scram, if I were you." Ruby's low voice comes from behind us. "Izzy can be pretty violent when it comes to bigots and bullies." He steps next to me and grins, winking. Where did he come from? Was he here the whole time? It wouldn't surprise me.

"Weirdos." One of the guys grumbles, but then they're off anyway, pushing their way through the crowd that has gathered around us.

Cheers break out again, and I look around, not really believing what just happened. Did this really just happen? Did Izzy just stand up for me? Did kind strangers from the convention stand up and scare off some bad guys?

Wow.

That was... *Wow.*

After the incident with the guys earlier, the rest of the afternoon was a lot calmer. We were asked to do a couple more photos with people, and during dinner time, we actually did a photo shoot with one of Izzy's friends, Justin. That was really fun, and I never expected how much I'd enjoy it.

We got some great shots of us doing some of the action poses from Magical Princess Club! and then also some sweet pictures, just sitting around, looking cute. It surprised me how much I really look like Aoi in the pictures, how *girly* I look.

After dinner, we quickly went to our rooms to freshen up, before we came down again for the ball. Some people have special outfits just for the ball, but I don't, I'm just in the same Aoi cosplay as before, but with some touched-up makeup and everything, since the heat really took a toll on the makeup.

Two of the big panel rooms have been converted into a single ballroom, with chairs on the outsides and even a bar, and there is already loud music coming from it. It's easy to spot Izzy and Jason, as they're dancing at the edge of the dance floor, both totally engrossed in the music and just joking with each other, having a great time. They're fun to watch.

"Let's go over to them." Mya smiles, guiding me to where Izzy and Jason are dancing, and I spot Ruby and some of the others sitting in chairs not far off. They're all here, some have changed into different outfits, but most of the cosplayers haven't. Izzy and I are both still dressed as Sakura and Aoi.

"Elliot! Mya!" Ruby waves at us. "Come here, you *have* to save us."

"From what?" But as soon as I reach them, someone grabs my wrist and Izzy is grinning at me, already slightly tugging on my arm.

"From her." Ruby laughs. "She's been wanting to dance with everyone since this started."

"Right…" I grin back at Izzy. That, I can probably deal with.

"Can I have this dance?" Izzy curtsies.

"Just this *one?*" I take her other hand too. "I'm not sure you understand the challenge."

"I don't?" Izzy steps closer, her eyes shining, laughing.

"Oh, no." I slide my hands down to her waist and pull her a little closer, our dresses bunching up between us. "You have no idea. You see, I don't do just *one* dance. Did nobody explain that to you?"

Izzy grins. "They must have forgotten to tell me." She wraps her arms around my neck.

"Are you up for it?" I love watching her laugh, the way her whole body moves with it, how joyful it looks.

"I guess we'll find out." She starts moving, almost pulling me along, until I step in line with her movements.

I wrap my arms around her waist tighter. She's so slim, I'm still surprised that she's not wearing a corset under the dress. Sakura's dress is tighter than Aoi's, and I don't think I'd have been able to pull it off without a corset or anything like that to tighten my waist, although, she does have some ribbons to tighten the dress at the back.

Izzy lets out a ringing laugh, so happy. Just so excited. I can't help but laugh too.

I let go a little of her, and she lets her arms slip from around my neck. Then I twirl her, and her dress flares out to the sides, showing the layers and layers of underskirts she's wearing, then she spins right back into my arms, and I catch her, still moving to the music as I keep her close.

Her eyes sparkle as she flashes me a mischievous grin. "Now your turn."

"What?" I let out a little squeak as she grabs my arm, but I still automatically follow her guide, not able, or wanting, to stop her.

The world spins for a couple of moments, until I'm back in Izzy's arms. I don't think I've been this giddy without any alcohol, or anything else, before, just drunk on life or something. No matter how cheesy that sounds. Every moment at Izzy's side is a surprise and makes me so happy, so giddy.

Before she can spin me again, I make sure to hold both my arms around her waist, and we spin together, round and round. Izzy's giggling is keeping me going and I'm not stopping.

Somewhere, I realise that people are staring at us, taking pictures. It must be quite the sight. Sakura and Aoi just twirling around the place, laughing, having fun. If we didn't want our pictures taken, we probably shouldn't have dressed up in such flashy cosplay anyway.

I think the spinning is getting to a point where things are getting a little less fun, though. My stomach is starting to object, just like my head.

When we pass by some abandoned chairs, I stop us and let us both fall onto the chairs. I can't stop my laughter, the feeling still bubbling up inside me, my cheeks aching from constantly smiling. This is crazy.

Izzy is taking deep breaths, still grinning, then she looks my way. "You weren't kidding about it being a challenge."

"No, not really." I wink at her. Once I start something, it's hard to make me stop. That's the advantage, or disadvantage, of being me.

"You're crazy. In a good way." She shakes her head, reaching out and touching my hand for a moment. "I demand another dance later."

"Later? Not now?" I grin.

"No." Izzy pulls a face, puffing out some breaths. "I need to recover first." She makes a great display of acting how tired she is.

Then Jason appears at our side, shaking his head as he's

grinning wide. "You are a miracle, Elliot. You may be the first person who can actually exhaust her." He kneels down next to Izzy, looking up at her. "Yep, first one."

Izzy glares at him. "It's just because I already danced with everyone else before he came in." Then she looks my way. "I still want that other dance later."

"Will do." I nod, taking a deep breath and standing up. "Do you want something to drink?"

Izzy nods. "Just a Coke or something." She smiles.

"Or something. Will do." Then I look at Jason. "You?"

"No thanks. I just had something." He stands up, looking around.

"Okay." I go over to the bar and get a Coke and a Sprite. Then I try to find Mya, maybe she'll want something to drink too, but I see her laughing with Kevin not too far off, already holding a drink. Nothing to worry about there, then. Mya really seems to enjoy herself with this group, maybe even more than she usually does with our other friends.

When I turn back to Izzy, I see her have a serious conversation with Jason and she looks... vulnerable. That's the right word. She looks vulnerable right now, and I don't know how to respond to it. She looked so strong today, filled with so much confidence, but to watch her like this now... I don't know, it feels strange.

When her eyes go over to me, I realise that I'm actually the cause of her looking like that, and that hurts. I don't want her to look like that. I don't want her to ever look like that because of me.

I smile her way, and she flashes me a tight smile back, pulling a mask into place which I can now recognise for what it is. *No!*

I go back over to her, handing her the glass with Coke.

"Feeling up for another dance yet?" I just want to make her laugh again, I want to see her smile again.

She shakes her head a little, averting her eyes. "Just a few more moments. I need to drink something first." She takes a sip, and I can't help but keep watching her every move. She's changed, somewhere between us dancing together and me getting us a drink, something changed.

When I try to catch Jason's eyes, I remember his warning. His warning not to hurt her, his warning that things haven't always been easy for Izzy, aren't always easy for her. That I can't hurt her.

How can I make her smile again? What happened? Why did she suddenly turn like this?

Why?

Why does it hurt so much to see that pain in her eyes? I just want to make it all better again.

But I have no idea how.

9
Izzy

Gender Dysphoria = Distress about the sex and/or gender assigned at birth. This is generally split into two types, physical gender dysphoria and social gender dysphoria. Physical dysphoria is about how you experience your own body and the problems with how your body looks/functions. Social dysphoria is about how others perceive you and respond to who you are, based on their gender assumptions. I don't get much social dysphoria these days, as people usually 'see' me as a girl, but the physical dysphoria can flare up from time to time, and it always catches me off guard. It's the physical side that's always the hardest for me…

When Jason came over to us, I was still laughing with Elliot. But as my heart slowed down, and as my need to touch Elliot became stronger, I knew I was in trouble.

I'm in big trouble. I want to touch Elliot. I want to touch him so badly, I want to kiss him… But that… That can't happen. It just can't.

I'm not sure if Jason realised it before I did, or if he was simply checking in on me after our crazy antics. But I know he felt the change in me too, felt it the moment things went wrong in my head. He knows. He's always been able to sense how I feel pretty easily, he's saved me from panic attacks and other things more than once. How can Jason read me so much easier than I can read myself? Why does he always know how I feel when I don't even know how to explain it to myself?

I think Elliot knows something is up too. He's quieter now, looking at me carefully, his eyes more guarded. I don't want him to look like that, but I don't know how to break him out of it. I don't know how to break him out of that mood without admitting to things I don't want to talk about. I don't even know why it just went bad in my head, and it's my head.

A really cool pair of boots appears in my view. "I'm going out for a smoke, do you want to join me?" Ruby's voice is low, calm, but I can still easily hear it over the music.

I nod, taking the last sips from my glass. "Yeah, I think that's a good idea." Going outside and not being locked in here will probably clear my head some. I turn to Elliot, who smiles carefully. "Are you coming too?" I don't know if it's a good idea to ask him, especially since he's the reason my brain is weird, but not asking him to come with us would be rude. And I still want him with me…

"Sure." He empties his glass too, and stands up. "Some fresh air would be nice."

"I don't know about *fresh*." I raise an eyebrow in Ruby's direction, who shrugs.

"It will be colder, cooler." Ruby smiles.

"Right," Elliot mumbles and then he touches his fingers to my arm. "It will at least be quieter, which is also nice."

My heart skips a beat and my whole body tenses. Quieter,

84

yes. Of all the things he could have said, I'm not sure if *quieter* makes me feel better, because quieter means that we can talk easier, we can hear each other better. And that's... That prospect is scary.

We make our way to the front, flashing our bracelets to the guy at the doors, and then we walk off a little, going to one of the further away picnic tables. Ruby and Jason are with us, but I'm only hyper-aware of Elliot walking next to me.

Before I can sit down, Elliot tugs on my arm. I turn to him, my stomach sinking, especially when I see the pained look in his eyes.

"Izzy?" He licks his lips, his beautiful lips...

I nod, not sure I can say much right now, my heart beating too loudly, my brain and body going weird just looking at him.

"Can I..." He eyes Jason and Ruby, before looking back at me. "Can I talk to you for a moment, alone?"

"Ehm..." Is this even a good idea? But I can't say no to that look in his eyes. I can't say no when everything in my mind and body is so hyper-aware of him and just wants to be close to him. "Sure."

Elliot nods, taking my hand carefully. "We'll be right back." He softly pulls me along, to a more secluded area, a little hidden away from the rest.

I tense up, no longer sure this is a good idea. "Elliot?" My voice is a little weird, and I clear my throat. I need him to look at me. I can protect myself if the worst happens, but I don't want that. I want to prevent getting in a situation that would force me to defend myself in the first place.

"Oh." Elliot turns back to me, his eyes filled with anxiety, then he looks around. "Of course. Sorry. This isn't..." He stops walking, his eyes still darting around. "Sorry. I didn't mean to...

I just wanted to..." He lets go of my hand, running it over the side of his neck. "I just wanted to talk to you, make sure you're okay." He doesn't look at me, his eyes constantly moving away from me, but I'm aware of how he's totally focused on me.

So he did see it. He saw my little break down earlier. I try to smile, try to comfort him, but I feel like he's looking right through it. "I'm okay. It's just been a long day. I'm just tired."

He nods. "Right." He reaches out and touches my arm, sliding his fingers down until they reach my hand, but he doesn't take it, letting me take the initiative for the last bit.

I want this, I want *him*. But I know that I can't do it. I can't do this. *I can't...* I can't go any further because he'll find out that I'm trans, and if he finds out he'll stop doing this, and I don't want that. I don't want to lose this.

But because of the stuff in my head, I don't respond fast enough, and he slowly pulls his hand back

"What's wrong?" There is a flash of emotion going through his eyes, but then something else happens, it's like a wall comes down between us and my heart aches. *No.* "I'm sorry. I just... I thought you... I thought that... Because they also crossdress... I thought that you'd... I'm sorry." The pain in his voice cuts into my heart.

We've been close and friendly all day, touching, hugging, joking around. So me not responding to him must confuse him now. I just wish it wasn't like this. I just wish that there was another way... But I feel it's almost better if he thinks this is about him and not my own problems, if he doesn't question things. *Almost better*, and I feel horrible even thinking it, to use his insecurity like this, but I don't know how to do this in a way that doesn't make it even more painful for the both of us... How to step away now and not hurt him. Or me. "You've got nothing to apologise for. We've had a great day, right?" I carefully take his hand, but I know that it's already broken. Whatever we had, we just broke it, and I let it, I didn't try to prevent the break.

No.

I don't want this. I don't want this to happen.

I don't know what I do want exactly but I know what I can't have, can never have. But I also don't want to have to push him away. It hurts.

"I guess I should..." Elliot moves his other hand nervously, but doesn't take his hand out of mine. That's got to count for something, right?

"Can you..." I don't want him to leave yet. If we leave here, I know that everything will be over. "I'd like to stay here for a while longer. Please?" Tears prick in my eyes, but I will them away. I can't cry now.

He nods. But the wall behind his eyes doesn't go away, it's still there, trying to protect him, trying to not show the pain I can see in his eyes.

If we were in an anime or a simpler world, I'd have kissed him. I'd have kissed him to show that even though I can't say anything, I don't hate him, I don't want to push him away. I'm acting like this *because* I like him. I'm acting like this because I want there to be more between us, and I know that there can't be, and I'm scared.

But I can't. I can't do that. No matter that Elliot is a crossdresser, I'm trans. I'm a girl, but I was born a boy, and no matter how openminded people are... That's usually enough reason for people to not want to be involved with me in anything more than just being friends. When people find out, they push me away, so it's better if we don't even start all of this. It's better if we only get our hearts broken a little bit, not a lot.

No matter how much I'd love to reach out, I can't push this on him, I can't do it. Elliot is cute, he'll find a girl who doesn't have the baggage I have... He'll find someone good.

He'll find someone who deserves him.

I slowly let go of his hand. This is better for both of us. I know it is.

I pretend like I can't see the flash of pain going over his face. I pretend like I can't see that broken look that stabs at my heart.

"Let's go back." I turn around before he can see my mask slip, before he can see these feelings inside, this pain.

When we're halfway back to the table with Jason and Ruby, Elliot touches my back softly. "I'm going back inside. I didn't tell Mya where I was going. I should check on her, make sure she's not worried."

I nod, not able to look at him. "Okay." I try to keep my voice steady. "I'll see you later, back inside." I don't look back at him, though I listen to his footsteps as he walks away, his heels clicking on the pavement.

I blink fast, clenching my jaw, my breathing irregular. This is for the best. Really. No matter how much it hurts.

When I get back to the picnic table, both Jason and Ruby frown as they look at me. I shake my head and sit down next to Jason, who wraps his arm around me and pulls me close. Tears prick in my eyes, and I don't want to cry. Not over this. Not over something so insignificant, not now. My head is starting to hurt from trying to keep myself together.

"What happened?" Jason's voice rumbles in his chest.

"Nothing," I whisper. Which is exactly why this is so hard. Nothing *can* happen. Not now, not ever. Nothing. "This just... This was stupid."

"Are you sure about that?" Ruby sounds serious, and when

I look his way, his eyes are filled with worry.

"Yeah." I nod. "You know I can't just... You *know*. It's not fair to him." I sigh. "This is for the better."

"For who?" Ruby doesn't let up. I know he doesn't agree with my 'don't date' rule, or even my 'no kissing' rule. But I've been hurt too often, even well before I even got to that stage. I don't want to have to go through that pain, or that fear, again. It's better that we now establish this as a friendship and nothing more, than get any further and get hurt down the road. But I don't know how to explain that to Ruby, he never understands.

"I'm going inside." I slip out of Jason's embrace. I can't be here, I need to curl up in bed and be alone for a while.

"Do you want me to come with you?" Jason looks up at me, but I shake my head.

"I'm going to bed. I think I'm just tired. This will probably all be better after I've had some sleep." I try to smile at them. I'm not sure how well that works, but that's okay. They know me, they know me well enough to understand why I have to do this. This will be okay.

I flash my bracelet at the guy at the door and go inside, walking through the front hall as my heart jumps a moment.

There, leaning against the wall next to the doorway to where the ball is taking place is Elliot. He looks upset, pained.

I clench my fists as he spots me, as he pushes himself off the wall, coming over, his eyes so confused.

No. Please, no. I don't know if I can do this again.

"Izzy..." He's getting closer. He's getting so much closer. Now, he's standing in front of me, holding out his hand to me.

And I slide my hand into his, but this time I'm the one tugging him along. I don't want to be out here in the open, it doesn't feel safe. I pull him along to where the elevators are, it's a little more secluded there.

"Izzy?" His voice is so sweet, but so filled with pain. "Please, talk to me. Please, tell me what went wrong. I know you don't want this either, I can see it."

I turn his way. "I want to kiss you." The words spill out, and I don't even regret saying them. It hurts too much just thinking them.

"Me too." Elliot steps closer, his voice dropping, his tongue slipping out over his lips, making them even more inviting.

"But we can't." I put my hands on his chest, suddenly aware of all the ways that we're the same and all the ways we're different. "We can't. You don't know enough about me. I'll disappoint you. You'll hate me later. You'll hate yourself later."

"Why would I?" He doesn't move, his heartbeat fast under my touch. "Who says that you won't be the one disappointed in me?"

Without him knowing it, *that's* what I'm afraid of the most, that I'll have given my heart to someone who will never accept me. Who will disappoint me. Who will hurt me. "There are so many things I have to tell you before we can do this." I really should, but the way he's looking at me, the way he's licking his lips... I have a hard time resisting him any longer.

I *just* want to be a girl. I *just* want to feel like a normal girl, a normal girl taking a chance on kissing a boy she likes.

"Do you already have a boyfriend, or a girlfriend, or a partner?" He looks like he's thinking, trying to come up with an explanation of why I can't do this.

I shake my head. I wish it were as easy as that.

"So, you're totally free to kiss me, technically? And I'm free to kiss you?" There is a spark of hope in his voice, and in his eyes.

I nod. Technically, yes. "But there are just things..." Things he should know, things that will ruin this forever.

"Things that would prevent this kiss from happening? Right now? Things that are standing in the way of a kiss? A simple kiss. A kiss that may be so bad that we may not even enjoy it, but we'll never know until we try?" He flashes a small smile. Like that could happen with him, like he could be a bad kisser...

I don't know how to explain it right now, my mind going a mess. I should tell him about myself, but what's the harm of one kiss? Just *one* kiss? It doesn't even have to mean that much. It's just a kiss.

It's just my first kiss…

Elliot's arms move, and slowly slide around my waist, he's not coming closer, just reaching out, just getting a little more contact. "Can I kiss you?"

I blink, looking at him, trying to find if he's joking or anything, but he looks so serious. I slowly slide my arms up his chest, wrapping them around his neck. "Yes." My voice is low, a sound I didn't expect. Too low for a woman, I think… Alarm bells start to slowly move in my head, not ringing yet, but close. "Please." Before things go wrong.

But before I can second guess what I've just agreed to, *I* step closer to *him*, and put my lips to his. Elliot's lips are warm and a little dry and patchy from wearing lipstick all day. It feels good, for a moment. So good. My first kiss, and it's with such a cute guy too.

Then his stubble scratches my chin and immediately the nagging of my body dysphoria flares up, alarm bells ringing now. *No. Not now.* I try to focus on how Elliot feels against me, how good he feels in my arms. But all I feel are the ways in which he is male and in which I'm still inadequate, and not a girl. All the ways in we're the same, exactly the same, and all the ways I'm not a girl. All the ways I'm not 'right' yet, all the ways I'm still 'wrong'.

My first kiss. It should have been so good, it should have been a happy moment.

Instead... I have a bad flare up of my dysphoria, the worst I've had in a long time, and panic settles in my stomach, making my hands shake, my chest tighten, my head crowd with bad thoughts.

Elliot pulls back, I can see the confusion in his eyes. "Izzy? What's wrong? Did I hurt you?"

I shake my head. He didn't hurt me, not in ways that he could have prevented anyway… He didn't do anything bad, my mind is good at hurting itself…

"Are you okay?" He sounds so worried.

"I need to go to bed." I step out of his arms, not able to look at him, I can't face his disappointment, not now. I can't do it. I need to…

I need to get to my room. I need to be safe. I can't do this. I really can't do this. I shouldn't have done this. I shouldn't have given into my instinct. I shouldn't have kissed him. Bad idea. Bad, bad idea.

"I'm—I'm sorry. It's not you. It's me. I've got... *issues*." I stumble over my words, sighing, still not looking at him. "I'm sorry." Then I make a beeline to the elevators, needing to get away from Elliot.

My dysphoria is fighting with the way my heart is breaking for what's huring the most right now.

This afternoon everything was fine, everything was fun. Now, I've ruined everything.

I wish I'd been born a girl, I wouldn't have had this same

92

problem if I'd actually been born a girl.

Elliot and I could have worked out if I'd been born a girl.

Another point for my messed up self to get in the way of actually doing fun things...

Will this ever go away? This pain? This sadness?

This wish?

10
Elliot

Fujoshi = Japanese for 'rotten girl' = A self-mocking nickname that women who love to read or watch Japanese romances between two men use. More than just a regular anime or Japanese media fan, the fujoshi is also often involved in 'shipping' boys from different media together to create boy love couples they enjoy. If they can't get their couples in canon, they will create them themselves.

I watch as Izzy flees. As soon I held her, she stiffened in my arms, and I could feel the panic settle inside her body. I kept wishing I could help her. But to see that happy girl from today, who I spent time with, who stood up to bullies for me, and to now to see her broken like that... How can I even combine the two? The two are like day and night, and I don't know what I can do.

When I came inside the hotel, I didn't go back to the ball, instead I just stood around, not knowing where to go, what to do. I don't know what I was waiting for, or who I was waiting for. But then Izzy came back inside too, and she looked so lost. I don't know why, but I had to go over to her. I wanted to make her feel better, needed to make sure she was okay.

And then she told me that she wanted to kiss me. Totally blowing me away. I've been feeling the same thing all day, at least all evening. And that kiss…

When she steps into the elevator, she finally looks back at me for a moment, tears sliding down her cheeks, her whole look and stance broken.

Why do I feel like I may never talk to her again? Why do I feel like we just messed up everything? Like we won't be able to go back to how we were all day?

And why does that hurt so much? Why does that thought hurt so much?

Not that I should have expected anything else. What girl would want to date a guy who crossdresses? What girl would want a guy like me, someone who likes dressing up as a girl in his free time?

She may be friends with a crossdresser, but being friends and dating are two totally different things. And you can be friends with people you'd never date… Maybe this is for the best. Maybe this happening now is for the best.

But it doesn't feel like that. It doesn't feel like it's right, because now I've had her in my arms, now I've felt her lips on mine… I only want more, and I'm sure she feels the same.

Low voices come into the hallway, and I recognise Ruby and Jason. *Crap.* Now what?

I guess I better face them right now ,rather than waiting until the morning. Better now, because bruises are easier to hide when they're a couple of hours old. That way you at least know how much you'll have to hide. Don't ask me how I know…

When Jason spots me, he doesn't look angry, just sad, and it takes me by surprise.

They come over to me, but it's Jason who talks first. "Did you see Izzy come in?"

I nod. "Yeah. We ran into each other just now."

He nods, looking troubled.

"She's on her way to the hotel room. She's... upset." I hurt her, I don't know how, but I hurt her, even though Ruby and Jason told me not to.

Jason nods again, I'm not sure how to read him, he's worried about her, but I don't know why exactly.

"We kissed." I don't even know why I offer up the information. "She kissed me, and then got really upset. I don't know why. I'm sorry." Even saying it, I feel bad.

Jason's eyes grow and he takes a quick breath. "Oh... F—" He stops himself. Then he looks at Ruby and again at me. "I think I should go check on her. Make sure she's okay. I'll see you two in the morning."

Ruby looks worried now too. "Yeah. I'll tell the others where you are."

"See you tomorrow." Jason waves at the both of us before he's off towards the elevators too. That was one quick change of pace, and it almost makes my head spin.

I thought that they'd get angry with me, I thought that they'd be really angry. I made Izzy cry after they'd told me not to hurt her.

"Elliot." Ruby's voice makes me look at him. "Some things are just... not easy to explain."

I nod. "I know... I didn't mean to hurt her. It just…" I made a girl cry with a kiss, how low can you go?

Ruby nods, his eyes going softer. "I know. It's just that, even the simplest of things can be really scary for Izzy. And... today has been one surprise after another. It may just have been a little too much for her." He sighs. "You coming back to the ball?"

I shake my head. "I'm going to my room. I think I've had enough of today." And I don't think I can deal with everyone's questioning looks now.

"Sounds like a plan." Ruby puts his hand on my shoulder, his grip firm. "Don't worry about it too much. It'll be okay." Then he walks off.

I don't know how I can't not worry about what just happened, but I guess that I'll just have to trust Ruby. I guess that I'll just have to try to get some sleep and see how everything is in the morning.

Right now, I don't even know if I want to come back out tomorrow. It just feels so scary. I have no idea what to expect next.

Great...

W A S D

I'm in jeans and a t-shirt as I'm having breakfast with Mya in the breakfast hall downstairs. I didn't feel like dressing up just yet. I barely slept last night, though I must have fallen asleep at some point, because when I woke up again, Mya was in her bed too, fast asleep. She seems to have really hit it off with Kevin, and I need to stop myself from letting it bother me. I need to not get jealous over something as silly as Mya having better luck with people than I have.

"You awake enough to talk yet?" Mya's voice is careful, and when she looks at me, I know that she's worried.

I shake my head. "You can try but I don't even know what I should say. There isn't really much to talk about."

"You went outside with Ruby, Jason and Izzy, and Ruby was the only one who came back in. Something must have happened." She keeps looking around the room, and I know she's trying to find Kevin or the others, though I haven't seen any of them yet.

"Yeah. Sort of. Can we just... not talk about this right now?" I poke at the egg on my plate, not feeling like eating anymore.

Mya sits up more. "There they are." She holds up her arm, waving, and when I look up, I immediately lock eyes with Izzy.

Izzy's eyes flare for a moment, but then she pulls her lower lip between her teeth and her face falls. She tugs on Jason's shirt, saying something to him, and then glances my way one last time before she turns around and leaves. No, she doesn't leave, she flees.

"Oh." Mya sounds disappointed. "She left."

"I'll be right back." I stand up. I need to talk to Izzy, I need to check that she's okay. I feel a little like a stalker, but this is the only way I can talk to her...

When I pass Jason by, he grabs my shirt for a moment. "Elliot." His voice stops me.

I glance at him. He has to know I want to talk to Izzy, he has to know I wouldn't hurt her.

"Check the hallways down the left side of the building, that's probably where she went." He lets go of me again. Then he looks up at Mya and waves at her, putting on a smile.

Okay. That's good, right? Right?

I leave the breakfast hall and take a turn left, to the downstairs hallways. When I look around, rounding a corner, Izzy is leaning against the wall in one of the hallways, surrounded by some, for now, empty conference rooms.

"Izzy." I carefully go to her.

98

Izzy stiffens, and then wipes at her eyes. My heart sinks just watching her, I don't want to hurt her. When she looks up, her eyes are red and puffy, and filled with tears. "Morning." Her voice is raw, and she looks away again.

"Morning." I step closer, close enough to touch her, but I keep my hands to myself.

"Why are you here?" She doesn't look at me as she talks.

"Making sure you're okay." I wish she'd look at me again. I wish she'd talk to me, really talk to me.

"I'm okay. You can go." She crosses her arms in front of herself, trying to protect herself, but it only pulls my attention to the 'fujoshi 4 ever' shirt she's wearing and the black and white striped skirt with long rainbow striped socks under them. She's not wearing any shoes. She looks adorable like this, a little like an anime character, a cute one too.

"Izzy..." I reach out, but then pull my hand back. "I didn't want to hurt you. I just want to make you happy." The last words slip out, but I can't take them back, I won't take them back.

Her face constricts. "It's not that easy."

"Why not?"

But she stays quiet.

"I liked the kiss." Until she froze up, that is. I liked the part where she pulled me to her and kissed me, before she shut me out.

Izzy reaches up, running her fingers through her hair, still looking away. "Me too..."

"Can I ask what happened?" Something, just give me something. Please?

"I got overwhelmed and did something impulsive." Her face and her neck colour a little. "And don't laugh at that."

Why would I laugh? She seems so pained by it. She seems

so pained by all of what happened. "Can we kiss again?"

Izzy's eyes shoot up to me, the need in them so strong, but then she shakes her head, a wall coming down. "It's better if we don't."

"Why?" I know she wants it.

"Because I'm not... I'm not who I look like. I just..." She shakes her head, hiding behind her hair. "It's better for both of us if we don't do this." There are tears in her voice, and it takes everything in me not to take her in my arms and try and comfort her.

"Why?"

"You could hurt me, even if you don't mean to. I could hurt you. This is just too much. I'm sorry." She looks up, her eyes filled with tears again, then she puts her hand on my chest, like she's trying to keep me away, but at the same time wants me close. "I wish I could explain it better. But this isn't the time or the place for that. I'm sorry."

Before she can pull back, I take her hand, keeping it to my chest, letting her feel how hard my heart is racing. "I wish you'd explain it. I really want to get to know you better." I step in closer and Izzy steps back against the wall. "You make my heart beat like crazy. Your smile means I can't not smile back. And your tears..." I reach up, slowly sliding my other hand over her cheek, her wet cheek. "They break my heart. I know it's crazy. We barely know each other. But I would like to get to know you better. From the moment I saw you... I knew I had to get to know you."

"Elliot..." Her voice is soft, but she doesn't look away anymore.

"You know about me dressing up in women's clothing. You know one of my biggest secrets. And it doesn't scare you off.

You accept me no matter what I look like. Right?"

Her face distorts, her lower lip wobbling, her breath irregular. I did something wrong, I said something wrong. She locks herself away from me, deeper this time. "I'm sorry. I don't... I don't know... I..." Izzy pulls away, her eyes going over me, then she wraps her arms around herself tightly. "I don't think this is a good idea. I'm sorry." And she flees again, to the elevators. Gone, again.

I look after her, my chest hurting. I wish I knew how to take that pain away for her. She's so beautiful, so amazing. I love her spark of life. But she keeps pushing me away. She keeps pulling me closer and then pushing me away again.

I take a deep breath and go back to the breakfast room. I can't even get to my hotel room right now. I need to get my keys, which I left on the table. But it also means facing Jason again, and Mya.

Am I making a mistake, a big mistake, by wanting Izzy?

When I get back to the table, it's just Jason, and I spot Mya getting herself some more coffee from the machine.

"Hey." I sit down, I guess I can stay here, it's not like the room is going to be any more fun.

"No Izzy with you?" Jason doesn't seem surprised.

I shake my head. "She told me that it's better if we... If we don't... I don't know." I put my arms on the table, putting my head on top of them. "Can you give me any indication if this is even a good idea? Am I reading her wrong?" I thought she really wanted me too. She didn't say that she *didn't* want me, or that she wanted me to stop. She just said that we *shouldn't*.

"She likes you." Jason sounds serious, and I almost want to look up at him. "Give her time. You're the first person she's ever kissed. Let her get used to that idea, give her a bit of time."

I sit up. "Her first?" Izzy? She seems so easy around people, a little flirty even.

"Yeah." Jason frowns at me, giving me a levelled look. "Her first."

"Ah, dammit." So that's what she meant by impulsive, that's why she got scared. "But you think that she may come around?"

"For you? Maybe." He shrugs. "That's all I've got. Sorry. She's my best friend, but there are things that we just…" He looks at his hands. "There are things that we've not gone through before. Izzy having a boyfriend is one of them."

I nod. Right. Not like Mya and I have. "Thanks."

If Jason thinks that we may have a chance, then maybe not everything is lost, yet.

Maybe…

11

Izzy

Transgender = A term for people whose gender does not match the sex they were assigned at birth. This can range from people feeling uncomfortable with their gender to people who really want to change their physical body to match a different gender or gender expression. I knew from a young age that I was a girl, not a boy, no matter what my birth certificate said. Luckily, my parents have always been very accepting of this and have always fought for my right to be who I am. I know that not everyone accepts it so easily though, and telling the wrong people can get me beaten up or worse… So I'm always a little scared when I want to tell someone.

I wrap my arms around myself closely as I'm curled up on the bed. I need to keep myself together. I need to do this. I can't break.

I can't give up on my own rules just for one cute guy with a cute smile, and really nice lips. And Elliot looked so sexy too, in his jeans and t-shirt. It suited him so well. Really, it doesn't matter how he dresses, but I already knew that. I already knew that he looked good either way...

There is knocking on the door, and someone opens it with a key.

"Izzy?" It's Jason.

"Yeah." I sit up, pulling on my clothes to get them to fit right, they've gotten all crumpled up.

"I got you some breakfast." He comes in with a tray. "I'd have brought a cute guy with it, but I don't know if you want to see him right now."

I glare his way. "Really?" *That's* what he's going to joke about?

"Yeah, really." Jason's voice is steady, and he puts the tray next to me on the bed. "He seems honest and real. I think..." He sighs, looking at me.

"I know." I look at the croissants and muffins on the plate, glaring at them more like it, because I shouldn't be glaring at Jason when he brings me good food. Like I don't know how honest Elliot looks, how caring. "I almost..." I eye Jason before looking back down at the food. "I almost told him." I swallow hard. "Last night. This morning. I almost told him. But I'm scared."

"I know." Jason reaches out and then pulls me closer, wrapping me in his arms, protecting me. "I know that you're scared. But I think you can trust him. You've trusted all of us. You've trusted the others. I think you can trust him too."

My heart does a little jumpy thing at the thought of Elliot knowing about me being transgender, at the thought of him accepting me, and not pushing me away... It would be so good, but can I chance it?

"Go have breakfast." Jason's voice is sweet. "We've got

outfits to get ready in. They're not going to be easy to put on."

"Yeah, yeah." I poke him in his side, making him jump a little. Then I get back over to the tray on the bed and start eating.

Jason is right, we've got outfits to wear today. We've got people to impress. I'm here for the convention, for the fun with my friends, I'm here for all of that. I don't have to let my weekend get sidetracked by a boy.

No matter how cute he is...

W A S D

A few weeks ago, Jason and I came up with the idea to not just cosplay, but to give our own twist to everything with an outfit that is inspired by magical girl anime outfits in general. Basically, the most generic and over-the-top magical girl outfit you can imagine. It was really fun to come up with, finding all the different elements we were going to use. A lot of layers of underskirts, lots of bows on everything, big hair and things like that, and, of course, everything is in the colour of sweets.

My mood has definitely lifted while we were getting ready. Remembering all the time we spent on designing and creating the outfits, finding our inspirations. Especially since we didn't show anyone what we were up to. It's going to be a surprise when people finally see us.

Jason did my make-up, frowning a little at the puffiness of my eyes. But I know that I can't help it, I cry easily and my eyes always go all red when I do. He just had to hide it a little with some makeup.

When we finally leave the hotel room, I feel a lot calmer and a lot stronger. I can do this. I can really do this. This weekend is for fun and hanging out with friends, and that's what I'm going to be doing, no more distractions from that.

When we get downstairs, Ruby is already waiting in the hallway, his eyes start to shine the moment he sees us. "I get why you kept this a secret." He grins as he looks us over. "Yeah... That's... That's something else." Then his eyes stay on me, softening. "How are you feeling?"

I carefully smile. "Tired. But I'll survive."

He nods. "Good. Now, let's get inside. I'm sure there are a couple of things we've not seen yet." He grins, and we get in line. Today is a lot faster, since we've got our bracelets and everything already, so we can just get into a separate line instead of having to wait at the main line.

With all the things that happened yesterday, I totally forgot to buy cool things at the stalls. It kind of totally got distracted by Elliot yesterday.

Ah, well. It's not like there are really so many things I want to buy anyway. Maybe just a fun t-shirt or a manga or something.

We walk through rows with stalls, greeting people we know, checking out what they're selling and such. I've been coming here for a couple years now, so I've gotten to know some sellers really well.

That, and then there is Emma with her own stall, Emma is also a Destruction of Elysium player and in the same guild as I'm in. So we talk to each other a lot, and I'm always so proud when I see people with the things that she makes herself. It's so cool to see someone create things that so many people love, some of her plushies and everything sell out in no time when she has them on her stall or her online store.

But as we approach Emma's stall, my heart drops. There, in front of the stall, is Elliot, talking to Emma, laughing with her. I don't know why, but I somehow hadn't expected to see him, at least not just yet... I stop, just staring.

"We can come back later." Ruby puts his hand on my back, but right then, Emma spots us and waves us over with a big smile on her face.

"Hey, everyone. I barely saw you yesterday, so crazy busy. How are you doing?" She's grinning, and I can't just walk away now, that would be rude.

"We're good." Jason steps behind the stall and hugs Emma. "How are the sales going?"

"Good. Really good. Already sold out all the plushies and things I made myself. So I've just got some manga and game swag left. I'll have to try to get more next year." Emma's eyes stay on me, raising an eyebrow. "I'd really love it if I could get help to make some more next year."

"From me?" I try to focus on what she's saying, but having Elliot so close next to me is throwing me off. "Why?"

"Because you're great and a really fast sewer?" She smiles. "I've seen you at work, remember?"

"Yeah, yeah." I smile back. "But you know that I'm busy with my own shop. Or, well, I will probably be again, right before con season." People often order underskirts and things like that right before con season, which means that I'm usually really busy with those on top of my own costumes.

"True." She shrugs. "Just think about it, please? It would really help me out."

"I know." I also step behind the stall, giving her a quick hug.

"Oh." Emma's eyes start to shine. "Elliot just showed me pictures of you two together yesterday. You looked awesome. Too bad I couldn't get my own pics of you two."

I nod, not sure what to answer now. How do I respond to that? To that spark of fun in her eyes?

"Maybe next time," Elliot answers instead.

Next time? My heart does a little floppy thing, and I finally look his way again, not sure if I should.

"Hey." His voice is soft, and I don't know how to read the look in his eyes. "Can I talk to you for a moment?"

I nod, he just makes me feel so much, I don't know how to act. I just wish things weren't so complicated.

Elliot reaches out to me, and I take his hand, his grip firm and warm. Then he pulls me along, away from everyone else, and crosses a food court before he sits down at one of the furthest away tables. A quiet table, quiet means a serious conversation, right?

When he looks at me, I just want to believe that this isn't going to end badly. I don't want this to end badly because I don't want what we have to end at all. I don't want…

I need to get real with myself… I really don't want this to end, I want to stay close to Elliot, even if it scares me. Maybe because this feeling inside scares me.

"I'm sorry." He runs his hand over the back of his neck, sighing. "I'm sorry if I scared you yesterday or this morning. I didn't mean to."

"You don't…" What do I want to say? He doesn't scare me? It's kind of obvious that he does. "I'm easily scared."

"Yeah." He smiles a little now. "I got that." He sighs again. "I guess I just wanted to say that I don't want you to be scared of me. And that…" He looks away, going quiet.

"What is it?" This guy…

"I think it's better if we take this slowly, really slowly." He carefully takes my hand, holding it like I'm precious. "I know that you have thousands of reasons why you think this will never work out. I know that already. I'm just asking… give me a chance, please? Nothing intense, just… trying to figure out where this

108

leads, if it even leads anywhere. Even if it's just friendship-plus or something."

My throat closes up, and my eyes start to burn. "I can't cry right now. The make-up." I'm still too raw for his sweet words.

Elliot smiles, his eyes a little watery too. "I'm not trying to make you cry. I'm trying to prevent it, honestly." He reaches up, and I realise he's got a napkin in his hand. Then he carefully runs it under my eyes. "I really want to get to know you. I think you're great and I'd like to get a chance to know how great. Even if it doesn't lead to much else, you're incredible and I'm… interested."

"I'm not that great," I grumble, but my heart is beating like crazy. That's like… basically a confession, right?

"I'm pretty sure that people always underestimate their own greatness. So…" He shrugs a little, still smiling. "I'm not asking for anything steady, just let's see where this goes."

"Until when are you staying at the hotel?" How much time do I have? Do we have?

"Tomorrow morning." He winks. "I learned early on that going back home on the same day as the end of the convention is a recipe for disaster, and it always makes the second day feel so rushed."

I nod. So, I've got a full day. A full day to get to know Elliot and figure out what and *if* I'm going to tell him anything. "Me too. We're leaving tomorrow too. For the same reason."

"Good." He squeezes my hand a little. "So, what about my proposal? Will you give me a chance?" Proposal?

I nod. A chance is only fair. It's only fair to get to know him better before I decide if I'm pushing him away or not. Only fair to him, *and to my own heart…*

I guess that one more day can't hurt. And if it doesn't work out, then maybe all this was supposed to be was just a con fling and nothing more. And I'm actually pretty good with that too, I think. Maybe.

"Can I still kiss you?" Elliot's eyes sparkle with mischief, his whole body relaxing now the hard part seems to be over.

"Sometimes." Because, *please, yes.*

"Will you freak out again?" *Like last night?*

"I can't promise anything." If we're going to be honest…

He takes a moment to think. "Fair enough. I'll take that chance." He leans in, and I close the last distance between us.

This time I'm prepared, this time I know what to expect, and even though the dysphoria nags at me, I hold his hands, his grip strong, and I focus on all the other sensations. On his scent, on the way he's so warm, on the way he looked at me right before I closed my eyes. It pushes the dysphoria away enough to enjoy the kiss this time.

When he pulls back, our breathing is hard, and I can feel all the ways that my body responds to the kiss. All the ways that he makes my body buzz, just being so close to him. It scares me a little, but it also makes me feel like I'm just a normal girl. Just a normal girl who's got a crush on a cute boy. A *really* cute boy.

Elliot smirks, his eyes sparkling.

"What?"

"I can see your blush through your makeup." He reaches out, carefully running his finger over my cheek. "It's cute."

I try to glare at him. "You're just making it worse." My cheeks are burning up, and I don't know how to make it stop anymore. This guy… He really doesn't know how to stop, does he? Does he even realise what he does to me? Does he even realise that it's not that easy for me to try and hide my feelings?

Though, seeing the look in his eyes, maybe he does know.

And I don't know which is worse. The thought of him not realising how he affects me, or him realising and still deciding to act like this? Teasing me? Teasing me with that look in his eyes…

And what about me? What about how I feel watching him like this?

This sucks.

This sucks, sucks, *sucks*!

12
Elliot

Canon = Official story content created by the creators of a story. Sometimes there is a difference between the original manga or light novel and the anime adaptation of it. And, depending on the creator's account of the story, it could be canon (for example a sweet scene in the anime that didn't show up in the previous work but still adds to the story) or it could not be canon (for example when it's just material to make the anime longer but doesn't add anything, also called filler). Fans can get really enthusiastic about something being canon or not.

I don't know if it was the best choice to make. To ask Izzy to take things slowly, to try and make this work, one tiny step at a time. I have no idea if this is going to work out for us, but seeing her upset like before, watching her flee and hide away. I hated it, I hated seeing her like that, and this seemed like the better plan. It has to be. Better for the both of us.

At least she's not crying anymore, and that's got to count for something... It has to. Right?

Every kiss from Izzy is so intoxicating that I don't know if I'll ever want to stop. I want to take her in my arms and hide away in a corner, just kissing her all day. It's been too long since I felt like this… No. I've never felt like this before, not this intense.

But I know that we've got to get back up soon. I know that I've got to be a friend to Izzy, well, more something between a friend and a lover. Like... trying to find the right place between the two for us. But I know that we'll have to get back to the others, or all I said was for nothing. It means we've got to get back to the rest of the event and be that combination of friends and 'maybe something more, trying something out'.

This is going to be a strange day, but I also know that if I don't want this connection with Izzy to fall apart, we're going to have to figure things out.

I slowly get up, away from Izzy's soft touches. "It's time to go back, people will get worried." Jason will start glaring at me if I keep her too long.

She nods, her eyes losing a little of that spark. "Yeah, I guess we should." She also stands up, straightening up her dress.

"You look great by the way." She so does. When I saw her just now, I got a little envious at her skill, at the way she just pulls this off.

I'll never get as good as her, but I guess that's to be expected. We've all got our own skills we're good at, and it's unfair to compare myself to her when we're different people and all. She can make and wear amazing things, and I'm better with words, usually.

But really, seeing her next to Jason and them both dressed like that, all matching... I know it's stupid, but I felt a little jealous. *I* wanted to be the one at her side. I wanted to match her outfit, again. I wanted to be her pairing. But, instead, the moment she saw me, her eyes changed, and she stopped looking happy. I'm the one who made her feel bad… *Sigh.*

I just hope that I won't make her look like that anymore, I hate it when she looks like that because of me. I hope that she can maybe smile again now.

"Thank you." Her smile grows. "You don't look too bad yourself."

It's sweet, but next to her, my dress pales in comparison… "Thanks." No matter how innocent she may look, she makes my heart beat faster anyway... And I'm pretty sure she knows that she does it too. I reach out to Izzy. "Let's enjoy the rest of today."

"Yeah." Her eyes shine, and she takes my hand, fishing her phone from somewhere in her skirt.

Pockets. Of course! "Before I forget, Jason said that you could teach me how to put pockets in dresses and skirts?" Hey, any excuse to see her again after this event ends.

Izzy smiles. "Yeah, I can teach you. It's not that hard." She shrugs a little, sending off a message, then she looks at me. "He told you about the pocket thing to get you to talk to me more, didn't he?"

I nod. "Probably."

She rolls her eyes, still smiling, shaking her head. "He really doesn't know how not to interfere with people's lives." Then she pulls me along, back to the busy areas between the stalls.

It's fun to watch her, to see her back in her element. To see her act like she did yesterday, much more open, much more happy. And she's holding my hand, she's still holding my hand, and that means the world to me.

Maybe it means a little too much to me, but what else can I

do with such an amazing and strong-willed girl at my side?

W A S D

The rest of the day is so much easier, and so much happier. We hang out as a group, talking to people from the stalls that show up at almost every event that we go to and meeting and getting to know new people.

And, of course, there are a lot of people who want to take pictures. Mostly of Izzy and Jason together, but also a lot of Izzy and me. Even though I'm just wearing a simple black and white goth dress, with only a single layer of underskirt to make it a little more poofy, nothing as extravagant as those two, but still, people want to take pictures of me too.

I don't know… I guess I'm used to it by now. Pictures happen all the time when I'm cosplaying guy characters at these events, but I never realised that it would happen the same while I was dressed as a girl. It feels different, this attention on me, especially since I'm not fully comfortable dressed like this yet.

At the end of the day, after the end performance and as most people have already left, we're all helping Emma pack away the last items from her stall.

"What are you guys going to do for dinner?" Emma looks around at us as she stands between her boxes.

"There is a restaurant around the corner, there will probably be a lot of con people there, but we can see if they've got some space for us." Jason shrugs.

"Or we get takeaway from them and eat it somewhere outside." Izzy looks around. "The weather is great, so we're not really dependent on sitting inside. And I really would like to sit outside right now, not stuffed into some building. We've done that all weekend." She grins a little.

"I can't disagree with that." Emma smiles too, wrapping her arm around Izzy's waist and pulling her into a hug. "I've been locked in here all weekend, I could use some fresh air. And it looks like it will be a perfect evening for dinner outside. We can even use the cloth I use as a table runner to sit on, not mess up everyone's clothes." Emma looks so excited about the idea, and Izzy looks so comfortable in her arms, so at ease. It's fun to watch Izzy be like this doll everyone keeps hugging, and she seems pretty happy with it too. A new thing I've learned about Izzy, she likes hugging, a lot.

"Outside it is. Let's get these into the car and then get some food. I'm hungry." I stand up, the box at my feet all nicely packed. Around us, it gets quieter, and I look at Izzy, who is now staring my way, a strange look in her eyes. "What is it? Did I tear my dress or something?" I look down at the dress, but can't seem to find an issue with it.

She shakes her head, her smile almost sad, her eyes darker. "No, nothing. Your dress is fine." Then she turns to Jason. "Can you get me a burger and fries? I... I'll be right back." Her voice is tense, then she looks at me again. "I kind of need to talk to you." Her smile is gone now, and she lets out a sigh.

Jason also looks serious at me, and that doesn't seem like a good sign.

I open my mouth, but I can't even think of what to say. Should I ask Jason to also get me something? And what would I want? And with the way Izzy looks... Will I even be coming back here with her? A heavy feeling settles in my stomach. Will I be coming back here with her? Something tells me that I may not...

"We'll wait with ordering until you're back. Go." Emma smiles encouragingly, though she also looks tense, and that really confuses me. What's going on?

"Okay." I go over to Izzy, my stomach in knots. "Where do you want to go?" Because this seems like a serious thing, very serious.

"Let's go outside. Somewhere quiet." She shrugs, not meeting my eyes anymore.

"Izzy, can you at least give me a clue? I'm kind of worried here." I follow her as she uses one of the side doors to get to the parking spaces, the heat flooding over us.

"I don't know how to without... without telling you everything." She glances at me, still tense, a tightness in her gaze that seems almost like fear.

"Not even if it's about a good or a bad thing?" Can I get that at least? Because this starts to feel a lot like this will be a 'bad' thing.

She shakes her head, walking away from the building, to an empty patch at the edge of the parking lot. "Good or bad depends on how you..." She's already upset, I hear the tears in her voice, even though she tries to hide them.

Okay, that's even more cryptic than I thought she could be. But I guess I'll have to wait until she tells me.

Izzy looks around, and then promptly sits down on the curb, her shoulders slumping, her arms wrapped around her knees, her chin leaning on one of the big bows from the dress. It would look cute, if she didn't look so devastated.

I carefully sit down next to her, trying to keep my dress as clean as possible, giving myself something to do to distract myself for a moment.

We're quiet for a while, and it only makes me more nervous. "What is it you needed to tell me?"

Izzy flinches a little, and I watch emotions go over her face. Fear, pain, anxiety and then, determination. "Remember when I told you that what you see, who I appear to be, it's not all of who I am?"

Again with that confusing sentence. "Yeah. You said that it wasn't the place to talk about what you meant, back then." Is she going to tell me now?

She nods. "It wasn't. And I wasn't even sure if I should or even could tell you this back then." She looks over the parking lot, the cars passing us by, the other con-goers and stall holders leaving after the busy weekend. Everyone looking exhausted.

I wait. I don't know what else to do, and I don't think anything I say will make this easier on her. Because I have no idea what she wants to tell me.

Izzy looks my way, almost reaching out, but she puts both her hands in her lap, stretching her legs. "It's really hard to say this, because I've never actually had to tell someone..." She glances up at my face, and back down to her feet, licking her lips. "I've never had to tell this to someone I like. My biggest fear has always been getting beaten up, not..." She shakes her head, wringing her hands together in her lap. "Not this."

Getting beaten up? Getting hurt? Why would someone want to hurt her?

She takes a breath, sitting up straighter. "When I say that what you see isn't all that I am, I mean..." She licks her lips again. "I was born a boy." She swallows hard, her hands shaking.

Wait. What? Just... *What?*

"I was born a boy. But from really young, as soon as I got any say about who I was, I've always lived as a girl." Her voice quiets now, her hands running over each other, still shaking.

I need to process that. I need to process what Izzy just said. Izzy, the beautiful and confident girl in front of me, was born a boy. And now she's shaking in fear telling me this. The confident

118

girl reduced to shaking hands and voice, telling me who she is.

I don't know what to think. But somewhere in me, I realise that we're similar in some small ways, even if her pain runs so much deeper than mine. And that if I'm too scared to tell my friends, who I've known for years, that I like to crossdress sometimes, how scary must it be for Izzy to tell me that she's transgender? Especially when we both know that there are feelings growing between us that are different than friendships. That's next level kind of scary.

I now understand her fear of being hurt, and I can imagine she's had her fair share of people actually hurting her too, physically or emotionally. *Damnit.* My heart breaks for her fear and pain, for the constant anxiety.

"Elliot?" Izzy's voice is soft, scared. She's scared for my reply, for how I'll react to her coming out, to her telling me such a personal thing about herself.

Of course! I should give her some reply. *Crap!* "Okay." I nod, trying to form a full thought. Trying to come up with something that will make her relax, that will make her smile again.

"Okay, what?" There is still the edge of fear in her voice.

"Thank you for telling me. Thank you for trusting me with this." It's like my mouth is saying things as my brain is catching up, but not really making much sense.

She nods, but her face falls, and she's biting her lip, trying to keep her tears inside. "Okay." Her voice is dejected, already teary, and she stands up, ready to walk away.

Whoa! *No!* Not what I was going for.

I stand up too, grabbing her wrist, and she flinches, but I keep holding her. "Izzy..." My brain is a mess, I don't mean to hurt her. I want to do anything but hurt her.

"You don't have to say anything. I get it. It's okay. I should have expected it." She's in pain. She thinks I rejected her.

"It's not like that." I tug on her arm carefully, hoping she'll turn back to me.

"Then what is it like?" Her voice breaks. She shakes her head, but finally turns to me, tears sliding down her cheeks, streaking her makeup.

I reach up, putting my fingers under her chin, reaching up with the other hand and wiping away her tears. I should have taken some spare napkins with me, or tissues. "I *like* you. I really like you." I hope she'll believe me. "As I said this morning, let's take things slow. I've never been with a trans girl, but I've also never been with someone who makes me feel as comfortable to be myself as I have been around you. This is all new for me, but… I *want* to explore things going forward with you."

There are a lot of bits of thoughts running through my head. Like, does this really change how I feel towards Izzy? What would it be like to *be* with her, physically? How am I supposed to stop wanting to hold her when she looks at me with those beautiful eyes of hers? And a running thread of shreds of questions that I don't even know how to voice now, or if I even should.

But most of the questions don't seem so significant as the one thought going over all of it, the one certainty in this all. Izzy is Izzy, and the girl I've gotten to know this weekend is the one who makes me feel so happy and makes me feel comfortable about being myself, and that's more important than anything.

"I've never been with *anyone* before, ever. I'm totally level zero when it comes to *exploration*." She swallows, and there is a spark of hope in her eyes.

I nod, I remember Jason telling me this morning. "We can

explore everything together." I lean a little closer, so relieved to still be able to do that. "You're going to have to tell me your boundaries, but..." I shrug. "That's the same for everyone you meet." Everyone has different boundaries, Izzy is no different in that.

She finally smiles a little again.

And, before I do something stupid again... "Last night, when we kissed, what scared you?" Maybe I can't do it again.

She nods, letting out a breath. Then she reaches up, running her fingers over my light stubble. "Facial hair, it... it messed things up in my head. I hadn't expected how it made me feel." Her voice is careful, but she's also calmer now.

I take her hand, holding it lightly as I put it against my cheek. "Does this scare you? Just be honest, I just want to know."

"A little." Her voice is breathy, and her cheeks are turning pink. Her tongue darts out to wet her lips.

"But?" Because something is going through her head.

"Can I kiss you again?" There is a flash of that mischievous smile again, and the way she's looking at me, a mixture of relief and interest, I think I'm turning to putty just being caught in it.

"Of course. Can I hold you?" Because I really want to feel her against me again.

"Yeah." Her smile grows as she wraps her arms around my neck and I slide my arms around her waist, pulling her closer.

Her lips are on mine in moments. Soft kisses, soft and careful kisses, slowly going longer as she gets more confident. She lets go of her reserve, no longer holding back, and I love it. I love how she's feeling a lot easier with herself now.

I never expected Izzy to be a trans girl, that that would be her secret, that that would be the reason she kept freaking out, panicking. But I'm glad that she told me. I'm so happy that she trusted me enough to tell me.

And I'm so happy that she felt confident enough to let me be the first person to share things with, to explore things.

Now I just have to make sure not to break that trust, now I have to live up to her faith in me.

I hope I can, because I don't want to let her go.

13

Izzy

Headcanon = Elements of a story or character that are not explicitly stated within the original content (so the canon content) but which is either something a fan themselves believes to be true, or which the fanbase at large believes to be true. This can range from shipping two characters who aren't explicitly involved with each other in the original content to a favourite food of a character based on their personality. Fans can get really enthusiastic about their headcanons.

My heart feels like it's going to break out of my chest, it's beating so hard. And at the same time, I feel a little floaty, so surprised at how easy I feel now.

I just told Elliot about being trans, about being born a boy but growing up a girl. I told him the scariest thing I can imagine ever telling someone I've only met a day ago, someone I don't even know that well yet.

And he didn't seem to be bothered by it. His lips are back on mine, his arms around me, and it feels so good. I can barely believe it!

I've never dated before, I've never even attempted it, because it's hard enough to find friends who are accepting, let alone finding someone who accepts me for who I am and who will still date me. To have Elliot accept me so easily...

Wow.

Double wow, as he tightens his arms around me and deepens the kiss, taking away my breath. This feels so good, so, so good.

I can hardly believe it. It's unreal. I've read so many stories about coming out as trans going wrong that I never really considered even attempting to date, not wanting to deal with all the hassle when I could have friends and I wouldn't have to worry about anything else.

After a while, I pull back. We're both out of breath, and I stare at Elliot, at the way he's looking at me. He doesn't seem scared, or repulsed, or anything like that, he seems simply interested, and turned on... Like he did before, like the way I feel when he holds me...

I swallow hard, stepping back a little, sliding my hands down his arms and taking his hands in mine. It's hot, sweaty, and we're sticky, but I still really like touching him.

Then, out of nowhere, my stomach grumbles, loud enough for Elliot to hear it too and he laughs.

"Maybe we should go back inside." He squeezes my hands a little. "I think they're all waiting to see what happened, and of course waiting to get food." He smiles, his eyes sparkling.

I nod, suddenly anxious again. Yeah, everyone is waiting to hear if Elliot freaked out about finding out about me being a trans girl or not. Great... "And what... How did we..." What do I even try to ask? *What are we to each other? What are we going to do going forward?*

Elliot's eyes soften, and he leans a little closer. "I'm thinking that something is going through your mind again." He gives me a quick kiss. "This doesn't change anything between us, at least, not anything different from what we talked about this morning. I still want to get to know you better, and take things slowly."

I nod. But I don't know how easy it is going to be. This is totally new for me, but I guess we'll see. I look at him, a smile tugging on my lips. "Let's get inside and get some food." I tug on his arm, and he follows me, his hand in mine comforting and steady.

As we walk into the hall, everyone is sitting around, waiting for us and a blush creeps up my cheeks. I feel like they're staring a little too much, but I know that they're also worried and protective, they want to make sure that I'm okay.

Jason stands up, grinning. "I guess it's time to go get food now. I'm hungry." He acts like nothing happened, like they were just waiting for us for no reason at all. I mentally thank him for acting so casual.

Emma also stands up, smiling. "Yeah, we've been waiting for long enough. Though... I guess I can *see* why it took so long." She raises her eyebrows and looks from me to Elliot and back, her eyes on me smug.

I look at Elliot too, and realise that his lipstick is a lot more shimmery than it was before, and I'm the one wearing a glittery lip gloss... Ah... Yeah... *Oops.*

I've got to ask Elliot the brand of lipstick he's wearing, though… That stuff stayed on well all day, and even through the kiss just now, and it's only my lip gloss which isn't exactly kiss-proof.

Elliot raises his eyebrows at me. "What is it?"

I reach up, running my thumb over his lower lip, showing it

to him. "Your lipstick has turned a little more shimmery than it was before."

Elliot laughs, the sound so comfortable and happy, wrapping his arms around me, pulling me against him. "We're going to have to match our lipsticks next time, saves on the staring."

I lean against him for a moment, happy with how easy this feels. "Maybe." Then I pull back again. "But first, food. I'm hungry!" I tug him along, my heart beating loudly, in a good way.

Maybe things don't have to be as scary as I keep imagining them. Maybe this can work out.

W A S D

We sit down on the grass next to the restaurant. Jason and Elliot went in to order our food, and the rest of us just made ourselves comfortable out here, not wanting to go in as one big group.

On our way out of the building earlier, we ran into Kevin and Mya, who both seemed a little flushed and very, very close as they came from the elevators, their clothes a lot more rumpled than they were when we saw them last. Well, good for them. And Ruby, Evelyn, Justin and Mark were already waiting for us out front.

As Jason and Elliot get back from their trip, they're carrying so much food. I can barely imagine that we'll be able to eat all of it, though, I know that some in our midst are pretty big eaters, myself included.

Elliot sits down on my one side and Jason on my other side, and suddenly I feel like a princess, surrounded by her bodyguards... Very handsome bodyguards, in pretty dresses.

It's so good being surrounded by people you like, by friends.

My burger is as good as I remember it, and next to me, Elliot is eating a burger too. I can't keep my eyes off him. I keep trying not to stare at him, but that's just... Yeah... I keep failing at it, still not used to him really knowing and still being here and still interested in me…

After all the food is gone, we don't move. The evening is much too nice, the light breeze takes the edge off the heat from the day, and being outside after spending most of the weekend inside is really good.

I listen in on some of the conversations going on around me. Listening to Jason talking to Ruby about some manga and Kevin and Mark discussing the next con they're attending and what they'll be cosplaying there.

Then Elliot's fingers play over my back, leaning close. "I don't know how to ask this..."

I look his way, he sounds... different. "What is it?" My heart skips a beat at the look in his eyes.

Then his eyes drop to the top of my dress, to my boobs. "Well... ehhh..." He runs his hand over the back of his neck, quickly looking up at my face and then away. "I was wondering... Like..."

"Yeah?" I can't help but smile a little at how awkward he seems.

"How do you like... fill the top of your dress? Like... How do you create *boobs* that are more than just a little padding?" He almost whispers the word boobs, his eyes darting away and his cheeks colouring.

I stare at him, for a moment not sure how to answer. But Jason breaks whatever awkwardness is going on as he bursts out laughing next to me.

"That's..." Jason keeps laughing. "Of all the things you ask her… That's a good one!"

I push at Jason, trying to push him over, rolling my eyes at him. "Stop being such a jerk."

Elliot awkwardly moves next to me. "I didn't want to..." He looks spooked, like he may have done something wrong. "I was just wondering, you know?" He looks down to his own dress. He looks a little lost and panicked.

I reach out to him, trying not to laugh too, and take his hand. "It's okay. It's not a bad question and Jason is just being a jerk." I glare at Jason, who finally stops laughing, then I look back at Elliot. "These are... Ehh... These are my real boobs. I don't have to *make* them anymore." I squeeze his hand again. "But I can teach you how I used to do it. Or show how I help Jason when he wants them." I glare at Jason for good measure, it's not like I've not helped him out with this exact question in the past too.

Elliot nods, still blushing. "Sorry. That was... It was a stupid question."

I shake my head. "Nah. I understand why you'd be curious. But yeah, these are real, these days" Hey, I've asked the same question before of people. When you can learn how to improve your cosplay directly from the source, you've gotta ask, even if it's awkward.

I see Elliot's eyes widen a little and he licks his lips, his eyes darking down again. "Right." His voice is different now, and I feel how the mood around us has changed a little, more charged.

Oops.

I bump my shoulder into Elliot's. "Don't worry about it. It's really hard to ask stupid questions, and we both have to kind of ehh... *feel* our way around things." I cringe even as I say it.

Elliot's cheeks go even darker, and I realise that, yeah... Maybe not the best choice of words in our current situation. Ah, whatever.

"I'm going to shut up before I say anything more stupid." I glance at Jason, who is trying really hard not to laugh again. "Are you done yet?"

Jason shrugs, letting his laugh out. "It doesn't often happen that you end up all tongue-tied." He shakes his head, then he looks at Elliot. "She can still help though, she's great at it. Just, you know, the moment of questioning was a little... funny and awkward."

From the other side of the group, Mya is looking at me curiously. *Oops.* She doesn't know yet...

I get up. Some things are better explained at a short distance, even if the rest of the people in the group already know about me. Some things you just don't yell over the crowd.

"What are they laughing at?" Mya eyes me, raising an eyebrow.

"Elliot asked... ehhh...." How can I explain it best without stuff going awkward? "He asked a question which could have been insensitive, and he didn't know how to ask it."

"Sounds like him, what was it?" She looks more confused now, though she's also smiling.

I think for a moment of how to word it best. "He asked me how I 'fill the top of my dress' when I cosplay." Still awkward, still odd, still doesn't make much sense without another piece of information about me.

Next to her, Kevin lets out a short laugh, eyeing the guys on the other side, amused.

"And that's a strange question, why?" Mya now looks between Kevin and me.

"I ehhh... I'm trans, a trans girl. So boobs aren't exactly a given feature for me." Could I have said it better? Sure, but it's better to just be blunt and get it over with.

"Trans?" She blinks, looking me over, more confused somehow.

"Born a boy." I try to help her out.

She grins, shaking her head a little, pulling a face. "I got that part. I'm not unknowing, I know what trans means. I'm just... surprised." She smiles now, her eyes softening. "Whatever, it's cool, you know." Then she looks in Elliot's direction. "But, yeah, that could have been a really insensitive question to ask. I'm sorry for my best friend not always knowing how to ask things, really sorry."

Kevin shakes his head, still grinning. "Too bad I missed it. He must have looked really awkward."

I smack him on his arm. "Kev, don't be mean. It's a valid question and pretty useful for guys crossplaying anime girls. You know that yourself."

"Yeah, yeah. I'm just imagining the horror on his face as he realised what he asked." He keeps grinning, holding up his hands to me. "Sorry. I'll stop." Then he leans close to Mya, who still seems a little like she's trying to figure stuff out. She doesn't seem upset or anything, so, that's good. But I would guess she's thinking the whole 'best friend dating a trans girl' thing over.

On the other side of the group, Elliot stands up and comes over, sitting behind the two of us. "What are you two talking about?" He's smiling, his eyes shining, happy.

Of course, Kevin has to butt in first. "You asked her about her *boobs*?"

Elliot narrows his eyes at Kevin, then he looks my way. "This is going to haunt me until the end of time, isn't it?" I'm glad he's taking it so well, as he's also smiling.

I nod, smiling too. "Probably."

Elliot seems to think this over, then shrugs. "There are

worse things to be known for." He leans to me, putting his head on my shoulder. "Hey, I was thinking, how about some ice cream?" Then he looks at Kevin, shooting a glare his way. "And we can leave these *troublemakers* behind."

"Sounds like a plan." I stand up, ready to move a little again.

We'll all be leaving for our own places tomorrow, so time with Elliot is limited. I better sneak in some alone time now.

"You going to ask more *boobie* questions?" Kevin turns to us, and I push at his shoulders, making him topple over.

"You're such a jerk sometimes." I shake out my dress, taking Elliot's hand. "I'm in for some ice cream. It's still way too hot out here, even this late in the day." I wave at Jason, who looks up at me. "We're going to have ice cream, will be back later."

"Sure!" He waves back. "Try to behave yourself, yeah? No weird questions out in public." He grins.

I just shake my head, pulling Elliot along. They can be such meanies. All of them. But it's also why I like them best.

Instead of going to the cafe that we just got our food from, we turn a corner into one of the streets going away from the convention building.

"I know a place where they have really nice ice cream. It's just down the road, found it last year." Elliot smiles. He seems pretty relaxed, but his hand is a little tight around mine.

"Sounds good." I tug on his arm a little, making him stop.

He turns to me, his eyes curious.

"I just wanted to say…" I shrug a little, now feeling awkward for even thinking this. "Thanks for not freaking out?" I know that not everyone would have responded as relaxed as he did.

He steps in closer, sliding his arms around my waist, as he keeps doing somehow, but it feels so nice. "I know it must have been scary for you to tell me. I understand that. But… I don't think thanking me for being a sane human being and not a jerk is really that much of a compliment." He winks and then leans closer, his lips near mine. "Plus, I don't think it matters."

I want to kiss him, but at the same time... "Why not?"

"I've seen you before, at other conventions, cosplaying and everything. To me, you've always been you. And I don't think that knowing you're trans really changes much for me." He sounds so serious, and I can barely hear myself think over the beating of my heart. Is this real?

"Really?"

"Yes, really." His voice is low, husky, and then his lips are on mine.

14
Elliot

Fanboy/fangirl = Someone who is a fan of a certain band, anime or other media. Fangirl is the better-known term of the two, since it's a word often used to belittle girls and their interests, but fanboy is getting used more and more. Some people use the word to make fun of other people, because they don't understand their passion, but I think it's cool. I think it's cool when you love something so much that you identify as a fan of something or someone as an essential part of your identity.

I don't like the way Izzy's surprised that I'm not acting like a jerk about who she is, but I guess I understand her fear if she's dealt with too many people not reacting well to her coming out. And that hurts. Knowing that she's been hurt like that, it hurts.

I don't know if I've fully realised what Izzy being a trans girl means yet, at least, what it would mean going forward in our... relationship? Is this a relationship yet? I don't know.

She feels so good in my arms, her body against mine, her arms around my shoulders as she deepens the kiss. This feels so good, so right. I've never been this head over heels for someone before, especially not so suddenly and I don't really know how to react to it. And even though that thought could be scary, it just feels right with Izzy.

Then she pulls back, her eyes mischievous. "I think we were on our way to get ice cream." She winks, and I want to kiss her again, but yeah, ice cream was what we were going to do.

"Yeah." My voice is low, a little rough. She does things to me that I can't hide from her.

"Let's go get it. Before we…" She smiles, winking.

Before we really start eating each other up in the middle of the street? Maybe.

I slowly let her go, taking her hand. "It's this way. It's not too far. They have delicious ice cream." Let's focus on the ice cream, that's a safe thing to think about. Let's not think about the way my body reacts to her being near, to us kissing… Let's focus on the ice cream.

We walk down the main street and into a side street Mya and I found last year. The small ice cream shop is still open. *Lucky!*

It's quieter here, so it's easier to think and easier to just be together. No people around keeping their eyes on us constantly, making sure I'm not going to hurt Izzy in some way. Here, it can just be the two of us, nobody else.

⎡W⎤ ⎡A⎤ ⎡S⎤ ⎡D⎤

Izzy takes another spoonful from the bowl of ice cream between us. We're sharing one bowl of ice cream, it was easier than deciding what to get each. Plus, more romantic. We've got strawberry, raspberry with vanilla, chocolate, and a lot of other flavours. Some of them we had no idea what to expect, but they had interesting colours so they went into the bowl too, like the black vanilla. Sadly enough, that was just a special colour, the flavour was like normal vanilla, nothing cool. *Bummer.*

Izzy looks so happy with the ice cream, her eyes sparkling as she tries each flavour, then she looks up at me. "Hey... Do you think Mya and Kevin are going to keep seeing each other after this is all over?" Random direction of the conversation…

I shrug. "Wouldn't be the first time that Mya has a con-fling. So I have no idea."

She nods. "Yeah, wouldn't be the first time for Kevin either." Then she falls quiet, taking a few more bites. I'm not saying anything either, just watching her think, watching the emotions on her face as she mulls things over. "And... what about us?" She looks down, not meeting my eyes, playing with her spoon over the table, not taking another bite.

My heart hurts a little at the question. She still thinks I'll push her aside, doesn't she? "I'd like to keep seeing you."

She nods again, not meeting my eyes. "Me too." Though there is no strength behind her voice, just anxiety.

"Then, let's do that." I reach out, putting my hand on hers. "Let's keep seeing each other. Just, what kind of travel times are we talking about, you know, from my place to yours, or the other way around?"

"I live in Utrecht." She shrugs a little.

"Groningen, for me." So, travel should be doable, should be.

"Oh." She smiles a little. "I've got friends who live there. They're all Destruction of Elysium players from the guild, I've been there a few times." I like how excited she gets when she talks about the game.

I can't help my smile either. "I guess that's a good thing,

then. Right?"

"Yeah. Though..." Her face falls again. "It'll be a pretty long trip and between classes and work and..." She lets out a sigh. Yeah, as students, this travelling thing can get pretty complicated, especially since Izzy has a very hands-on kind of study direction.

I squeeze her hand slightly. "We're on summer break right now, right? No classes."

She nods. "Yeah, true. It's just... I don't... I don't have a lot of money to travel. This con has taken up most of my savings. And I…" Her face falls.

"That's okay. I can travel for free during summer break." The advantage of living close to my university is that I don't need to use my student travel card to get to classes during the week, so I've got free travel during the weekends instead, and during some of the breaks and holidays.

She nods again.

"So? Are we doing this?" I try to get her to look at me, to hopefully take the worry away. "Am I going to come visit you?"

She finally relaxes. "Yeah." A smile spreads over her face, slowly. "I guess being the one in their home environment is a good thing, not as scary."

"Definitely." I can't help my own smile. "That means I can totally dig around your closets and you can teach me about making even better cosplay outfits."

"Not that I'll be able to teach you that much. You're pretty good already." She starts taking a few bites of the ice cream again. "And there is, of course, the problem with you raiding my closet. You'll find out all my dirty secrets."

"Dirty secrets? You leave your dirty socks at the bottom of your closet because you keep forgetting about them? Or is that just me?” I grin, glad that everything feels easier again.

Izzy laughs, shaking her head. “Not exactly... But I’ve got about ten unfinished dresses hiding there.”

“Why? That seems like a waste of space and too bad about pretty dresses.”

“I, ehh...” A blush spreads over her cheeks. “I grew out of them.” Her voice is low, like she’s embarrassed.

“Grew out of them? They’re that old?”

“N—No. Ehm...” She points her spoon at her chest. “These have been on a growth spurt a lot in the last two years. I started some of the dresses at the end of last summer, and never finished them because I got into autumn fashion, and when I tried them on again a couple of months later... I’d grown out of them.” She looks shy and frustrated at the same time.

“That’s... an interesting issue.” I can’t help my laugh. She can’t fit into the dresses she started because her body is now more the way she’s supposed to look and she has outgrown them. Kind of an interesting issue to have, really.

“Although...” She looks me over.

“What?”

“You may be able to fit into them.”

“What? I’m taller than you are. And I’m pretty sure I’m broader in my shoulders.”

“The length isn’t much of an issue with these, and the shoulder thing should be fine. That’s easier to adjust than adding boob size and curves for them.” She keeps looking at me.

“I just...” Now *my* cheeks are on fire. “I may look like this here, at the con, but I don’t usually look like this when I go out. Not as extravagant.”

“I know, and that’s okay.” She smiles. “It just gives me an excuse to finish them, and I even get to see someone cute other than me wear them." She winks.

"Right." I shake my head a little, grinning. This girl's brain has some interesting places it goes to sometimes. But it's also refreshing. I love how Izzy isn't afraid to be herself and say what she wants to say, especially when it's just the two of us. "Well, then, I guess that means I'll *have* to visit your place soon, right? Can't let you keep all those unfinished clothes clogging up your closet, taking up precious space."

"No, you really can't." She winks. Then she takes a spoon full of the ice cream and holds it out to me.

I wrap my lips around the spoon, eating the ice cream. Part strawberry and part chocolate, not bad, but not the best combination that you can get from the bowl. "Hey, you said that you play Destruction of Elysium. Do you play it a lot?"

Izzy colours again. "What's a lot? I play when I can, mostly."

I grin. "I'm dating a gamer who's also a fashion designer. Impressive." Because both of those things are seriously time-consuming.

"Dating?"

"If you'd like to call it that?" Did I say something wrong?

"Yeah." She looks up, her cheeks an interesting shade of red. "I'd like that. It sounds nice."

"Yes, it does." It sounds very nice.

At the start of the weekend I was worried about people reacting badly to me crossdressing, and now I've got a girlfriend who not only knows about it but who seems to have her own plans for dressing me up in the future. A weekend can change a lot of things.

I was worried I'd be missing the friends I usually hang out with at anime and gaming cons, but if they'd been here, I'd never have met Izzy as easily as I did, and that wouldn't have been as

138

much fun. I guess this really was a lucky thing to happen.

W A S D

Our final evening is over way too soon, but after exchanging phone numbers and friending each other on Discord, we both had to go to our own rooms for the night. I hope I'll still see Izzy in the morning at breakfast, but after this weekend, maybe we'll both be sleeping in. We did sort of agree that I'd come over to her place next weekend, if her parents were okay with it, taking a couple of days of rest before we see each other again, or, you know, some time to wash a bag a clothes before I'm off again.

I'm sitting on my bed, already wearing jeans and a shirt as I've packed most of my bags, not wanting to deal with it tomorrow morning.

"You're in looooove." Mya looks at me as she leans back on her bed, scrolling on her phone.

"Hush." I pretend to glare at her, but I can't help grinning. Just thinking of Izzy makes my heart beat faster.

"It's loooove..." She sits up more, her eyes soft as she smiles. "From fanboy to boyfriend in just a weekend. Impressive."

"We're taking things slow. Not like you and that Kevin guy." I raise my eyebrows at her.

"Hey. The sex is good, and he's funny, most of the time." She lets out a short laugh. "But I don't think there's more to us than that. Not like the totally smitten way you two have been acting, all gooey."

"What do you think of her?" I've known Mya for so long that I trust her on these things. Better the opinion of a second person and all.

"She's nice. And totally nerdy. And that same obsessive type of fan that you are when it comes to anime." Then her smile turns more serious. "I'm just surprised that she's trans. That really caught me off guard me when she told me."

"Yeah, me too. When she told me that she had to tell me something, and she looked all serious, I guess that I was more worried that it would be something really big or bad. But when she told me that she was trans, I don't know..." Thoughts about what it will mean for doing physical things with her kind of come in waves, but other than that... I don't know. I guess I'm still too much in the 'rose coloured glasses' stage of everything.

"It didn't scare you?"

I shake my head. "Not really. I was just glad she wasn't dying or had some rare destructive illness or something, you know?"

Mya snorts. "Of course, that would be totally you. Think big and destructive and everything." Then she takes a deep breath. "It's not going to be easy, dating Izzy, not because of who she is, but there will be people out there who will give you, or her, crap for her being trans when they find out."

I nod. "Yeah." I remember the way that those guys had been nasty yesterday after the competition, and that was just about some crossplaying. I remember how that scared me. But I also remember the way that Izzy stood up for me, so strong. I'll need to be that for her sometimes too. We may have to protect each other like that sometimes. "But I think she's worth it."

"I'd think you insane if you didn't think that. All of them are amazing, and I think that they're cool people to hang out with again. Also, that Ruby, he's got a wicked sense of humour."

I grin. "He has. And he's very protective of Izzy."

"They all are. After you two left for ice cream, we all talked, and I realised that you do not want to mess with these people. But they're awesome, and I guess that friendships like that are rare." She leans back, looking at her phone. "Oh." Her eyebrows go up. "It... ehh... It seems I *am* meeting Kevin this week again." A smile goes over her face and she keeps looking down at her phone.

So much for being the cool and collected one of us. She's definitely into him more than just the chemistry they have with their clothes off. "Congrats. Seems I'm not the only one who made *special* friends."

"Hush." She makes a sweeping motion in my direction with her hand. "I haven't even accepted the invitation yet."

"You're going to, though. I know you." I grab my own phone, opening a direct message chat with Izzy on Discord. 'Kevin asked Mya to meet up this week.'

It takes only moments before I get a reply and it's a whole row of smilies with hearts for eyes. 'YES!'

I laugh.

'She's said yes, right? And Jason said to tell her to not accept coffee if Kevin offers it, he makes it way too weak, Jason says it's like tea.'

I burst out laughing. 'No worries, I don't think she'll realise it with him around.'

"What are you laughing at?" Mya sits down next to me on the bed.

"Nothing. Just told Izzy about your invitation." I push my shoulder into hers. "She's happy for you."

"Tell her that I accepted and that I'll try to avoid the coffee." Mya looks down at my phone, reading the exchange.

"Will do." I grin.

This is good.

Not just meeting Izzy and the others, but Mya liking them too. It's not always easy for Mya to make new friends and her being friendly with Izzy is definitely a plus.

Your best female friend being friends with your girlfriend is definitely not a given in most situations, but it seems to be the case here.

This weekend only seems to be getting better.

15
Izzy

Otaku = Japanese word often used to describe people obsessed with anime, manga and video games. This word has a negative tone, though it's being used more and more as a point of pride. Being an otaku means that you have a great passion for something, even if it's unconventional or if others think you're too passionate about it. In the West, people tend to refer to themselves as otakus when their interest are mostly in the area of Japanese anime, manga and games, unlike geek or nerd which tend to be more focused on Western media.

This weekend was interesting, with all its ups and downs. I'm totally exhausted, but I don't know how easily I'll fall asleep tonight. The butterflies in my stomach keep me way too awake and active and just knowing that I'll be seeing Elliot again next weekend already makes me nervous.

Going from just being at the event and not even thinking or considering finding someone I'd fall in love with, to having a boyfriend and already having plans to see each other again... It's a lot.

I can't help my constant smile and no matter how scary the prospect of doing anything more than just kissing with Elliot is, it doesn't spiral me into panic, and that's a good thing.

Jason comes out of the bathroom, wearing sweats and a shirt, and he's still drying his hair from the shower. When he looks at me, he smiles. "You're not going to keep me awake all night with your tossing and turning, right?"

I shrug. "I don't know."

This is new. This whole boyfriend-thing is something new for me, and I have no idea how I'm supposed to act or how I'm supposed to calm down again. I've had my fair share of crushes, but this is different. This is not just a crush, Elliot is actually interested in me too.

"Fair enough." He grins. "We add two people to the con group, and suddenly we've got six people in relationships instead of just Evelyn and Mark. That's got to be some special convention magic right there." He sits on his bed, his eyes softer as he smiles. "Are you okay?"

I nod.

"Anxious?"

I nod again.

"I know you'll be fine."

"You'd be the one who'd know, because I don't." I smile at him. Jason would know, we've been close for years, and he's one of the few people who I feel really understands me.

After one of my parents' friend's daughter, who was also trans, committed suicide, we moved from the small town I'd grown up to Utrecht. My parents believed that if I wasn't constantly reminded of the ways in which I was different from other kids around me by people who'd seen me grow up, I may be able to be myself more. And if I could be myself, maybe I wouldn't always feel bad, maybe I'd be happier. They weren't wrong. Though, not all the darkness in my head had to do with who I was, or was supposed to be, we also found out that I have problems with depression, totally separate from all of that. But moving and being able to start over somewhere else, somewhere where I could be myself and present myself however I wanted to, it did help a lot to reduce depression triggers.

The first day of class, I showed up in a lolita gothic dress, very nervous, but Jason complimented me on it immediately. Back then, he was more into the androgynous look, though he definitely went more experimental as we got to know each other better. I told him about me being trans pretty early on, just because it felt better that he knew, that it wouldn't somehow surprise him and to explain some things that I did. He accepted it easily and I soon after found out that he was into the whole crossdressing thing, even back then.

At the time, I was just on hormone blockers so I wouldn't get facial hair and my voice wouldn't drop and stuff like that. Doctors don't start giving you cross-sex hormones until you're much older. I was so frustrated by it, especially since the girls around me were getting boobs and I was still flat as a pancake. But with Jason at my side, I was able to experiment a lot, and I got good at giving myself fake-but-realistic boobs pretty fast. The best thing about being friends with Jason was that he never treated me as anyone other than just another girl.

We didn't have many other friends at school, but that didn't matter. We had each other and later on we met others online and at conventions who were also into anime and cosplaying and everything. And, of course, I had my gaming friends online, who just cared about how good I was at my class and nothing else, mostly.

"And I'll be right." Jason winks. "And because I'll be right, you'll be able to sleep tonight."

"I'm not so sure about that." I grin at him. "But I'll try." Luckily, we won't have that long to travel tomorrow, and we don't have too many bags with us, for us anyway. It's still four bags each for all our outfits.

"Please do try. We need to leave tomorrow, and I kind of would like to actually have some of my day or energy left when we return home." He turns to his side, ready to fall asleep.

I guess sleeping is a good idea now... Probably. Likely.

But those butterflies inside just won't calm down.

⬚W⬚ ⬚A⬚ ⬚S⬚ ⬚D⬚

The next morning, I don't see Elliot or Mya at breakfast, and when I message Elliot, he's apparently just waking up and they have to hurry to catch the train home.

I'm a little disappointed, but I guess it's not a bad thing that I don't see him today. I don't know how to feel about saying goodbye and everything again. But it's also a little sad, I would still have liked to see him one last time.

After breakfast, Jason and I also finish packing our bags and as we're packing the last things up, there is a knock on the door. My heart skips a beat, not just from the surprise but also because it could be Elliot. Maybe?

But as I open the door, it's Ruby instead. "Hey." He grins.

"Hey." I smile, but I guess my disappointment is visible.

"Not who you hoped for?" He looks at me, winking.

"Not who I expected, but you're always a welcome distraction." I step to the side. "You all packed yet?"

"Yeah, I'm ready to go home." He comes inside, looking over to Jason. "Morning."

"Morning." Jason sits down on his bed.

"I was just checking in, seeing if you're all good to go, and to invite you to a party in a couple of weeks." Ruby grins again.

"Party?" I look to him.

"Yep. Birthday party, I'm turning twenty-two and thought it would probably be a good time to celebrate and all."

"Nice." I always forget that Ruby is not that much older than the rest of us, he just looks older because he's just so tall and broad and everything. "When is it?"

"Not exactly sure yet. Start of September." Then he eyes me. "You can take your boyfriend, if you want to." He winks.

My face heats up. Of course, he *now* reminds me of that... "Thanks. I'll try to remember that."

"Good." He nods. "Well, just wanted to tell you face-to-face. And see that you'll be off well." He looks at me, his eyes soft. "Did you have a good weekend?"

I nod, my cheeks still hot. "Yeah. It was good. It was different, but good."

"I'm happy. And I'm happy you've decided to not stick to your 'no kissing and no dating' rule. It's good to see you like this. It's adorable."

I'm not sure what to answer.

"Elliot seems like a good guy and happy to be with you, so, that's a definite plus in my book." Ruby comes closer. "Now, I'm giving you a quick hug and then I need to grab my things to leave."

I look up at Ruby, smiling. "I'll probably talk to you tonight or whenever." I open my arms, and he gives me a tight hug.

"Yeah. I'll talk to you soon." When he lets go of me, I don't know what to think about the way he looks at me. It's almost like he's a big brother or something, protective of his little sister.

Then he goes over to Jason, giving him a hug too. "Make sure to get her out of her room once in a while and that you don't get locked into your room either."

Jason laughs. "You're telling *us*? Pretty sure it was you who hadn't seen the sun in weeks before coming here."

Ruby shrugs. "Maybe." He steps back, giving a small wave. "Okay. I'm out of here. Time to go home."

"Talk to you soon." I wave back at him.

When the door closes behind Ruby, Jason looks at me. "We should finish up soon too and check out."

Yeah. Going home. Leaving this weekend, this place, behind us again.

Time to face the real world and the things that that means, whatever it means anymore. How can it feel like so much has changed, even if it's not really a big thing?

So I got a boyfriend. No big deal, right?

It still feels like a big deal.

W A S D

The trip home isn't too long, luckily, just a short bus trip to the train station, and then a train to Utrecht before we take the bus into the city. Jason and I both still live with our parents, and just a block away from each other. We can almost see the other's house, if Jason's place hadn't been just around a corner, right out of view.

That was the best part of becoming friends with him. We live so close together that we could always hang out, and our parents didn't care. They even hang out together when we're not around. I guess both having gender non-conforming kids means that they've got something to talk about. That, and Jason's parents are as easy in letting us do things as my parents are.

We've gotten into a lot of trouble together, but nothing too major, really. Just silly stuff.

"Need me to help you carry stuff upstairs?" Jason looks at me as we're standing in front of my house.

"Nah, I'll be fine." I grin. "I'll let Mum do it."

Jason lets out a short laugh. "You're the worst sometimes."

"I know." I shrug a little, my grin not faltering. "Nah, I think I'm gonna wanna go in on my own. They're going to want to, you know, *know* about things that happened."

"Ah, yeah. You're going to get *the talk*, finally." He's far too giddy about the idea.

"Potentially." I can't help my own smile.

Jason's eyes soften. "You look happy. You look happy and in love."

I nod, swallowing hard. "Yeah. I think I feel like that too. It's still a little confusing."

He quickly wraps an arm around my shoulders. "Hey, you're fine. Your first boyfriend. That's a pretty normal teenager experience, including the anxiety that comes with it. I would know, you saw me when I had my first girlfriend."

I nod, leaning against him. "I guess."

"You're a beautiful girl, someone was bound to fall for you at some point. I'm just surprised it took so long."

My heart falls a little. "Why?"

"Because you're amazing. You're smart, cool and way too funny. That, and you're cute."

"It's because everyone always assumes that you're my boyfriend." But his words do me well.

I know that people see me as a girl, I look like what most people expect girls to look like. But I'm always scared and awkward around people I like. And it's not that nobody ever confessed to me, but I've never felt safe enough to accept their feelings. Something that I really don't feel scared about with Elliot for some reason, not too much anyway.

"Well, that's a stupid reason for not trying to get to know you. If they're only out to be your boyfriend and not your friend and they fail to get to really know you. That's their loss."

"Just boys?" I smile a little.

Jason lets out another short laugh. "Girls are more awkward anyway. Girls flirting with other girls... It's always funny to watch or to hear about. What is it about girls flirting with each other and not knowing if it's flirting or not? Why is that such a thing?"

"I don't know." I remember seeing my friend Alex with her new girlfriend a couple of weeks back.

They'd met in Destruction of Elysium, and for the longest time, they didn't confess their feelings to each other. Too awkward and unsure if what the other was doing was flirting. But seeing them together at Alex' birthday party. It was hard not to see it. That attraction, that look in their eyes. They were head over heels. I wonder if Elliot and I looked like that this weekend.

"I've got to admit." Jason tightens his arm around me a little. "Sometimes I wasn't sure if I was watching two girls awkwardly flirt anyway this weekend. The way you and Elliot were acting towards each other... It reminded me of things."

I try to move my arm to poke him in his side, but the way he's got his arm tightened around my shoulders prevents me from doing anything. "Meany."

"Nah." He lets me go, smiling. "It was good to watch. I know you've been worried, and I know you've wanted to try dating someone for a long time, even if you didn't admit it to yourself. I'm just happy for you. I'm just happy you've found someone. And he seems really happy to have found you too."

I nod. "Yeah. He makes me happy."

"And that's all that I care about." He steps back. "Okay. I'm off. I need to use the loo like crazy, and you've got to face the parents."

"I know." I take a deep breath. "Talk to you as soon as they let me go."

"I want to know everything." Jason grins, pulling his backpack higher on his shoulders and grabbing his other bags. Then he turns around. "Later." And he walks off.

"Later." I watch him for a moment and then grab my own things, getting them over to the door before I open it. "I'm home!" I step inside, the cool house welcoming after the summer heat outside.

"Welcome home," Mum calls from the kitchen. "How was it? Did you have a good trip?" I hear some movement and then she steps into the hallway, carrying a plate with sandwiches. "I was about to have lunch. Are you hungry?"

"I'm good." I put my bags down and close the door behind me.

"Okay. Tell me *everything*. Did you have a good time at AmAnime?" She motions for me to follow her back into the kitchen. "I was sitting out back."

"I had a good time." I follow her and grab one of the bottles of water from the counter, opening it and taking a sip. Then I watch Mum sitting down in one of the chairs out back. "You may want to wait with that." I eye her as she was about to take a bite from her sandwich.

She puts it down as she frowns my way. "Why?"

"I... ehh..." How am I going to tell her?

"It's nothing serious, right?" She's frowning more.

"No. It's not. It's good." I almost fall over my words. "I...

I've got a boyfriend." The grin spreading over my face makes my cheeks ache.

Mum blinks a moment. "A boyfriend?"

I nod.

"Really?" Is that excitement in her voice?

"Really. His name is Elliot, and we met at AmAnime. He was cosplaying Aoi from Magical Princess Club!" I sit down on the other chair, my heart beating fast.

"Genderswapped?" My mum knows these things, and she knows my friends. This is a totally valid question.

"No. Crossplay. He looked really good. We won the first price in the competition together." My cheeks ache from my grinning.

"Congrats. And, of course, congratulations on the boyfriend too." She's also grinning, her eyes sparkling. "So, tell me more about him. What I'm hearing, I like him already. Aoi is a great cosplay choice."

I nod, my heart beating fast and I need to purposefully stretch my cheeks so they stop aching for a moment.

"You should see the pictures of us." I grab my phone, scrolling through the ones I took this weekend. "Look. These aren't all of them, Justin has some really nice ones too."

Finally someone to share my excitement with who hasn't seen him yet. Finally something typically teenager to share with my mum.

Moments like this, when I feel like what I think a typical girl feels like, it makes everything worth it. When I feel 'normal'.

16
Elliot

Shipping = The (fan) act of envisioning two characters from a series of manga, anime or other media to be together in a relation*ship*. Shipping is a common part of fan culture, where fans are dedicated to a specific 'ship', aka two characters being together in a relationship. Sometimes this can become a 'shipping war' where the shipping of one couple will automatically void another couple and fans will argue who the best 'ship' is. I don't tend to get involved in these things often, but after last weekend, I'm definitely one-hundred per cent behind a Sakura/Aoi ship, or Aoi/Sakura, I'm not picky.

I dump my bags next to the door and let myself fall on my bed. I'm tired, really tired. There is something about a weekend at a convention and then the travelling home that just exhausts me. Taking the train back was simple, and nothing happened to slow us down, and the bus to my place was right on time too. But now I'm back home, I feel like I could sleep for days.

I reach out, turning my computer on. I have no idea what I'm going to do with the rest of my day, but I should probably check the cosplayer forums and see what the other guys have been up to while I was away. I've stayed off Discord and other places most of the weekend, too busy with enjoying myself at the con, and especially too busy with Izzy.

Just thinking of her gives me these butterflies in my stomach and I grab my phone, looking at the pictures we took. She's beautiful, and I don't know how to act around her most of the time. A girl like her, so cute and adorable and sweet, why would she even look at me? Like... It's like a dream come true, and dreams usually aren't in any way related to reality. You wake up from them and realise that things aren't as fun or good as they seemed. But that hasn't happened yet.

My phone dings and a notification shows up at the top of my screen. 'You home yet?' It's Benji, one of the friends who couldn't come to AmAnime because he was saving up for another event later this year.

'Yeah. Why?' I send a message back.

'You haven't posted anything last weekend. You got lost or something? Lost your phone?'

'Nah. Just got busy, forgot to post.' I usually do post quite a lot of pictures on Twitter or other places during cons, but with me all dressed up as Aoi or in the goth dress, I didn't want to show that off until I was sure I was comfortable with doing so.

'Did you compete in the cosplay competition? I couldn't see you on the website.'

'Yeah, I did. Will show later.' When I get the courage to do so... *If* I get the courage.

I sit up again, sliding behind my computer and I log on. I first check my Twitter, it's easier to browse on a large screen instead of my phone and find that Izzy, Jason and some of the others are now following me there. Cool.

154

Clicking on Izzy's profile, I see that she's already posted a couple of pictures from the weekend. Just of her or her and her friends, none of us two together, but I guess that's not unexpected. She knows that I wasn't comfortable yet and I guess it's up to me to post the first picture of myself in a skirt.

I smile when I see a picture posted by Jason of Izzy asleep on the train. They didn't even have to go that far, and she still managed to sleep? That's skills. Though, the way she's got her face angled to the window, the sun on her face, she looks adorable, like an anime character. And she's not even all dressed up as one, just in a regular t-shirt and jeans.

I hit the reply button to the tweet. 'Obviously a sleeping princess, exhausted after a weekend of ruling over her kingdom.. #PostConBlues #SleepingPrincess'

Then I take a shot of all my bags in a heap on the floor and send out a tweet myself. 'Finally back home. Crazy weekend. Lots of fun. Made loads of new friends. Now alone. #PostConBlues #ReadyForConCrud #TooTiredToUnpack'

I look at the other pictures on my phone and decide against posting any of them just yet. I need to come back down to earth first and consider how I feel about being open about my crossdressing. It's not uncommon to crossdress, heck, I've just spent most of the weekend surrounded by people who were crossdressing, but it's new *for me*, and that scares me.

I get a notification of a reply to my tweet and click on it. It's from Mya. 'Just surprised you got everything home safe in the first place. Next time I'm not carrying all of that again...'

I grin. Well, she's got a point, really. I should probably invest in big sturdy suitcases or something. Dresses take up a lot of space, especially all the layers of the under skirts. *If* I'm doing this again, that is. Though, I'm pretty sure that I probably will. It was amazing, no matter how scary it was sometimes.

And I met Izzy. I wouldn't have spoken to her that easily if we hadn't both dressed up as characters from Magical Princess Club!, so that was definitely a good thing.

Now to get the courage to share this part of myself with people outside of those who were actually at the con...

Maybe later.

Maybe.

⟦W⟧⟦A⟧⟦S⟧⟦D⟧

I put the pan with pasta on the table as Mum looks at me curiously. Since I was at home anyway, I decided to cook dinner, but I'm pretty sure that's not why I'm getting the questioning looks.

"What?" I finally sit down, waiting for Mum to start scooping pasta and sauce onto her plate.

"You look... happy." She raises an eyebrow at me. "*Differently* happy than normal when you get back from a con."

"So?" I shrug, grabbing a spoon since she's apparently not going to do anything and Dad is also looking at me. I scoop pasta onto my plate, but stop before I get the sauce, too nervous about their staring.

"Did you have a good time at the convention?" Dad keeps his eyes on me, reading my reaction.

"Yes, I did." And I squeeze my lips together to hide the smile trying to form on my lips.

"I *knew* it." Mum grins. "You've got that fluttery thing going on. You've *met* someone."

"I may have." I focus on the sauce, looking at it so I can maybe hide my blushing.

"And you weren't going to tell us?" When I look at Dad,

he's grinning.

"I was waiting for you to realise what was going on." I wink at them. "I don't have to immediately tell you everything, you know. A guy can have *some* secrets."

"Right..." Mum smiles too. "But you're not very good at hiding 'secrets' like this."

Dad also starts scooping things onto his plate. "Who are they?"

"She's called Izzy. She lives in Utrecht and studies fashion. We also both cosplayed characters from the same anime on Saturday."

"So, she's good at making clothes, and she's into geeky things..." Dad shrugs. "Sounds like a great match." He doesn't say the rest, but I know that my parents, especially my dad, think that I don't date the right type of girls, that I always seem to date girls who don't share my hobbies. It's just not that easy to find girls who are into the same things as I am, like anime and manga, at least, not that I've found. They exist, of course, I meet so many at cons, but that doesn't always mean that we get along well...

"We are." I nod. "We've spent most of the weekend together, to be honest."

"I hope you didn't leave Mya all on her own, did you?" Mum looks at me.

"No. Izzy had some cool friends and Mya hit it off pretty well with one of them. She's seeing him again later this week." I didn't leave her all alone, if anything, it was the other way around more... Kevin and Mya were off together, just the two of them, pretty often, you don't need a lot of imagination to figure out why.

"And you?" Mum grins.

"I'm going to visit Izzy next weekend. You know, after the

unpacking and some good sleep." I take a bite of my dinner.

"Sounds like you had a great time. Anything else happen this weekend, apart from being stuck to a girl the whole time?"

"Not the whole time," I grumble. We weren't that bad, not really... "Anyway, Izzy and I competed together in the cosplay competition, and we won first place."

"Congratulations." Mum beams. "Do you have a picture of you two together? I've seen your cosplay, but if you won, hers has got to be good too."

I shrug, pulling out my phone and showing them a few pictures from the first day.

"She's cute." Mum smiles, but I can see something else in her gaze, something more reserved. "I get why you like her. But it's still a little strange to see you all dressed up like that. Just a skirt or dress around the house is one thing, but fully dressed up as a female anime character, that's a totally different look. It's hard to recognise it's you under all of that."

I shrug, an unease settling in my stomach. I already know that, I know that they think me dressing 'like a girl' is odd, even though they won't say a bad word about it. I know that they're still getting used to the idea of me doing this. And that makes me think of Izzy and how my parents may react to finding out Izzy is trans... I don't know. Not that they have to know about it right now, or that I'd have to tell them, but they're still getting used to me crossdressing, and I know that they've got a lot of questions that they won't ask. Adding even more to that, right now, doesn't seem like a good idea, especially since even Izzy isn't fully open about it to everyone, what I've seen this weekend anyway.

Like the way my parents asked about me having met 'someone' and who 'they' were, it's no longer automatically 'girl' and 'her'. They're trying to be inclusive, but by not asking and just presuming things about me now, it's going the opposite of that. It's like I've somehow changed my sexuality too, just because I changed my wardrobe choices. They've been acting like I've changed in more ways than just one and I don't even know how to talk to them about it, about their assumptions. They won't ask me things, and I don't know how to really bring it up in a way that doesn't seem like I'm not grateful that they're trying…

And, somewhere, I'm scared. I'm scared that if I tell them about Izzy being trans, that they're going to expect that I want that too. That I'll also want to become a girl.

Because that's what makes them the most uncomfortable, that I look so much like a girl in the cosplay pictures. I've seen them look at them with that questioning look, like they want to ask me if I want to live like that all the time, but they don't dare to actually ask me.

So, instead, they've started to use words that could apply to more than just a single gender. Like they feel that they have to be super inclusive or something just to keep me comfortable.

It's frustrating, but I also don't want to explain every last detail to them. Yes, I like dressing up in dresses and skirts, and I've got wigs with long hair, and Mya has been teaching me about putting on makeup. But I'm also still the same guy I've always been. I like girls, especially cute girls with long hair, and my sexuality or my gender hasn't changed just because I now dress differently.

But I guess that my biggest fear is that they'll feel like my crossdressing is just a 'phase' between being a boy and wanting to live as a girl. And no matter the thoughts going through my head since Izzy told me about herself, none of them have been that *I* wanted to be a girl. There have been a lot of thoughts about asking her fashion tips and of how to get a more feminine shape under clothes, hence my stupid question about her boobs, but none of them have been any more involved than that.

I don't know. I guess I'm scared that people will assume that I am trans too, like Izzy, or that I'll want to be different, when they find out about my crossdressing and that it will change things for me that I don't want to change. That people will treat me differently.

And that feels stupid. That worry feels so stupid, no matter how strong it is.

Being different isn't bad, but I've never really been *different*, so this is so new to me that I don't know how to deal with it…

17

Izzy

Scanlation = A combination of the words scanning and translation. When it comes to Japanese media, this usually refers to the original Japanese manga being scanned by fans and then translated into English or other languages. Scanlations are fan-based projects and often a group effort. Apart from the scanner and the translator, who are often not the same person, there are cleaners and typesetters involved, just like in any other manga or comic creation. The cleaners take out the original Japanese text and clean up any edges and other irregularities while typesetters put in the new English or other language text. This is dedication, as scanlation groups do this for free, just so others can also read certain manga that aren't available in a language they can read. And in more explicit manga, which in Japanese are often censored, there can be someone involved who will be redrawing certain body parts.

My bedroom is huge, and used to be really spacious too, used to be. When we moved here a couple of years ago, my parents remodelled the whole attic and made it into one big room for me. Sure, the ceilings are sloped, and I'm living right under the roof, which is really hot in the summer. But it's still huge in comparison to what most people have.

The door to my bedroom is on the floor below, right next to the bathroom, and after going up the stairs, with walls all covered in anime and J-pop posters, you arrive at the first 'section' of my room.

It's got a TV with a Wii and a PlayStation connected to it and a couch and two beanbags to hang out in. Jason and I love sitting on the beanbags when we play videogames together, it's almost perfection when it comes to gaming setups.

Then next, there is my 'crafts' part of my bedroom. Most of this space is dominated by two huge tables, to make laying out patterns easier, and two mannequins, one standard one, though it's still pretty fancy, and one that was designed specifically for me, although, it needs more boob size now, as it's a couple of years out of date, but it still works.

I've used some shelves to sort of separate the 'parts' of my bedroom and give extra storage space, since sloped roofs do not allow for many more traditional locations for shelves. The shelves of the 'craft' part are all filled with fabrics and things that I need when making cosplays. And everything that doesn't fit on my shelves here usually ends up in the storage behind the panels that line the sides of my room.

And the final 'part' of my bedroom is where I actually have my bed, and my computer, and my manga, and my anime, and things like that, anything not gaming or crafts related. It's a little separate from the rest because I easily get distracted and this way I can't do something else when I'm supposed to go to sleep. Apart from of course my computer, which is also here, but it just didn't fit anywhere else.

It sounds really big, and it's bigger than most people would be used to, but it's actually pretty crowded up here. Especially since I have a habit of collecting so many things and come up with a new hobby to try out about five times a year… But it's my room, my space, and my parents let me do whatever I want here, as long I don't break things, which is awesome.

But as I stand at the top of the stairs, dropping my bag on the floor next to me, I look at it with different eyes. I try to look at it the way Elliot would see it if he came over. The mess, the clothes and fabric all over the place, the big anime girls and boys on the walls, some of them wearing very little clothing… I look like such an otaku, really. I don't know, I guess that's just who I am, underneath it all.

I go over to my sleeping area, stepping over two dirty loads of laundry on the floor, one black and one that needs sorting, and finally flop down on my bed, taking a deep breath. I'm home, I'm finally home again. I love going to conventions, but getting back home after it is the best feeling ever.

I grab my phone and look at the pictures from the weekend, looking at everyone's happy faces. But especially, looking at one person in particular, looking at Elliot. Butterflies start fluttering in my stomach just thinking of him, and I get a little nervous imagining him coming here in a couple of days...

Now I actually have to make my room presentable before he comes over... Always fun.

But not today, today I'm not moving from my bed again, no way. Too tired.

Friday afternoon sort of came around before I even realised it…

For the last couple of days, I've been playing Destruction of Elysium with the guild, catching up on all that I missed this summer, did all my laundry, it turned into six loads to wash and fold in total, and even tried to neaten up my bedroom, not easy, especially when you get distracted by every new thing you find. It was quite the advanture, finding all sorts of projects from the last year.

But, of course, I totally got inspiration for a new dress last night, and I had to find the right fabric for it, which I was sure I still had, and that resulted in almost all my fabric being dumped on the floor to sort through. So, all the work on cleaning up my room was for nothing, basically.

I'm waiting in the main hall at Utrecht Central station. It's a pretty new station, and they've redesigned the whole thing a couple of years ago. It's super open and modern and bright these days. The rails and platforms are on the level below, and the main hall is basically this huge arch built right over it. It's got all sorts of little shops for food or drinks or just things you may need or want when you travel. It's clean and modern but I prefer the look of old stations like Amsterdam Central or Groningen Central, they're so much more iconic, but at least Utrecht is easier to navigate now, and it feels safer with more space and light. Upsides and downsides of each.

I'm so nervous. People are crowding all around me, coming and going, as I keep my eyes on the board that tells me what trains have arrived. It's ten past two, so Elliot's train should arrive in another two minutes, if there are no delays...

My phone buzzes and I pull it out, hoping it's not Elliot telling me he's late, but instead it's Jason. 'Your boy here yet?'

I sigh. 'I'm still waiting. He should be here soon.'

Jason sends me a broadly smiling smilie and then another

message. 'I'll come annoy you two as much as possible this weekend.'

'No!' He's not allowed to do that!

'Of course, I should. Maybe I should come borrow some manga or videogames or something. I'm trying to come up with something really embarrassing to ask for now.'

'No. You can't do that. That's not fair.' I frown at my phone, like that's going to help anything. Jason can be so mean!

"Izzy!" I almost jump as Elliot's voice is suddenly really close.

I look up and Elliot is standing a couple of feet away, grinning at me. He's wearing black jeans, a shirt with Deimos from the Destruction of Elysium anime on it and really big shoes, probably New Rock or something similar. He looks really sexy like this.

"Is your phone not working right?" He comes closer, still smiling.

"*Jason* is not working right." I sigh.

"Ah. He never is." Elliot grins again, then he cocks his head to the side. "Hug?"

I nod, stepping in close, and I wrap my arms around him. He feels so good to hug, and I love how his arms tighten around me. "So good to see you again." Lame, but whatever.

Elliot lets out a laugh. "You too. That's a different look from before." He steps back a little and looks me up and down. I'm wearing a black jeans skirt with a frilly lavender top, and I put on my cutest, while still pretty comfortable, pair of sandals I could find.

"I'm not the only one." I wink and then look around. "You want to go to the city centre first or drop your things off at my place? It's really fast to get back to the city centre from my place, so not too bad, no matter what we decide on." I'm starting to ramble, I'm so nervous.

Elliot smiles, sliding his hand into mine, squeezing a little. "I think that dropping my bag off first is a good idea. I don't really want to lug my laptop all over the place, you know?"

"Okay." My heart is in my throat. Going to my place first means that he'll see my room very soon... *Eep*. "Then we need to get to the busses down those stairs. Unless you'd like to walk." I glance at him.

Elliot shakes his head. "Walking is fine, normally, but no thank you, not today. It's way too hot."

I start tugging him along. "Maybe you shouldn't have put on those shoes then. They look really warm."

He laughs again. "Yeah, I should have thought of that too, but they're not too bad, and they're too comfortable. It's mostly the jeans and the backpack that are an issue. Plus, I had to find something to impress you."

"Colour me impressed. For daring to wear them in this heat." I step onto the escalator and Elliot steps really close next to me, pressing to my side. I don't think my heart will calm down at all this weekend, not when I keep feeling like this every time he comes near me.

Elliot leans in close. "You're grinning."

"I can't help it." I stretch my cheeks. "Stop staring at me."

He lets out another laugh, and we get off the escalator.

I quickly navigate us to the right bus stop, and we have to wait there for a couple of minutes. There is a bus to my place every five minutes, but we just missed it, I saw it pass as we stepped on the escalator.

"So..." Elliot leans against the glass wall of the bus stop pulling me to him, his arms around my waist, as he looks at me.

166

"What is your place like?"

"My *parents'* place is kind of old, but in a neighbourhood with pretty big and old houses. Ehh, what else?" I stare at him, at the way he smiles and then pulls his teeth over his lower lip before he answers me.

"How thin are the walls?" He smirks, and my cheeks heat up fast.

"Really?" My voice is more of a squeak. "That's... That's..."

Elliot reaches up, running his fingers over my lower lip. "I'm kidding. Though, I did hear something about Dance Dance Revolution, so I do hope not too thin." He winks, and I flash him a quick glare.

"Meanie." I look up, trying to see when the next bus will arrive. It looks like it'll take another couple of minutes. "Instead of being mean to me, what did your parents say about you coming here today?" I step out of his embrace because if I stay that close, I may get too distracted, and I'll want to kiss him, and then we'll miss the next bus. That seems to be a real danger right now, especially with the way I keep wanting to lean into him.

"They were curious about the girl I liked enough to travel two hours for. And my mum totally loved your cosplay. She's the one who taught me how to make clothes, so it's kind of something we have in common." He's smiling sweetly now, a different side to him. "They were surprised that I met someone at AmAnime, but they were like 'you're old enough to choose these things, so whatever'." He shrugs a little. "What about your parents?"

I let out a breath before I try to shrug too, but fail. "They were happy for me. Though a little wary. But, yeah..." I look at my feet before I start rambling and saying nonsense things.

"Will they be there when we get to the house?"

I shake my head. "They're both at work. But they'll be home by dinner."

"Okay." Elliot's voice is soft. "I'll promise I'll *try* to behave, then." When I look up at him, he's smiling again, and I shake my head again.

"*Everything* is behaviour, even bad behaviour." I raise an eyebrow at him.

He flashes me a grin. "You got me."

I can't believe he's so silly… It'll be fine. It will all be fine. I don't have to worry about anything. Not about Elliot or about my parents. It's not that scary.

Even though it totally is.

Bringing home your first boyfriend... I just think that that's scary anyway, no matter who you are. And then there's me being a huge fangirl and my room being covered in posters and such. What if I'm too much of an otaku for Elliot to handle? Maybe I should have covered up or taken down some of my posters... Maybe.

Maybe.

I don't know anymore. Why does this have to be so confusing?

18
Elliot

Light novel = A type of book in Japan which is characterised by having manga-style images in combination with regular story text. This type of media isn't really that popular in the West, and doesn't get scanlated or translated very often, which is too bad, because a lot of light novels do get turned into anime or manga, but you always lose some of the original content that way. My Japanese isn't good enough to read them, so I can never read the books that some of my favourite anime are based on, sadly enough.

The bus ride to Izzy's place is pretty short and I like the view, both next to me and out of the window. Izzy was right when she said that she lived in a pretty old neighbourhood, these houses are seriously *old*. Though, probably just as old as some of the areas in the city centre of Groningen, so I'm pretty used to it. It's interesting to see the different styles of houses between the two cities, though.

The inside of Izzy's house is pretty nicely decorated, though not overwhelmingly so. And after she quickly points me to the living room, the kitchen and a couple of other small rooms on the ground floor, we go up the stairs, and then we stop in front of another door.

"My room is upstairs, don't mind the mess, I *tried* cleaning it." She lets out an awkward laugh, and I reach out, putting my fingers to her cheek, leaning in.

I want to kiss her, she looks adorable when she's a little nervous. Her eyes grow, and she looks everywhere but me, the tip of her tongue darting out and sliding over her lips.

"Oh, and don't pay too much attention to the posters and stuff." Her cheeks colour as she says it. Interesting.

"The posters?" I raise an eyebrow, but can't help smiling.

"Yeah. The posters, you'll see what I mean." She lets out a sigh and then opens the door.

Behind the door is a set of stairs but the most obvious thing is the poster of Yuri!!! on Ice right in view as we step inside. Ah, that's what she meant with not minding the posters.

Izzy walks ahead of me, and I close the door behind me. Every little piece of wall in here is covered in posters or cards, almost all of anime, though I recognise a couple of games and even some bands.

"This is my room." She steps to the side, and as I take the last couple of steps, I look around.

The place is huge, and very full. In a way, it makes total sense that this is Izzy's room. It's cluttered, busy and very cheerfully coloured.

"This is my gaming corner." She points to a TV and a couch. "Then there is my atelier, and behind that my bed." She shrugs. "That's kind of it."

"Right. 'Kind of it?'" I take her hand and pull her to me. "Before anything else, I'd like to kiss you now."

Her eyes grow. "Oh." She almost sounds surprised.

"Can I?" I slide my arms around her waist, and her arms slip around my neck.

"Yeah." She smiles now, leaning closer. "I'd like that."

"Good." I nervously lick my lips and then cover the last distance between us. Her lips are soft and warm, giving in as I push on a little. Sparks go through my body from every point where we touch, sparks that set my whole body on fire.

When she stills in my arms a moment, I pull back.

"You okay?" I try to see if I made her uncomfortable.

She's smiling still, but looks awkward. "I'm good. Just..." She shrugs a little. "Still not used to it." She runs her tongue over her lower lip. "And it's so hot."

"Yeah, I can't do anything about the heat, sorry." I pull her away from the stairs, finding a safer place to stand around, a place where one misstep doesn't end this weekend on a fun trip to the hospital with multiple broken bones.

"I know." She sighs.

I sit down on the couch, tugging on Izzy's hand to come sit down too, and she nervously climbs on the couch next to me, pulling the skirt over her legs to make it more comfortable. The silence between us turns awkward fast. "Am I the first guy who's been here who you've wanted to kiss?" Extra points to asking awkward things when trying to break an even more awkward silence.

Izzy flashes me a grin. "You're the first *person* who's been here who I've wanted to kiss like that."

"First boy or girl?"

She shrugs a little. "First boy, girl, non-binary, anyone. I've not... I've not done this before."

I bump my shoulder into hers. "It's an honour then, to be

the first."

Izzy lets out a snort and looks at me, her eyes sparkling. "You're silly."

"And you're smiling again." I pull on her arm, trying to get her to sit on my lap. This couch feels like the perfect place to make out.

After a couple of awkward moments, she's on my lap, straddling me, her skirt fanning out around us. I put my arms around her waist, holding her comfortably, but not too tightly.

I play with my thumbs over her back, trying to distract myself from the fact that I've got a beautiful girl in my lap and my body is definitely responding to it. My jeans are getting tight right where she's sitting, and I'm pretty sure that she can feel it too.

She keeps looking at me, a mixture of nervousness and curiosity on her stunning features. Then she leans in and starts kissing me again, her arms around my neck. This time she's much more active and aggressive with her kisses. Not just with her lips, but also with her tongue, and she's even nibbling on my lower lip, taking total control over what we're doing.

I try to keep up with her, but my head is filled with so many sensations. and it all feels so good. I let out a soft moan, and Izzy stills in my arms, stopping her kiss. *Not good.* "Izzy?" I open my eyes, looking at her. "What's wrong?" My voice is quiet, trying not to spook her even more.

"I don't know if I can do this." It sounds like she's about to cry and I pull back further, lessening my grip around her even more, making sure not to keep her in a way that makes her feel trapped.

"Can't do what?" I reach up with one hand, running my thumb over her cheek. She may not be crying right now, but she

172

looks about to.

She opens her mouth, her lips forming words but nothing comes out. Then she takes a deep breath. "I don't know if I can do more than kissing. I don't know. I..." She shakes her head, tears now forming on her lashes. "I know that you'll probably... You'll want to… But..." She shakes her head, almost climbing off my lap. "I don't know. I don't know if I can."

I take her hand in mine, hoping that it will keep her from fleeing. She can pull away easily, but it still keeps us connected without trapping her. Giving her control over what happens next. If she climbs off now, she'll flee, and we'll probably not get a chance to bring this up again without it becoming even more awkward. "Izzy," I whisper, sliding my hand into her hair, softly stroking it. "Izzy, Izzy."

She looks at me, anxiety in her eyes, anxiety and fear.

"I like kissing you. I'd love to kiss you all weekend long." I slide my hand down her neck, my fingers playing over the exposed skin there. "I've said it before. I'm okay with taking things as slow as you want me to. Really."

"But you're already..." She looks down between us. Towards where my hard-on is caught in my jeans.

"I know. And just because my body reacts like that doesn't mean that we *have* to do anything."

She frowns, confused now. "Don't you want to?"

I can't help my smile. No matter how I've got no idea how to go about doing 'things' with Izzy that involve more than what you can do over people's clothes... I did look things up this week, 'how to have sex with a trans girl', but most of the advise came down to 'do whatever you're both comfortable with', on top of some physical things that seemed pretty obvious when you're dealing with people who have parts like ours. But while I'm a total noob on *how* to have sex with a trans girl, like I do already have experiences with cis girls, I totally want to do all sorts of 'dirty' things with Izzy. That's not the problem. "I *do* want to. But I don't want *you* to be uncomfortable. I can deal with mister happy, he really doesn't need the be entertained every time he's awake." I'm totally blabbing now, making silly voices because I'm also not that comfortable talking about sex and bits, but Izzy burst out laughing.

"'Mister happy'?" She shakes her head. "Is that his name?"

I grin. "Only to make cute girls laugh." I slowly slide my hand up her neck again, into her hair and tug on her a little, pulling her closer. "But I'm serious. I'm not looking to do things you're not comfortable with. You get to set the pace, we're going your speed." Because as long as I get to hold her and be with her, any speed is good with me.

She nods and then puts her lips on mine again, kissing me hard before pulling back. "You're really okay with me? With *me*? My body?" She's frowning again, worrying.

"I am. You're beautiful, and you're amazing. The rest we'll figure out when we get to it." I keep my voice light. I really don't want to scare her off, even though I feel like I keep doing exactly that, scaring her off.

Or maybe it's just that she doesn't really believe me yet. Maybe she doesn't really believe that I really do want and like her. But that means I have to keep convincing her until she does believe it, until she'll trust me.

No matter how long that takes.

W A S D

Izzy is dozing off, her head on my shoulder, as we're watching an old season of Cardcaptor Sakura.

We've both not seen it for a long time, but my eyes kept being pulled to the poster of a very intimate, but fully clothed, display between Sakura and Tomoyo on the wall opposite the couch. We may have had plans to go into the city centre today, but I don't think they're going to happen any time soon. Staying inside and watching anime is both the more couple-y and the saner option, as it's really, really hot outside today.

I hear sounds from the floors below, and then the door downstairs opens.

"Izzy?" It's a woman's voice. "You home?"

"Yeah," Izzy calls out sleepily, not moving away, though I can feel her tense up a little. "Up here."

There are footsteps on the stairs, and I see a woman who looks a lot like an older version of Izzy, just with lighter hair and a slightly sterner face. As she sees me, she smiles. "Ah, he's here. Hi, I'm Izzy's mum." She waves a little at me.

I wave back. "Elliot. But I'm pretty sure you already knew that." I smile back.

"I guessed as much." She takes the last couple of steps and looks at the TV. "Ah. It's been a while since I've seen Sakura." Then she looks back at us, her eyes soft. "I'm ordering pizza. Do you have anything you really like or can't have?"

I shrug as best as I can with Izzy stuck to my shoulder. "I don't prefer fish on my pizza. But I love peppers or chilis, and I like cheese?"

"I want a cheese pizza." Izzy looks at her mum. "Sliced, please."

Izzy's mum grins. "Coming right up. You want to continue watching that downstairs or do you want to watch something else?"

Izzy thinks for a moment, then she looks at me, sitting up. "Do you want to watch anime downstairs or a TV series or something? We're watching Bones right now. Like, me, Mum and Dad are, and Jason, when he's here."

"I'm good with anything." I look between them.

Then Izzy's mum nods, before looking at Izzy. "Is Jason joining us?"

"I don't know." Izzy frowns a little, eyeing me. "If he's joining us, he'll probably stay a while. We can watch more anime or play games or something after dinner. I don't know." She's obviously not used to him not being around all the time, and maybe having a bit of a buffer will make her feel less awkward around me. Plus, the guy's pretty cool.

"Sure. Maybe I can beat him at Soulcalibur or something. He *did* challenge me to a game at AmAnime, telling me that I wouldn't be able to beat him with Kilik." I smile and Izzy's grinning too.

"I'll message him and tell him to bring his GameCube over." She grabs her phone.

"And I'll order the pizzas. I'll see you two downstairs in a while." Izzy's mum goes down the stairs. Before she's out of sight, she looks back, smiling.

Well, that seems to be one parent who's approved of me. Good. One down, one to go... And to not mess up things with Jason, of course.

"Jason is coming right over. He said he's looking forward to kicking your butt." Izzy turns to me, grinning, her eyes sparkling.

"What?" I raise an eyebrow at her, and she grins more.

"I don't know. Jason is really good, you know." She shrugs a little.

"And so am I. I should take my save game with me next time." Next time. *If* there is a next time and *if* that goes well too.

That's a lot of ifs, but it also feels really exciting to think of, so that's good. Right?

19
Izzy

Shoujo = Means young woman in Japanese. This term is used to describe media like manga and anime focused on teen girls. The most common theme in them is romantic relationships and a high focus on the emotions of the characters. I love reading them because they can give you that gooey feeling inside and that makes me happy.

I'm stuck between Jason and Elliot on the couch in the living room. We're eating pizza and watching an episode of the new Frankenstein series with Sean Bean. Apparently, not everyone was into Bones and the gore that comes with it. Though, I'm not sure that Frankenstein is a much better choice on that front. But I don't care. I'm happy right where I am, and that's all that counts right now.

Elliot coming over was scary, and then the whole making out, and me freaking out a little during that making out thing, that wasn't good. but it's good now. Now Elliot is here a little longer, I'm not as nervous anymore, and I'm not going to make out with him right in front of my parents. That's not something I want to do, really.

But just being here with everyone around, it's very calming, and I guess I could get used to this.

Dad looked a little odd as he saw Elliot, but they hit it off when Elliot said something about a book he'd read or was reading or something, and that seemed to make my dad like him. Figures.

When I'm alone with Elliot, I keep wanting to touch him, I keep wanting to kiss him and everything. I never thought I was someone like that, someone who just couldn't stop touching the person they liked, but apparently, I am. It's just that, with my body not exactly being the way that I feel like I should be, I don't really know how to *do* things with him. What does he expect from me? What do I want him to do? What do I *not* want him to do? I don't know. And that's the frustrating part.

I have no idea. I have no idea how to do all these things that most couples do, and I don't know if it's any use to ask Jason or someone else. They're cis couples, and my problems are more related to me being trans. But who can I talk to? Sure, I've got trans friends online, but that just feels so awkward. Just... I don't know. I don't even know who I should ask, or how, or if my feelings are even normal, or if I'm just overthinking things. That last one is a real possibility too.

Elliot's fingers trail over my arm, his touch warm. I glance his way, not sure how to react to him, how to act now. But he's just smiling, happy. Then his eyes go back to the TV, and I slide my hand along his, entwining our fingers. Touching him makes the butterflies in my stomach only worse. But it also feels good, and he's so warm, but not too sticky in this hot weather.

After the episode ends, I get up, looking at the two guys on the couch. "I think there is a Soulcalibur contest to be played. Right?"

Jason and Elliot look at each other and then they both nod. Elliot stands up first, stepping close to me. "Of course." He's grinning, and I can't help my own grin.

"Did Izzy warn you yet? I am quite good at it." Jason also stands up, putting the empty pizza boxes on top of each other on the table.

"That's what everyone says." Elliot laughs, and we go back up to my room. I'm walking between Jason, who is in front of me, and Elliot, who is behind me, and I'm just hoping that their friendly banter really is friendly and not just them trying to be nice to each other because I'm around... That would be a bad thing.

It's not like Jason and I have any more to our friendships than being friends, we're not romantically involved, or sexually, we're just really close friends who share most of their lives together. But I know that some girls Jason dated would see me as 'competition' or something. We just hang out a lot, always having fun. He's my best friend, we understand each other in ways that many others never do, although, maybe Elliot does too, understand the way we are.

Jason did joke at one point that I was more likely to start hitting on one of the girls he dated than I'd ever see him in a sexual or romantic way, and he wasn't wrong. Though, he'd never say it when the girls were around, some people do not take jokes like that lightly, especially people who would worry about me trying to 'steal' him away in the first place.

I grab Jason's bag with the GameCube, go over to my TV and turn it on, looking over to the guys. "Where do you want to sit?" I start unpacking the old console, connecting the cables to my TV on autopilot. I don't have a GameCube, but Jason brings his over often enough for me to do this at least a couple of times a month.

"Beanbag for me." Jason flops down into one.

"Eh, I guess for me too." When I look back, Elliot is looking a little awkward, standing in the middle of the room. "It's easier with the cables and stuff." He shrugs.

I smile a little. "I'm good with anything. You're going to be competing against each other, I'm just watching." I connect the controllers to the machine and then step over to them, giving them both a controller. Then I go to the back of my room and grab my fluffy blanket before I go back to them. It may be really warm today, but I prefer to sit on this and not just on the couch, always, no matter the weather.

When I get back, they've already chosen their characters. Jason is Ivy and Elliot is Kilik, of course. That was to be expected with these two.

"You ready?" Jason looks back at me. "Going to watch how I kick your boyfriend's butt in this game?"

"Hey." Elliot almost sounds offended, but then he grins. "I'm going to be the one wiping the floor with you. Watch me."

I let out a short sigh and then flop down on the couch, making myself comfortable. "All words. I want to see action. Come on, action!"

They both grin as they turn back to the game and Jason starts the battle.

They immediately go for it, hitting each other, using special moves. It's great fun to watch, since they're pretty evenly matched. I just lean back, watching what is going on on the screen and not worrying about the rest too much. This is much better than constantly worrying about what I'm doing or supposed to be doing, much much better. This, I know.

Playing videogames and competing against each other, or just watching others do it, are things I know how to do.

It's late when Jason finally leaves, way past midnight, and when he closes the door to my room, things immediately get more uncomfortable. Elliot and I are alone again, and we're going to be sleeping soon... We're going to be sleeping in the same room, and we'll have to change in other clothes to get to bed and everything...

I bite my lip, trying to not let the panic grab me. I don't even change my clothes in front of Jason, I don't ever let anyone see me without clothes. I don't, simple.

"Izzy?" Elliot comes closer, his eyes soft, and also filled with sleepiness. "Did you have fun?"

I nod. "Yeah." After they finished playing Soulcalibur for a couple of rounds, and ended up with equal scores, we played Mario Kart instead, because we could all play that together and at least I was more in the mood for it than Soulcalibur.

"Good." He smiles, reaching out and doing that thing where he softly touches my face, like I'm precious or something. But it's not the touch that makes the emotions shoot through me, it's the look in his eyes, that protective look. That doting look that I've only ever seen people give people who aren't me.

"I think we should go to sleep." I break eye contact with him, my cheeks heating up.

"Probably." His voice is lower now. "Where do you want me to sleep?"

Where do I want him to sleep? I blink. "What?"

"I can sleep on the couch, or an extra mattress or something. I don't know if you..." His face is now colouring too.

Oh. I presumed he'd want to sleep in my bed.

"Unless you want me to?" He's so careful, giving me the option to back out before I even have to come up with an awkward way to turn him down.

"I..." I shrug, a little overwhelmed, and my brain fuzzy from exhaustion. "I don't know."

"Okay." He smiles, shrugging. "We still need to change anyway, so we can decide later." He looks around for his bag. "Do you want to get changed first?"

"Yeah." My voice is quiet, my heart beating really fast, my whole body on high alert.

I turn and go over to my closet, picking out a cute top and pyjama shorts, since a full pyjama is much too hot in this weather. I'm really aware of Elliot being close by, and I grab a different pair of underwear, one that's more comfortable to sleep in. Then I go down the stairs, to the bathroom and lock the door behind me, taking a couple of deep breaths.

Elliot sleeping in my bed, or sleeping on a mattress nearby, or something else? What can I do? What would be the right thing? Would he expect anything from me if I let him sleep in my bed? And what if we end up pushed against each other and I get a bodily response? Would that freak him out? Would that freak him out in the morning?

Would *I* freak out if he had a response like that to me being next to him in bed? If I woke up and felt him against me like that?

I let out a groan, not liking all these things going through my head at all. Why is this all so complicated? This is one of those moments where I wished I was just 'normal', no matter how unlikely that thought even is. I wished I didn't have to go through all of this stress just because I like someone.

I wished I didn't have to go through so much stress, period.

I quickly strip down and put my night clothes on. Then I brush my teeth and grab the clothes I was wearing before.

Time to face Elliot, time to decide what I want to do for the night, because I still have no idea...

I get back up the stairs, and Elliot is sitting on the couch, looking at me, his smile growing even more when he sees me.

"That's an adorable pair of pj's." He stands up, coming over to me and then trails his fingers over my bare shoulder. I may have chosen something that is cute and a little sexy at the same time. I didn't want to wear something totally unsexy, I *am* going to be sleeping in the same room as the guy I like, you know. I get to dress up a little for that…

"Thanks." My face heats up. "Ordered them from Japan. They were too cute to resist."

"I can imagine." He lets out a laugh, and when I look up at him he flashes me a grin. "I'll be right back." He gives me a quick kiss on my bare shoulder before he dashes off with a stack of clothes in his hands.

I put my clothes on a chair and then go over to my bed, looking around. I could put a mattress on the floor next to the bed, I have the space and the spare for it, but also... My bed is big enough, and we could just sleep on either side of the bed, or something like that.

I don't know. I really have no idea. This is hard.

184

I like the idea of being able to touch him and everything, but then what happens next? I know he keeps saying that I'm the one who decides what happens, what we're going to do, but what if I don't have a clue either? What if I don't even know what I want myself? Then what?

Arg!

20
Elliot

Shoujo-ai/Yuri = Two related media genres in Japan where the main plot is a love relationship between two girls or women. Shoujo-ai means girl-love and generally is of a more innocent nature. It doesn't mean that the characters are girls, it's mainly to differentiate that there is little to no sexual content in the stories. Yuri means lily in Japanese and is of a more sexual nature, not just focusing on romantic love. I enjoy reading both of them, at different times.

When I get back to Izzy's bedroom and look around, I can't help but smile. Izzy is such a geek and fan of all things Japanese, I love it. I already knew that she was, of course, but to actually see the things around me, to see how nerdy she is exactly, it's different. It's no longer imagining or wondering just how much we're alike but knowing that she really is on the same level as me in this way. It makes me calm down around her in ways that I've never been able to do before. Finding a girl who is as nerdy as you are, it's rare. Especially when it's nerdy in the same ways.

Izzy is sitting on her bed. The pink frilly top with cute bows where the shoulder straps connect to the front of her top suits her so well, especially with the pink shorts with bows on them she's wearing.

I'm just wearing one of my anime shirts with sweat shorts, simple and practical. I'd packed them because I was pretty sure that there would be no naked sleeping, not even half-naked sleeping, on this trip and I was right.

I carefully sit next to her on the bed. "Am I sleeping on a mattress on the floor or in the same bed as you?" I don't want her to think that I don't respect her boundaries, but I also don't want her to think that I don't wish I could sleep in the same bed as her...

It's a fine line to walk and a little confusing sometimes, as I've found out, but it's worth it. I want her to feel safe, but I also don't want her to feel like I'm treating her any differently than how I'd treat other girls I've dated in the past.

"Ehm..." She lets out a sigh, then she looks at me, and I can see the frustration on her face. "What would you like best?"

"What would *I* like?" This is up to me?

"Yeah." She sighs again, letting out a little growl of frustration that almost makes me smile. "Because I don't know anymore."

"I'd like to sleep in the same bed as you. If you're okay with that?" I try to read her body, the way she reacts to that.

But she just nods, relaxing some. "Okay." She flashes me an shaky smile and moves aside. "But you're sleeping on the wall side." She points to the other side of the bed.

"I'm good with that." I smile, climbing over to the appointed side and stay on top of the covers. "I'm not going under there, though. It's too hot." The temperature in here is almost like an oven, and I'm not sleeping under the covers tonight, getting all sticky and stuff, when I know that Izzy isn't even that sure about this all. This makes a perfect and not-awkward excuse to give her some extra space.

"Fine." She grins a little, then climbs under a single layer of sheets herself, staying on her back, her arms folded over herself. She looks happy, but also nervous, and no matter how cool I try to look, I'm a little anxious too. It's not easy to know how to act the first time you're sleeping over at someone's place, and that has everything to do with trying to seem cool for the one you like.

I lie down too, turning to my side so I can watch her. I love looking at her, just watching her every emotion go over her face, or the way her whole face lights up when she smiles when she gets excited about something. I slide my hand to the space between us. "Can I hold your hand while we sleep?"

"It's totally sticky though. It's so hot and humid in here." She eyes me for a moment but then turns to her side too, reaching out, and I take her hand in mine. She's right, it's too hot, but I don't know how comfortable she is with me spooning her and everything, both because of the body stuff and because of the heat.

"I'm okay with that." I grin, kissing her fingers a few times as I keep looking at her. Her eyes go wide for a moment, and I can hear the way her breath catches, see the way she swallows as her eyes are stuck on what I'm doing.

"Elliot..." she whispers, her voice a little rough.

"Yeah?" I whisper back.

"I would like to kiss you now." She smiles a little, but there is also a tension in her voice.

"I wouldn't be against that." I reach out to her with my other arm, tugging on her shoulder a little. "Come here."

She nods, sliding closer and I move my arm under her head as I take her in my arms. And then she's close, pressed up against me, and her lips are only a breath away from mine. She feels so good against me, especially as she wraps her arm around my waist too and then angles her head up a little.

The next moment, her lips are on mine. The first kisses tentative, mostly just exploring what we're doing, but as we keep going, she gets bolder, and her kisses get harder, feistier.

I can't help my grin, but before she can ask me anything, I push closer and slide my tongue along hers, pulling a soft happy sound from her. She's so responsive, so adorable. It makes my stomach flutter in all sorts of ways.

Her fingers tighten at the back of my shirt, and suddenly she's taking control of the kiss, taking my breath away. A rush of feelings coursing through me.

I could do this all night. Kissing her, holding her, I could do it all night and never tire of it.

W A S D

When I wake up, Izzy is still in my arms, her head against my chest, her hair tickling my nose and her arm still wrapped around my waist. All the while, she's under the covers and I'm on the outside, the extra barrier between us still in place. I don't exactly know when we fell asleep, but it was really dark outside, and now it's really bright out. Which, in the middle of summer could either mean seven or ten in the morning. But I don't really mind.

I smile a little, taking a deep breath as I tighten my arm around her shoulder a little, the other one is asleep under her head and is going to be painful and tingly when she moves later, but for now, she can stay where she is. Having her here with me is the best thing ever, and I'm not letting her go yet. I normally don't know what to do, but with Izzy, just staying here, right where I am, is all that I really want.

As I look around the room, at all the little things that make Izzy Izzy, my mind goes to a place it's been going a couple of times these last days. A place that I don't really like for it to be going, but it still happens.

In a different world, one where I didn't have friends who pulled a disgusted face each time I showed interest in something that was 'girly', a world where 'boy' and 'girl' things weren't so strictly separate, would I be like Izzy? Would I be wishing to have a different body too? Would I be wishing to be a girl too?

I don't feel like that now, in this world. I just like dressing in different types of clothes, depending on my mood, but mostly depending on my courage. But would that be different? If things weren't so strict, would I have been trying things out sooner? Are my parents right in worrying that I want 'more' than dressing differently?

I don't know the answer to that question, and I don't know if I would like to know the answer either. Somewhere it feels disrespectful to Izzy to wonder about these things. To wonder about all the things that seem to scare me, but which Izzy has had to face for years. To idly think about things that Izzy has probably struggled with for a long time, while I'm 'safe' in my own bubble of cis-ness, of identifying with the sex that was assigned to me at birth, at least mostly.

Considering all those things, I don't know, and I also don't know if I would even have the courage to be different, even in that world, even in a 'safer' world.

"You're sighing." Izzy's voice is a little rough from sleep, and she pushes her head to my chest more, letting out a small content sound, before pulling back. "Why are you sighing?"

I give her a quick kiss on her forehead, not wanting to chance morning-breath kissing just yet. "Nothing you have to worry about." Because all of this is just in my head. I push all the thoughts away, instead focusing on the beautiful girl in my arms. "Good morning."

"Morning." She smiles a little. "You're really warm."

"So are you." I grin.

"But I don't want to move." She sighs now, lightly frowning.

"Then, don't?"

Izzy lets out a laugh, slowly untangling herself from around me. "I have to. Need to use the bathroom." She slowly climbs from the bed, her body moving in that wobbly 'just waking up' way. One of the straps from her top slides down a little, but she quickly pulls it back up before it can reveal anything she doesn't want me to see. Then she pads off, her footsteps soft on the wooden floors.

She's beautiful, no matter what time of day I see her.

But this gives me the opportunity to make myself a little more comfortable in my boxer briefs, having her so close to me makes things happen in my body. I was worried that it may freak her out, feeling my morning wood when we woke up, but she seemed fine. So, that's good, right?

I sit up, my eyes going over the spines of her mangas on the shelves. I recognise the titles of almost all of them, and some of them I don't need to recognise because the publisher name on the spine alone tells me enough about what type of manga it is.

Most of the titles here are either magical girl mangas or romantic or slice-of-life shoujo mangas, but I recognise some publishers who I know publish BL, boy's love, manga too. And then there are a couple I don't recognise at all, and I'm too curious not to snoop.

I slide out of bed, and I pull one of the unknown titles off the shelf and am faced with two very busty girls having a very intimate moment. I don't need any more explanation to know what these are, yuri. It seems that Izzy really is into just about anything, as long as it's sweet or has romantic subplots.

"You want to borrow one of those?" Izzy's voice startles me, but when I look at her, she's grinning. "They're not easy to get your hands on here. You really do need connections. But you can always borrow some of mine." There is a mischievous sparkle in her eyes as she steps next to me. "If you're not used to reading much yuri, you may be more interested in reading this series."

She reaches up and takes a book from a shelf higher up, sliding her beautiful body against mine, and I close my eyes for a moment, wanting to do something definitely inappropriate to her right now.

When she stands back straight, she holds up a book I actually recognise the title of, Citrus. I grin. "I know those ones. I've already read them."

"Good." She grins, but doesn't put it back immediately. "If you hadn't, I would have made sure that you'd have read at least the first one before the end of the weekend."

"Why is that?" I step closer and slide my arms around her waist, putting my head on her shoulder, and she leans back against me, into my embrace.

"Because it's a classic. If you're into girl on girl stuff, you should have read it at least once." She opens the book, flipping through it, pausing on some pages, probably reading some parts, before going on. "I'd read a lot of girl-on-girl doujinshi before I even found this series, but these are easier to get around here, since it's better known."

"I don't have a lot of mangas, I don't have space for them." I like having Izzy in my arms like this, when we're just being comfortable and talking and just being together. "Where do you get yours?"

"Emma gets them for me. She'll tell me if she has something new she may be able to get her hands on. Both for the yuri and the yaoi that is. Most of the regular mangas I just get through more official channels, gotta make sure they keep translating them and stuff." She lets out a laugh, which turns into a cute giggle. "And then, of course, there are the ones not on this shelf." She steps out of my embrace, putting the manga down, and going over to one of the panels on the side of her room. "These I don't keep out in the open, for obvious reasons." She slides it open and pulls out a plastic tub full of what looks like magazines.

When I get closer, I totally get why she doesn't leave these out on her shelves. They are definitely XXX rated.

I laugh, shaking my head. Another surprising side to her.

I'm learning a lot about Izzy this weekend, including that she has a lot of interests that you wouldn't expect from a girl who looks this cute...

21
Izzy

Shounen-ai/Yaoi = Are two related media genres in Japan where there is a relationship between two boys or men. Shounen-ai means boy-love and is the more romantic version of the two. Yaoi is harder to translate as it's more of an acronym than a real word, but in origin its meaning comes down to sex stories between two men without much of a plot otherwise. Another term used a lot more these days is BL, or boys love, both in Japan as well as outside of Japan as a way to combine both of these types of stories under a single term. They're both genres I read and watch a lot, even if some of it is so over the top that it's kind of silly, but that's half the fun of it.

After showing Elliot my stash of 'porn' on impulse, we went downstairs to have breakfast, and I couldn't help my cheeks heating up from time to time, just remembering what I'd just done. Elliot didn't seem particularly shocked to find some of the more explicit stuff on my shelves, but showing him *that*... I don't know. That may have been overdoing it a little. Maybe.

Potentially.

Mum and Dad were already out of the house by the time we came down, having left a note that they went to visit my aunt, since she'd just bought a new house, and they were going to help with painting and stuff. I don't know, it sounded suspiciously like they were trying to give us the place to ourselves... But I didn't mind much, it just meant that we didn't have to worry about waking anyone up and we could just be silly while getting our breakfasts.

When we went back upstairs, we sat down in front of the TV and watched some more episodes of Cardcaptor Sakura while eating our breakfast. Luckily, we're watching the Japanese version, and not the butchered American version they normally show in the Netherlands... What they did to that show... It's a crime, it's a crime to all things artistic and translations.

Elliot bumps his shoulder into mine. "Have you cosplayed Sakura yet?"

"Which one?" I flash a grin at him. Both the main character in Cardcaptor Sakura and Magical Princess Club! are called Sakura.

He points at the TV. "That one." He raises an eyebrow at me, a smile on his lips.

I shake my head, grinning more. "Nah. There are enough other shows to cosplay from and a lot of people do Sakura already anyway. Plus, you'd need a really, really good Tomoyo if you're going to cosplay Sakura, it's not the same without her. They're a unit, you can't really do one without the other."

Elliot lets out a laugh, putting his plate to the side. "To get the full effect, definitely. But have you never thought about doing it? It would totally fit your style."

I shrug a little. "A few times. But there are always enough

Sakuras around at cons, doing something else at least makes you stand out."

"True." Then he turns to me, his fingers playing over my bare shoulder. "I guess I'm lucky that you think like that, or I may never have been able to talk to you." There is a soft look in his eyes that makes my stomach all fluttery.

"Maybe," I whisper, swallowing hard as his fingers leave traces of fire on my skin. "But maybe I'd have talked to you anyway, depending on your cosplay."

He grins. "You would have had to be the one doing that then, because I never dared to come even close to you. You were just... too impressive." His cheeks colour a little. "We all have those we look up to."

My own cheeks flare up, my heart beating fast. "Even now? After knowing me?"

His gaze is soft as he nods. "Yeah." His voice is soft too. "Maybe even more than I did before." Then he comes closer, putting his lips on my shoulder for a moment. "For many different reasons, but mostly because you're awesome." His lips tickle my skin, making my heart beat even faster. Why does he keep doing this? Being all sweet and charming? It keeps my heart beating so fast that I don't know what else to do.

"Oh." I glance down at my hands, totally blanking out on anything else.

"Izzy, Izzy, Izzy," he sing-songs. "I'm just complimenting you, and I will keep doing it, because it's true." Then he slides one of his arms around my waist and turns me so I'm with my back to his chest, and puts his head on my shoulder. "And because it makes you blush so adorably."

I try to jab my elbow back into his side, but he quickly grabs my arms, stopping me, as he laughs.

Then he lets out a deep breath and relaxes against me. "Hmmm. I like this." He sounds a little different now, and since I can't see his face, I don't know what to read into it.

"You like what?" I look at his hands on my arms, the soft and comforting touch.

"Joking with you. Holding you. Just being with you. It's easy, and good." He slides his arms around my waist, and I put my hands over his.

It still feels a little odd, but more in the 'I'm not used to this' way than the 'this is strange' way.

I guess I'm bound to get used to this with Elliot around, aren't I? Because it does feel really good.

W A S D

Elliot looks around the shelves and shelves of fabrics as I hunt down one of my recent projects. Everything is in bags, but, of course, I tend to forget to label them, so I have to keep looking in each one to find the one I'm looking for. I finally have the right bag and pull it out, putting it on the table.

"This one. I think this is probably the most complicated dress I've ever made." I slide the delicate fabric out of the bag and align the different elements on the table. Not only is the fabric hard to work with, it's silk, but the pattern asks for a lot of pleats and fancy things on it. The end result will be beautiful, but for now, I've been loving and cursing it in equal measures.

Elliot comes over, looking at the dress, reaching out to it and running his fingers over the fabric. "Wow." He grins. "Brave."

I shrug a little. "Kind of. But I like it too much not to try it out. Also, it lets me learn new techniques, and that's always cool." I look at the dress. It's all black, and I don't even know when I'd ever wear it, but that hasn't stopped me from trying new things before. A black silken dress with has like all of these different moving elements to it, yeah… Not really something that would be day-wear appropriate, and I don't get a lot of evening-wear situations to try it out at.

"How many projects do you have going at a time?" Elliot looks at the stack behind me.

I look at the stack too and laugh. "Lots of those bags are just filled with leftovers from a project. Stuff I still need to sort out but haven't yet. Or…" I grab the top bag and open it. "This one holds pieces of fabric that are too small to store elsewhere but that I can still make something fun out of like bows, or that I can use for panels or other things in new projects."

Elliot reaches into the bag, pulling out a strip of bright pink fabric. "This is from your Sakura cosplay." He runs it through his fingers, letting out a short laugh. "This stuff is so slippery though, I cursed so often when I used it for the Aoi costume. Ugh."

"Oh!" Him talking about the Aoi costume reminds me of something I told him when we were at the con. "I have something I want to show you." I put the dress back into the bag and put it back onto the pile, together with the leftover bag, then I reach behind one of the panels in my room, pulling out three other bags, all filled with projects. Dresses I wanted to make, but where adding bigger boobs into the top would be way too much of a hassle. "These!" I put all three bags onto the table.

Elliot raises an eyebrow at me. Has he forgotten already?

I pull the first dress out of the bag. It's a beautiful white dress with big red flowers on it. The skirt is full, the top a little tight, but it gives a great silhouette. "These aren't finished yet. But I also don't really know if I should finish them for myself."

198

"You wanted to dress me in them?" He's smiling, but I can also see some nervousness now.

"I can try." I shrug. "I can't give them to Jason, he will never fit into them, and I think they'd look really good on you."

"Really?" His cheeks flush, his breath quickening. This is making him nervous, talking about cosplaying is one thing, but crossdressing makes him more nervous. Hmm.

"Yeah." I nod. I pick up the dress, holding it so that the skirt shows well and turn it a few times. "There is no zipper in it yet, so I can add panels easily. It's just that..." I shrug. "It's easier to flatten the front more than to make it boobier."

He slowly reaches out, the nerves still in his eyes, but also a curiosity, and something like adoration. As I expected, this is his style. Which I kind of had expected already, with how our styles match in general.

"Take your shirt off. You can try it on." I look at Elliot, and after a moment, he swallows hard and then nods decisively.

He takes a step back and pulls his shirt over his head in one movement. I feel all tight inside as I look at his bare chest, he looks so sexy like this. Then he puts his thumbs into the pockets of his jeans and broadens his shoulders a little, a teasing look in his eyes now. "Like what you see?"

I smile, nodding. "Definitely." Emboldened by his actions, I reach out and run my fingers over his chest down, over his belly button and the light trail of hairs going down into his jeans. Hmm... But before I do something that startles either of us, I push the dress at him. "Now, put this on."

He lets out a soft laugh and then pulls the dress over his head. It takes him a couple of moments, but then he's got it pulled down all the way. He runs his hands over the top and then the skirt. "This is a really comfortable fabric."

I nod, trying to look at the dress and how it fits him, instead of seeing how sexy and sweet he looks in the dress. Come on, brain, get out of that gutter.

I step around him, pulling the dress closed as far as I can at the back, checking if it will fit and how it would look. It doesn't fully close at the back, Elliot is a little broader in his shoulders and chest than I am. But with a few changes, it would still work. Then I let him go. "Come check in the mirror." I turn one of the panels on my shelves, revealing a huge mirror.

He steps in front of it, his eyes going over the fit of the dress as he fiddles with the front of the top. But I can also see the interest, the curiosity, the joy, in his eyes. "It's beautiful." His voice is filled with awe.

I nod, stepping back behind him, pulling the dress to the correct fit and then look at him in the mirror over his shoulder. "Do you want it? I can get your measurements and change the front, and you can have it. It will only take an hour or two-three to finish it."

"Are you sure?" His voice is breathy. "It's way too nice."

I meet his eyes in the mirror, smiling. "I'm not wearing it, and it would be a shame to leave it at the bottom of some closet, all unfinished. Of course, you can have it. It looks good on you."

He nods, his eyes going back to himself in the mirror, I can see that he's interested, but also scared. "You don't think it's weird?"

"What is?" I turn around trying to locate my tape measurer.

"Giving me a dress you made for yourself. Giving your *boyfriend* your dress?" There is that tension in his voice again, like some fear, but I also know that no matter how he sees me, how he sees me as just a girl, crossdressing is still something that he's not confident in for himself.

200

I turn back to him, meeting his eyes in the mirror, and then I kiss his shoulder, the way he did for me earlier. "And what's supposed to be strange about that? Don't you share your 'boy' t-shirts with other people? With girls sometimes? Why would this be different?"

I slide my arms around his waist, pulling him close as I put my head on his shoulder, still looking at him. "I have a beautiful dress that I'm not going to destroy by trying to fit the front to my new boob size, so it's just going to remain unfinished. But I also have a cute boyfriend who looks really good in that dress, and for who making a few adjustments to the fit will be much easier. So, if he wants the dress, he can have it. It's no different than giving away a t-shirt that fits someone else better, or jeans, or anything. Just because it's a dress doesn't make it any different."

He takes a deep breath, letting it out slowly and then nods, his eyes watery. Then he puts his hands over my arms. "See? This is why you're so amazing." He smiles, tightening his grip on my arms a little.

And I have tears in my eyes myself, all emotional. "I'm just normal, you just make my amazing side come out."

Gender and clothes have often been hard for me, trying to fit in one way or another. But I guess that it's also gotten so much easier in the last few years, now I'm more comfortable with myself, and I guess that some of that is rubbing off on Elliot.

On my *boyfriend*. My *boyfriend* who looks great in jeans but without a shirt and also in a dress that hugs his body in the sexiest way possible.

I'm the luckiest girl in the world.

22
Elliot

I stare at the screen of my own TV in front of me, taking a couple of moments to register why the game is no longer playing and why it's telling me that Nightmare has won.

"Elliot!" Mya growls, pushing my shoulder. "Seriously. This

is the third time you've died in a row. What's up with you today?"

We're playing Soulcalibur V on the PlayStation, playing against each other like we always do. But my head isn't here with the game. Instead, it's still with Izzy and the weekend we had.

I was so nervous when I went over there, but it all turned out so much better than I expected. The only problem is that I still can't get the thoughts out of my head. While I was there, Izzy finished the white and red dress, and it's currently hanging in my closet, within reach, if I just open the door. But no matter how confident I felt when I was over at Izzy's, that confidence is gone again, and I just don't know anymore. It's like being with Izzy is a different world from this one, a different me.

I don't know why it keeps going through my head, the idea that it's not right that she gave me her dress, even though I totally get that there is nothing wrong about it... Like she said herself, it's just clothes. But a dress is a different type of 'just clothes' than a t-shirt would have been...

And then the way she looked at me... Like she really didn't see a problem with it, like she really didn't see me differently from the person I was in jeans just because I was wearing a dress.

And then the way she'd touched me after I'd taken off my shirt... I don't know. It almost looked like lust, just her fingers travelling over my skin... Just the light touch and the look, but then she still looked at me like that when I was wearing the dress...

It messes with my head. It constantly messes with my head because I've always convinced myself that nobody would be interested in a guy who likes to dress up in girls' clothes, and if they were okay with it, I should probably not show it to them too often. But Izzy didn't seem to see any difference with it, and she even seemed to *want* to dress me up or something. While I was with her, being myself was easier but now I'm back at home… I don't know anymore. I guess I'm just really confused.

"Elliot?" Mya now looks at me with worry in her eyes. "What's going on? You've been off all day. Did something happen?"

I shake my head, not sure how I can even explain it to her, even though she's always been the one I trust with things like this.

That makes her turn to me more, putting the controller away, all her attention now on me. "Is it something Izzy said? Did she say something bad?" There is a fire in her voice, her wanting to protect me.

I almost let out a laugh. If Izzy had said something bad, it would probably be a lot easier to deal with. But she hasn't, and that makes it harder for me to know what to think, somehow. "Maybe it would have been easier if she had…" I close my eyes, sighing.

"Now you've lost me… What *didn't* she say?"

I lean back, looking up at the ceiling, running my teeth over my lip a few moments, trying to collect my thoughts. "She gave me a dress. It's in the closet."

"She gave you a *dress*?" I hear Mya stand up, opening the closet and taking a look. "Oh, that's beautiful! Did she make that herself?"

I nod. "She already had most of it, but last weekend she finished it and gave it to me. Well, she had most of it finished already, but then altered it so that it would fit me."

Mya flops down next to me. "So, what is the issue?"

"She didn't even blink when she offered it. Like… Like it was no big deal. Like…" I shake my head again. "I guess it would have been easier if she *did* think it weird that I wore dresses. That,

I could understand and deal with…"

"Why? Didn't you say yourself that you find it hard when Izzy acts like she expects people to be nasty to her for being trans? Why is Izzy being cool with your crossdressing any different?"

She's got a point. "Because it's *me*? I don't know."

"You *don't* deserve to be treated normally no matter what you wear?" I know that she's now glaring at me, I can hear it in her voice.

"That's not… It's not the same."

"What are you really worrying about?"

I put my hand over my face, not able to say this any other way. "What if she expects me to become like her? What if she only puts up with the 'normal' me because I also wear dresses at other times?" What if she expects me to want to become a girl too, so she's just waiting it out?

"Elliot…" Mya's voice drops low, an edge of danger to it. "You're not saying what I think you're saying, right?"

"Is 'I don't know' a right answer, still?" Because now I've said the words, I don't know if I can ever take them back, or how I even could. It doesn't feel right to think it or say any of it, but my brain keeps going back to these thoughts, going around in circles, over and over, going back to the bad thoughts.

"Izzy doesn't like you just because you wear dresses. I also don't believe she would be 'expecting' you to 'become like her', ever. And why would you even think that? Did she say anything?"

"She didn't. It's just…" I sigh. "It's everywhere."

"What is?"

"The things people think about crossdressing and being trans. 'There is a bigger chance that people who crossdress have gender identity issues.' 'Crossdressing is just the stage before they admit that they're actually trans.' Things like that." I sit back up, staring down at my hands, sighing deeply.

"Are you? Trans? Having gender identity issues?" Mya's questions never stop, but then… it's always been like that, she's good at asking things I otherwise don't want to answer.

"I don't think so. But what does that matter when other people *do* think that? When they treat me differently just because they do think those things?"

"Then they're jerks and should keep their eyes on their own paper and not say shitty things to others." Mya reaches out, putting her hand on mine. "Is that really happening? Are people saying that?"

I shrug. "I can hear it in their voice, I can see it when I just hang out online. When you're crossdressing, it's just 'one step away from coming out as trans'."

"Would that be bad, being trans?"

I shake my head, my eyes still on my hands. "But I'm *not*, I don't think so. Am I?" I look up at her now. The words are finally out of my mouth, out in the open. I can't stop it anymore. This fearful feeling in me that has been growing. Am I just not seeing things, am I just blind to things going on with myself? Am I just denying something about myself that's so obvious to others?

"Why are you asking me?" Mya raises an eyebrow. "This isn't about me."

"But you know me best. Am I just blind? Am I just blind to what everyone else thinks is so obvious?"

Mya shakes her head, her eyes sad. "All this over a dress?"

I shake my head too. "All this over a girl running her fingers over my abs before handing me a dress and telling me to put it on. All this over my parents looking at me like I've totally changed in the last months. All this over…" I shrug. "All this over liking to wear dresses and not wanting everything to change because I'm finally brave enough to actually do it."

Mya smirks, like she's just heard something funny. "Izzy touched you and then told you to put on the dress?" She looks at closet, which is now closed again.

My cheeks heat up, remembering the heated look in Izzy's eyes when she did. "Yeah. I'd taken off my shirt because she wanted me to try the dress on, and then she trailed her fingers over me before basically forcing the dress at me." It had been so confusing.

Mya bursts out laughing.

"What?" I don't think there is anything funny about my anxiety.

She shakes her head, her eyes sparkling with joy. "You're here, freaking out about what *you think* Izzy thinks your gender should be, while the poor girl may just have tried to hide her own arousal at seeing you without a shirt, at seeing you partially naked. It may have been the only way she knew how to put some distance between how inviting you looked and her own body's reaction at seeing you like that."

"Oh." I blink. That actually makes sense, a lot of sense. I'd never thought of that. I'd never thought about how Izzy might have felt seeing me undressed, at the things she may have felt at seeing me partially naked… I groan. "I've been *so* stupid."

"Nah." Mya lets out a breath. "You were dealing with other things in your head. And I can understand that dealing with a girl who really doesn't care how you dress, as long as it looks good on you, may be very different from what you're used to." She raises an eyebrow at me. "Right?" A few beats later, she shrugs.

"And I don't count. You're not in a romantic or sexual relationship with me."

I nod. "I guess."

Showing even a little bit too much interest in something 'girly' has gotten strange looks from girls I've dated in the past, let alone them knowing that I full on dress as a girl sometimes, with wigs and makeup and everything added too. Mya even looked oddly when I told her, but she soon became my number one source of help and information, and now I'm dating a girl who really doesn't care, who will make me dresses just because she thinks that they look nice on me. A girl who probably knows many ways to help me look even more like a girl, just because she has experiences with doing it herself.

I sigh. "But what about the 'just a first step to admitting being trans' thing?"

"So what?" Mya levels a look at me. "*So what?* Your identity is yours. You are the one who will know best about who you are, and even then, it's never fixed in place, your identity changes over time. But *your* identity is nobody else's business. Not mine, not from random strangers on the internet, or your parents'. Not even Izzy's. Only yours."

I nod. Not sure if I feel like that, but she's still right. It doesn't make it easier though, not in my head, not yet.

"Hey." Mya pushes my arm a little. "I'm serious. You don't think that Izzy has always been worried about this herself? Or that Jason or any of the others who crossdress have been wondering or worried about this? It's not so simple that you can say 'sure, this will never happen', but would it really be that bad? If it *is* an in-between stage, would that be bad?"

"No." My voice is harder than I mean it to be. I think of Izzy, of how happy and comfortable she is. How much she loves

208

being herself. If that is a future for me, it wouldn't really matter, right? Just as long as you're happy and comfortable, what does it really matter?

"Well then." Mya grins. "Now, stop freaking out about it. Some people just don't get it when you don't neatly fit into the 'cis, always cis, never wearing clothes of another gender' box or the 'trans, wanting to fully change into a different gender' box, and especially if you don't fit into the rigid binary 'boy' or 'girl' box. They don't understand the shades of dressing and gender. But after everything from the last weeks, haven't you gotten more comfortable just doing whatever you like?"

I shrug. "Maybe." And seeing Jason at Izzy's, not in a dress, just himself in another clothing style, but still obviously himself, I guess I get that distinction. "It's still annoying when people are being mean though." When they presume all sorts of things.

"Of course." Mya nods. "But I'm here with you. If anyone needs butt-kicking, I'll do it. Stupid people are stupid." She stands up again, smiling. "Hey, show that dress off. You've actually made me curious. And I want to see something 'normal' that Izzy has made." She grins now, reaching out to me.

I take her hand, pulling myself up. "Sure." I open the closet, taking the dress out, running my fingers over the fine cotton, the vibrant colours, then I eye Mya. "I could ask Izzy to make you one too."

Mya grins back. "Three matching colours. Oh! No! Four! Also one for Jason. Or maybe a suit version for Kevin!" Somehow, she's all excited now.

"I'm not sure I can get that all from my girlfriend for free." I pull my shirt off, throwing it on the bed. "I'm afraid you may have to order that from her and actually pay for it." I zip open the dress and start pulling it over my head.

"Meany. What's the use of having a best friend dating someone who is into fashion if I can't use it?" I can hear her pout.

"Well, I could maybe get you a boyfriend's-best-friend-discount code?" I'm finally through the dress and pull it down properly.

When Mya looks me over as I zip the dress up, I see she's got the same look int her eyes as I had when I saw it for the first time. The design and the fabric are stunning together.

Yeah, Izzy's skill can't be denied, and she's great at making people looking their best.

I guess I'm really lucky for that. Really lucky.

23

Izzy

Baka = Japanese for jerk or idiot. A pretty common Japanese insult that tends to get thrown around in anime and manga a lot. It's often used in shoujo anime and manga when the girl would try to get the boy she likes to do something sweet for her and he doesn't seem to act the way she wants him to. 'Baka!' Before she storms off, all upset.

The new school year is only a day away, and I'm dreading it already. I don't want to think about having to go to classes, or having to do group projects or things like that. But at the same time, it will give more structure to my weeks again and I get to learn new cool techniques. And I've got a class about making more 'commercial' type of fashion and clothes, I don't know why exactly, but I'm looking forward to it. I can do big and outrageous dresses, but something you can actually wear every day… That's harder. Especially when it's not for myself.

I don't like that I can't see Elliot this weekend though. He's got other things he has to take care of at his place this weekend, and it wouldn't work out. I talked to him last night, but I still miss him. I miss having him with me. I feel a little silly about it, but I guess it can't be helped. I just like him a lot.

Even Jason has been saying that I've been 'sighing' a lot lately. But I just think he's a little envious, his last relationship ended right before summer started, so he's been alone since.

I'm on my way to meet Jason and some of our friends for a day of just hanging out in the city centre and watch people while drinking fizzy drinks and probably getting a sunburn. Jason left ahead of me because I wanted to finish a dungeon with the guild and that ran a little longer than expected.

Which, I guess, is totally normal for our guild. And playing today gave me serious relationship envy. Seeing the relationship of Alex and Fleur grow even more while they've turned into this healer and tank power couple… I hope that Elliot and I can be like that one day. Not worrying, just trusting each other, just having fun together but always aware of how the other is doing. I didn't see Alex and Fleur's relationship when it started, too busy with school and work at the end of the school year, but these days… They've got what relationship goals are made of. I never thought that I'd be thinking that *I* would like a connection like that with someone, not just wanting a relationship with anyone, but that I would want my relationship with a specific someone to be like that, with Elliot.

But still… Living a couple of hours away by train from each other, and both being swamped in homework and such as soon as classes start again… That's going to put even more strain on us, and I'm not looking forward to it, not looking forward to talking to him even less… It's already starting to make edged of my brain feel weird.

Just then, my phone buzzes, and when I look at it, I find it's
212

from Elliot. 'What are you up to? I bet it's better than having to visit family you don't want to actually visit… <3'

I grin. No, my day is definitely better than that. 'Going into town with Jason and some friends. Why are you visiting family?' He hadn't said anything about that before.

'Apparently, my parents want me to go to my grandfather's birthday. I thought I could get out of it…'

'But, no?'

'No. They thought it was even more important than getting my stuff for school ready or cleaning up around my room before classes start. I have no idea what this is about anymore, dragging me all over the place this weekend.'

'Poor you.' I do feel for him, my family is decently close, but they wouldn't make me do things like that.

'I wish I could have been with you this weekend. Just hang out and have fun. Kick Jason's butt at Soulcalibur and show you the new skirt I made last night.'

Oh! That's something I do like thinking about! 'You made a skirt? I need pictures!'

'No pictures yet. When I get back home, I promise.'

'Really?'

'Yes. Really.' He sends me a list of emoticons, all smiling and grinning. 'So, what are you and Jason going to do?'

'Hanging out. Not much else.' I just like being with my friends, but I also really miss Elliot. 'Maybe you can join us next weekend.'

'I do hope so. I miss you.'

My heart skips a beat. 'I miss you too.' Then I see the stop I have to get off. 'Got to go. Good luck today.'

'You have fun! <3'

'<3' I grin as I put my phone in my pocket. I swipe the travel card and get off the bus, immediately hit by the suffocating heat.

Summer break is almost over, and now I feel like I don't know what comes next. What happens next.

How do you go from summer-relationship to during-school-time-relationship?

W A S D

I wince as I carefully put the aftersun on my sunburns. We definitely overdid it today. We sat around, as we usually do when we all hang out, just talking, joking around. And even though I missed Elliot the whole time, I still enjoyed myself. But now that it's the evening, I don't think it was such a good idea… At least not if I want to be able to sleep for the next couple of nights.

A notification pops up on my monitor, it's a voice call from Elliot.

I put on my headset, wincing at the movements, and then accept the call. "Hey." I smile, my heart beating fast.

"Hey." Elliot's voice is not as upbeat as I expect it.

My own heart calms down too. "What's wrong?"

"Nothing much. Just… parents and stuff. It's not important. I just wanted to hear your voice." He does sound like he's starting to relax a little as he talks more.

"You wanted to flatter me with words?" I smile again, carefully leaning back but I still let out a hiss as my back hits the chair.

"That doesn't sound good, what did *you* do?"

"Sit in the sun, but not wearing sunscreen."

"Ah, smart move."

"Hey, you can't be mean to me. I'm in pain." Though, I'm mostly just annoyed with myself for forgetting the sunscreen in the first place.

"I'm sorry. It's horrible that that happened to you. I agree."
Though, he's still mocking me, I'm sure.

"Change of topic. Are you looking forward to Monday yet?"
Elliot makes a noncommittal sound.

"No?"

"I don't know. It will be fun to learn new things, but my classmates are meh. So, I guess, it depends on what part of Monday you're referring to."

"Ah, yeah." That makes sense. Most of my classmates are fine, but I know that I'm just very lucky with that.

"Another change of topic." There is now a smile in Elliot's voice. "What are you doing the first weekend of November? There is a gaming convention, and I was wondering if you were going to go too?"

"Probably." I try to remember what events I've still got coming up. "Likely?"

"Would you…" His voice wavers a little, filling with uncertainty. "Would you like to go together? Also, match our outfits and stuff?"

I feel my skin heat up, but this time it's not just from the sunburn. "Are you sure?"

"Yeah. I'd like to go together, if you want to. I really liked it at AmAnime, so I think we can come up with something new for this one. And we can even work on the cosplays together. Which would really be an advantage for me."

"Why is that?"

"Your room is bigger, so we'll have more space to work in."
He sounds so sweet, and a little naughty.

"You've not seen it during the school year." I laugh.

"I can't believe it would be that bad, honestly."

"Hmm, hmm. It's bad." I suck at keeping my room

uncluttered and, most weeks, I can barely get to my bed.

"I can't believe anything you do can be bad…" The teasing in his voice makes me smile, but also makes my heart flutter. He does seem to think the best of me… Somehow. It's sweet, even if it's a little funny too. I really do have bad sides to me, but he somehow seems to refuse to believe them.

I guess it's nice, but it also feels like that makes everything so much more fragile. And that makes me scared.

[W] [A] [S] [D]

I feed the fabric through the machine, my brain going off in its own direction as I hem the skirt. This isn't the most interesting part of making clothes, this is just the finishing up after all the fun stuff is finished. I got an order in this week for a skirt with three layers of underskirts. The underskirts were finished fairly easily, but the top skirt gave me a couple of problems with sizing and pattern fitting.

The first week of classes has mostly been getting to know the teachers and just getting to know what will be expected of us this semester. I've had all the teachers before, and I sort of know what they will be looking for. But what I didn't expect was some of the theory we've got to read, and then there was the whole 'we expect you to make things outside of your normal style this year', and of course all the teachers would look at me when they said that. It really annoyed me.

I can do different styles, that's why I chose the classes that I did, I wanted to be challenged, but apparently, not all teachers believed that I'd be able to pull it off. I'll show them, I'm sure of that!

A blip from my phone makes me look up from the machine, eyeing the screen. It's from Elliot. 'I'm sorry. I can't come over tomorrow. They've given us a lot of homework, and it's unfair to you if I just sit there working on it instead of paying attention to you.'

My heart sinks. I'd been looking forward to seeing him this weekend. We were going to spend the weekend coming up with cosplay ideas. I reach out, unlocking my phone, and send a message back. 'Too bad. I'm fine with you working here, though. I've got things to do too.' Or I can always come up with ways to entertain myself when he's working on his things, that's not really an issue.

'I'd love to. But I wouldn't get anything done with you around, you'd be a very special type of distraction, and I won't be much fun when I'm grumpy from having to work. I promise you.'

'Okay.' The idea of just going over to his place for the weekend pops into my head. But there we'd have the same issue. I'd still need to do work, and I wouldn't have my supplies with me, and I still need to finish this commission, and then I also have a design to start on for class for next week. Plus the reading…

'I'm really sorry. I wish I could just come over. I've missed you so much.' I know that he's telling the truth, but my heart still hurts. Is this how it will always be?

'I miss you too. I guess we'll have to see about next weekend?' I push away from the table, taking my phone. I don't want to think about having to spend another weekend here on my own. I won't be alone, but in a way, it still feels like that. Like I'll be alone without Elliot.

'Next weekend! I promise!' Then another message comes in. '1000000 promises.'

I smile a little, but then drop onto my bed, letting out a deep sigh. 'I'll keep you to that!'

'That's the plan!'

Then I get an idea. 'Even if it's just an afternoon, I just really want to see you. Maybe we can have dinner or something halfway between here and there?'

'Sounds like a better idea, actually. Let's do that. What about Thursday or Wednesday?'

'In the middle of the week?' I know that he has a weekend card for cheap travel, not a weekday one, so he'd actually have to pay for this. Would he do that, just for me?

'It's sooner. I miss you that much.' *Oh!*

I nod, my heart filling with emotions. 'I'll check my schedule for next week! BRB!'

I go over to my desk, pulling up my classes and workshops for next week. If we can make this work, maybe it will help us get through this without driving both of us crazy. If our schedules are this busy right away, I don't know what the rest of the semester will bring...

If we can even survive this.

24
Elliot

Kawaii = Japanese word for 'cute' which has started to be used by Western fans of Japanese culture too. Things that are kawaii aren't just cute, but more likely to be cutesy or even over the top cute, often fluffy or squishy, like kittens or baby rabbits. Kawaii isn't simply a description, it's a feeling.

I sit down at the back of the classroom, a good spot to see what's going on, and to sometimes even get a little thinking in while the professors are doing stuff on the board. The first week was nerve-wracking, getting my assignments, trying to catch up on the reading I have to do each week for my classes, especially catching up on reading Shakespeare, which I never had to do before. And then we were also grouped up for some projects where we have to work together on writing and accessing and editing each other's works, it sounded fun, but with my group, I'm not entirely sure anymore.

I've spent all weekend reading Shakespeare and writing my first article to be 'critiqued' by my classmates. All the while wishing I could just be with Izzy, wondering what she was doing, wanting to be with her. I would have gone over there, if I thought that I would have gotten any work done with her around… Now I'm not so sure that staying at home was a good idea or if I was actually more distracted than usual because I was thinking of Izzy the whole time and being frustrated that I wasn't with her.

"Morning." Jacob, one guy from the assigned group, sits down in the seat in front of me. "Did you finish your article?"

"Yeah. Finished it last night." I pull the copies from under my notebook before stashing them back.

"Cool. I forgot mine at home. So we'll have to do yours or one of the others first this week. I'm hoping that it doesn't matter much, we'll probably be done with the class before anyone notices that I didn't bring anything in anyway." He grins.

"That's not a good start of the year." The words leave my mouth before I can stop them. I know that this guy is a slacker, but I also know that it's no use arguing with him about it.

"Pff. Like that matters. One week is not an issue. My girlfriend came over and we got distracted. You know?" He shrugs like it's the most typical excuse not to do work.

"Right…" I look away, not feeling like this discussion is going to go anywhere.

"What would you know about that? I bet you think education goes before everything, that girlfriends don't matter until you're like… a professor or something."

"I've got a girlfriend." Why do I let him rile me up? I regret saying anything immediately.

"Really? Good for you. And does she like… actually exist in physical form, or is she just on the computer?" The grin he's giving me is starting to really piss me off now.

"She's real."

"Oh! Can I see a picture of her?" He leans against my table.

"A picture of who?" Harper, our other group mate, sits down next to him.

"Elliot's girlfriend."

Harper snickers. "Is she nerdy like you? A study like you? Always her nose in some book?"

"I'm not doing this." I take my phone, putting my earphones in.

Jacob tugs on one of the earphones, so it falls back out. "You're just going to ignore us? We just want to make conversation, get to know the guy we're working with. We're just curious. You don't have to be so stuck up."

"And I don't have to make conversation with you. The class hasn't started yet." I put the earphones back in, drowning them out. I can still see them talk from the corner of my eyes, but I do my best not to actually listen to what they're saying.

It was the same last year. According to some classmates, I'm 'too serious' and 'nerdy' and apparently a great subject of their jokes and jabs.

I'm sorry for caring about my education and finishing this degree with good grades…

W A S D

After two days of classes, I'm so ready to see Izzy again. I'm walking from the university building to the train station, my heart already beating fast at the thought of seeing Izzy soon.

'About to step on the train. What about you?' I finally feel a little happier, knowing that I'll be able to hold her soon.

It takes a while before her reply comes in. 'I should be ready to leave soon. Professors are being confusing about something with this assignment and homework. I'll let you know as soon as I'm leaving.'

Izzy and I are meeting at a small cafe in Zwolle, close to the station. So, even if I'm early, I can get some work done before she's there. Although, with this weather, I'll probably just sit outside or something, get some more reading in. The weather is really nice, and not as hot anymore as it was over the summer.

I'm still only halfway through this article I have to read before class tomorrow, and it's not the most fun thing to read either, very information-dense. Not exactly being-excited-about-date-reading-material. But it has to get done.

I cross the market, it's so loud with all the stalls, although... I can't help myself. I've got enough time to make it to the train, I can take just a little peek.

Today some stalls sell fabric on the market, and I haven't checked them out in a couple of weeks. I turn onto the market, past the fruit and vegetable stalls, and on my right, also a bread and cheese stall. Then I find the first stall with fabrics. They have all sorts of types and colours, and I'm not specifically looking for something, just looking for inspiration.

Then my eyes fall on on a fabric that has a pattern on it like it's made of old pictures and designs. It's in sepia with some light pink, and as I get closer, I think this would look great as a skirt of some sort. I run my fingers over the fabric, it's soft and smooth, and pretty heavy too. Interesting.

I snap a quick picture of it and send it to Izzy, maybe she has some ideas for it. It would be too bad not to do anything with this fabric.

Then I look around a few more stalls, but nothing catches my eye like that fabric had. I'll have to see if they have some left over next week, because I can't buy it right now, I can't keep carrying it around on our date. And if I don't have a purpose for it, I don't know if I'll buy enough of it or not.

I slowly make my way back to the side of the market I came from and then walk down the street to the station. This area is always pretty busy, it's the main road between the station and the markets and the university buildings. There are some really cute clothing shops around, I always check the windows to get some inspiration. I should go shopping here with Izzy soon, she'd love it. She'd love the little alternative shops we've got.

I pass the museum, the strange multicoloured tiles on the outside as odd as ever. I guess that's what you get when you ask some strange artist to design a museum, but at least it's unique and not just some old building that's been repurposed because it was old and 'important' and people didn't want to break it down. At least you know what you'll get when you see this building, loads of eclectic art and stuff, almost all of it modern.

As I cross the bus stops in front of the station, my phone starts ringing.

Frowning, I accept the call, it's Izzy. "Hey." I start grinning, which somehow always happens when I think of her.

"Hey." Izzy doesn't sound so happy though.

"What's wrong?" My stomach drops, this is not good, right?

"I can't come. I'm sorry." She actually sounds upset as she says it.

"Why not?" There goes my lovely afternoon with my girlfriend.

"The professor gave me a bad mark, and if I want to hand it in again, it has to be before five this afternoon. I'm so sorry." Although I'm disappointed, I know that this can't be helped.

"Will you be okay?"

"Yeah." She sighs. "It'll be fine when I hand it in again. I just... I really wanted to see you."

"Me too. But school is important too." I stop walking, looking around, not sure why this hurts so much. The train I was supposed to take to go see Izzy is arriving at the station right now and I know that it's no use to go over to it anymore.

"Yeah. We'll have to meet next weekend. I promise." Things keep coming between us meeting up again, but I guess that's normal when you live this far apart. And with our schedules, we can't just go over to each other for an evening or something, the trains don't go early enough for that most of the time...

"Yeah. We'll see each other on the weekend. That will be longer too." I try to hold onto that idea, hoping it will be better then. Hoping things will work out this weekend...

"Yeah, I'll be able to see you longer too." There is a small smile in her voice again. "Okay, I have to get back to my assignment. I just wanted to make sure you hadn't actually gotten on the train yet. You haven't, right?" *Now* she remembers to ask that?

"No, I haven't. I was just on my way to the station. I hadn't gotten on a train yet."

"Good." The relief in her voice is obvious. "I'll talk to you tonight."

"I'll talk to you later. Good luck with the assignment."

"Thanks. Still, sorry about this."

"It's okay. It can't be helped. Go wow the professor with your work." I smile a little. I know all about trying to avoid getting work done when you don't want to do something, and what Izzy is doing now is exactly that. "We'll talk later."

"Later." Then she disconnects the line.

I take a deep breath. There goes my afternoon. I'd been looking forward to it so much, the idea got me through the last couple of days, and now it didn't happen anyway. This dark feeling of disappointment pushes on my mind, frustrating me even more.

I don't want to go home yet, so I send Mya a message. 'You done with classes yet? Want to meet up?'

Then I walk back to the centre of the city, at least I can entertain myself a while there.

Mya's message doesn't take very long to come back. 'Done with classes. But I thought you were going to see Izzy?'

'She had to hand in an assignment again, so she can't come.'

'Oh, I'm sorry.' I watch as the program tells me she's typing more. 'Meet me in front of the Martini tower in 10 minutes?'

'Near the museum now, so I may take a few minutes more, but I'm on my way.' At least I get to spend the day with one of my best friends. Although, no offence to Mya, but yeah, it would have been more fun if Izzy had been here too. I turn my music on high, put my earphones in and pocket my phone.

I don't know why I have this feeling. Why I'm so annoyed when I can't see Izzy. I never used to be like this. I've often dated girls who were in university or higher professional education and we often had to work around schedules, but I'm just missing Izzy more when she's not here. It feels a little silly, even though I know that's no use, it keeps happening.

When I cross the street to the Martini tower, I spot Mya already standing there, grinning as she's doing something on her phone.

"Hey." I get closer, taking out my earphones.

"Hey." Mya grins, giving me a quick hug. "What do you want to do? Go home or hang out somewhere around here?"

I shake my head. "Up to you. I'm good with anything."

"Cool." Mya nods. "I've got a couple of stores I want to

check out, and we can go to my place after that. Order a pizza or something. Sounds good?"

"Sure." I nod. "Where do you want to go first?"

"I have to pick up some notebooks and stuff." She sighs and starts walking. "Do your professors have like... strange things they want you to do or pick up just because that's the way they do things, instead of what you prefer? One of my professors 'isn't a fan' of computers in the classroom, so now we have to take notes in notebooks. Ugh." She shakes her head. "Oh. And I need to check a makeup store, there is a new line from one of the makeup brands that I want to check out. It looked really pretty online. But it was all glittery, so you never know with those."

"Glitter?" I eye her, not sure I'd be interested in a makeup line like that.

"Yes. Glitter." She looks at me with a grin. "I was actually hoping to test it on you..."

"I don't think... Nope, no glitter." I shake my head.

"I'll ask you again when you see the colours. Don't say no just yet." She tugs on my arm, helping me avoid crashing into a bike coming down the street the wrong way.

I guess there are some similarities between Izzy and Mya. One of them being that they both seem to have no problem with putting dresses or makeup on me. Not that I'd be complaining, but it's still a fun comparison to make between the two. Although, I suspect that in the case of Mya, it's also partially the fact that she can try makeup on me instead of having to try it on herself, she seems to enjoy that part the most.

And now I miss Izzy again...

25

Izzy

Ecchi = Describes things that are sexual but not directly sex-act related. Dirty jokes or panty shots in anime are examples of this. It's more lewd than really overtly sexual. Ecchi content tends to show up in a lot of manga and anime that are for teens and older, while they aren't exactly sexy in general, but it does tend to show up as fan service type of content.

I don't want to be here. I don't want to still be on campus because I was supposed to be with Elliot right now. We were supposed to go out for dinner so that we'd at least see each other once in a while, but that's not happening. Not today apparently.

I run the seam of the skirt through the machine. Slowly, carefully, making sure to keep the fabric straight and preventing it from curling up.

The teacher gave me a bad grade over something stupid like the end of the seam not looking finished enough and the patterns not matching perfectly. I hadn't realised that that had been so important for this assignment. So I hadn't paid too much attention to it, but now I'm in the sewing room with four others, all trying to fix the same issues. I was lucky that making the pattern match was only a small adjustment for me, but it had meant taking apart the whole skirt and redoing all the seams.

One of the other girls, Sophia, had to redo a couple of the panels of her skirt because they'd been too off to fix, she had to redraw and recut them and everything. And she's only now starting putting the panels together again. Poor girl. The same thing had happened to me last year on a dress assignment, and that had been hell.

I lean back, stretching my shoulders and back, trying to get the stiffness out of them.

"Hey, Izz!" Another girl, Cloe, comes over, leaning on the table before coming down and looking up at me over the edge of the table, making puppy eyes at me.

"Yes?" I smile, looking at her.

"You still need to show me those pictures from the con that you took. I saw some on social media, but not as much as normal. I know you have them. Also, we *need* a step by step for the Sakura cosplay, of course." Cloe became a fan of my work after we talked at the start of the first year and she saw some of my cosplays. Now she loves looking at the cosplays, even though she's not into anime or cosplaying at all, she just likes looking at them.

"You and what army?" I raise my eyebrow at her and continue with the seam of the skirt. The reason I hadn't posted all of them was that Elliot was in a lot of them, and I wasn't so sure he would have been totally comfortable with me showing them around.

"The rest of the class? Right, Sophia? We need more step-by-step pictures of how the Sakura cosplay was made, right?"

228

"Oh! You won first place with it, I think? Of course we want to see how you pulled it off." Sophia grins as she goes back to her skirt.

"See?" Cloe looks at me triumphantly.

"I'll have to see about that." I grin. "I'll just have to check with some people first, and then find the time to actually write everything out. Yeah?"

"Yeah. Cool." She stands up. "Okay, letting you get back to the skirt. Don't want you to fail this class." She sighs.

"You done with yours yet?" I look over to her table.

"Yeah, as much as I can fix it." She shrugs. "Otherwise, I'll have to make up for it some other way."

I nod. Yeah, that was my idea too. If this doesn't work out, I'll have to make sure I'll get extra good grades for the rest of the semester. "Good luck."

"Thanks. See you tomorrow." She sighs and then picks up her skirt from her table. "Time to face the music." She pulls a face and then leaves the room.

I check the time, it's just past four. I have less than an hour to finish this. *Ugh.* Can this be over yet?

I want to go home already, I want to talk to Elliot. I hate that we had to cancel over this. But he was right, it couldn't be helped.

Now to just make sure it doesn't happen again.

I'm on my bed, a notebook on my lap, scribbling design ideas in it for an assignment we have to do for next week. We have to use odd shapes in a piece of clothing but still make it wearable. It's kind of frustrating because I have no idea where to start that stands out from things I've made in the last years...

Over my headset, the notification for the voice call comes through, and I connect the call with Elliot. When I came home today, he'd been at Mya's place so I couldn't talk to him, but now we're both at home.

"Hey." His voice is low, giving me good shivers in my body. "What are you doing?"

"Designing. You?" I smile, putting the notebook aside and instead making myself comfortable on the bed.

"Making sure I don't miss out on my homework for tomorrow." Then he's quiet for a few moments. I'm about to say something, when his quiet voice reaches me. "I miss you."

"I miss you too." Tears spring to my eyes and I wipe them away, not wanting to cry. How did I get used to having him with me so fast?

"We're going to have to come up with a better system." He lets out a sigh.

"Like what?" In the last couple of days, with the stress putting so much pressure on my brain, my head has been doing not-good things, like wondering if this thing with Elliot is maybe just not meant to be. I know it's all in my head, and that it's just fear talking, but even if your own brain keeps telling you the same thing over and over, you start to wonder if there is some truth to it.

"Calling each other more?" We already do that, we talk every evening, and most mornings too.

"If we'd call more, we're going to have to call during our sleep." I smile a little, but I don't feel like we can come up with a solution that really works.

"True. And, although you snore really cutely, it's not going to be very effective."

"I don't snore." I glare into nothingness.

230

"I said cutely?"

"Still no." I take a deep breath. "Maybe I can come to your place this weekend?"

"Are you sure? Don't you have like... work to do?"

"I just have to make sure I leave on time on Sunday. It should work, right?" I want to see him so badly.

"I think it should. I don't see why not. And you get to meet my parents."

Uh-oh. "Yay?" I don't know what to think of that, I'd forgotten about that, I'd somehow forgotten about Elliot also still living at home. I'm not sure why, but I had...

Elliot laughs. "It will be fine. They'll be good, I promise."

"Good?"

"I'll try to get them not to make stupid bad jokes. Stuff like that." He's laughing now, and I smile too, relaxing a little.

"Do your parents know, about me?"

"About what? You being my girlfriend?" Although, the tone of his voice tells me that he knows what I mean. "No, they don't know yet, and I don't see why they'd have to. Maybe if it ever comes up, but it's not really something they have to know. Just like they don't have to know if you have or haven't had boyfriends or girlfriends before. I don't think they have to know about you being trans. I can do it if you think I should tell them?"

"I don't know." I think for a moment, and Elliot stays quiet too. "If they knew, would they react weird?"

"They may act a little ignorant. It's something they don't know too much about yet. They're still trying to get their head around me crossdressing. But I don't think they would react weirdly or badly." I like how honest he is, instead of trying to simply comfort me. "You can tell them, or not tell them. I can tell them, or not. You're my girlfriend, you're not a drug addict or whatever else they may need to know about upfront. So, I don't see an immediate reason to tell them. If you're comfortable with that."

"Yeah." My heart is beating fast, but what he's saying also makes sense. They don't have to know, at least not yet.

"Are you sure? I'm not trying to hide it, or you. I'm just..." He's stumbling over his words, which is kind of cute.

"I know. They're not involved with me, they don't have to know. Most people don't know, some people I've known for years don't even know."

"Really?" That seems to surprise him.

"Yeah. My classmates don't know. At least, most of them don't. And apart from my friends, I don't think anyone at the conventions knows." At least, I'm pretty sure about that.

"I didn't know until you'd told me. I don't think that anyone I know knows either. Mya now knows, but that's because you told her. Yeah..." His voice trails off in surprise. "I guess it's something that's not easy to just put in a conversation, right?"

I smile. "Yeah, no. It doesn't tend to come up in conversations easily, at least not for me, and I just... I don't really want people to know. I'm me, I've always been me. Nobody else needs to know about my bits or things like that."

"I agree." Elliot laughs. "I'd prefer it if people would keep out of your bits too, you know?"

My mouth falls open at his bad attempt at a joke.

"That's a really really bad joke, right? Yeah. Not a good one." He laughs again, awkwardly.

"Yeah. That was... bad." I shake my head, laughing too. "But I agree. I don't want to share your bits with anyone else either."

"Good." Elliot snickers. "At least we agree on that."

Whenever I talk with Elliot, I feel so happy, but I also know that my brain is doing messy things with me lately. And even if I joke around, a slight darkness is slowly starting to settle in my brain, in my heart. This is not good, but I'm not so sure how to stop it.

And the problems with meeting up with Elliot is not helping any of that. It only makes the thoughts worse, the darkness creeping up.

Ⓦ Ⓐ Ⓢ Ⓓ

As the train rolls into Groningen station, I put my book away, having read enough for one of my classes. I've been reading the whole time on my way here. As I watch the station halls come into view, the old and new parts of it so separate, so disjointed, as always, it feels strange to come here to see Elliot and not my friends. I've been here quite a few times, but that was always to meet Alex or one of the others from the guild, and I'm not dragging my whole computer with me this time either.

I stand up, checking that I've got everything with me, and then wait in the section with the doors until they open. The butterflies in my stomach are going all over the place, making me nervous and a little uncomfortable.

The train stops and the doors open. As I step into the heat, I look around, trying to find Elliot. We were supposed to meet up at this platform, but since there are so many people around, I have no idea where he is.

"Izzy!" Elliot calls for me and then I see him standing a while off.

A grin immediately pulls on my cheeks, and my heart does one of those jumps it tends to do when I see Elliot.

Then he's next to me, and his arms are around me.

"It's so good to see you." His voice is soft, his lips close to my neck. "You look great."

"I look like I travelled hours by train after having been in class all day." I grin, tightening my own arms around him. "But, thanks."

Elliot lets me go, grinning at me. "Are you hungry or do you want to go to my place first?"

I shrug, not really sure. I just wanted to see Elliot, I don't really care what we're going to do while I'm here. My brain only had two modes for the last days, making sure I stay up to date with my coursework and wanting to see Elliot again, that was it. There wasn't space for anything else.

"Okay." He winks. "Maybe, let's go to my place first. I'll let Mum know that we're probably eating at home, and we can always go out again later to go to a bar or something. Or just stay at home and play games, I'm pretty easy on that part." He takes my hand, weaving his fingers through mine, holding on tightly.

"Sounds like a plan." I am tired, this week has been so busy, and just being with Elliot, touching him, holding or being held by him, it all sounds really good right now.

"Good." He starts tugging on my arm. "Let's get to the bus and then we'll see about more after that."

I nod, not really sure what to say or if I should even say anything. I'm just hoping that this weekend is going to be as easy as Elliot coming over to my place was, I really hope so, because I don't know if I'll be able to deal otherwise.

My tears are right under the surface, they have been all week, and I don't want to break down over nothing in front of Elliot and his family. I just want to be the funny and cute girl, not the dark and depressed girl. I can do that when I get back home, but right now I just want to enjoy things, I want to enjoy being with Elliot, I want to have fun, not worry about my brain for a while.

But I'm not so sure how easy that's going to be…

26
Elliot

Chibi = Japanese word for short, often used as an insult on the same level as 'baka' (idiot). Within otaku culture also used to describe anime or manga characters who are not just very short but tend to have a deformed body type with a very large head (sometimes up to half their full body size) and a small body. The style tends to have very few details, only emphasising details that are distinctive of that character. These chibi versions of characters tend to be even cuter than their original, and within a larger context (for example anime episodes or manga chapters) they tend to act more childish than their regular sized bodied counterparts. It can be really cute, or really annoying, depending on how it's pulled off.

I really loved seeing Izzy at the station. She made my heart beat faster the moment she stepped off the train. Though she did look a little hesitant, like something was bothering her, like she wasn't entirely sure that she should be here.

I'm just hoping that it was some anxiety about meeting my

parents or something and not anything worse than that. I don't really want to think about her being unhappy, but I can understand if she'd be nervous. At the same time, I know that things aren't always easy in her head and that she can't help it when that happens either.

The bus is pretty empty, which is uncommon for Friday afternoon, but we're probably right between two waves of students getting out of class or coming home for the weekend. A couple of minutes into the drive, Izzy starts talking about her friends who live around here too, and going to gaming parties and things like that at their places. And my fear of something being wrong with Izzy eases. She seems a lot more like herself again, which is good, maybe it was just the nerves.

It's fun to hear about her friends, and I think we may need to have a big friends get-together when we can because the way she's talking, everyone may mix pretty well. Although, as I understood it, these are not the same people as the people from the con, somehow. I don't know, she has a lot of friends, all doing different things and not all of them overlapping, it's kind of funny and interesting.

When we get to the street where I live, Izzy looks around, surprised. She may live in some old building, I live in the total opposite, a brand new house, built only in the last decade or so. I don't remember exactly when, we only moved into it three years ago. My parents wanted to live a little 'bigger' and a little further outside the city centre, now that I was 'mostly grown up'.

Although, I think it was mostly because the houses here have a bigger garden and you can get onto a small stream, right from the edge of the gardens. It makes my parents feel luxurious and rich or something like that. I don't know. I tend to be either in my bedroom or out with friends, not really out in the garden or 'enjoying the house' the way my parents do. But it's their place, not mine, so it's all up to them.

I stand up, taking Izzy's hand. "We're here."

She nods, her eyes going over everything, the houses, the gardens, the cars at the side of the road, jumping around as we get off. "It's pretty here. Very new?" Her hand is a little sweaty, and I'm not sure if it's from the weather or her nerves.

"Very, very new. Come on, this is me." I tug her along, trying not to run or race. I'm just... a little excited, I guess?

I open the door, and it's quiet inside, really quiet. It's almost like there's nobody home, until I spot my mum in the garden, sitting in one of those big lounge chairs and reading a book in the sun.

I stop, turning to Izzy, nervous and excited about having her with me again. "Do you want something to drink?"

She shrugs a little, and I don't know what it is, but something is different in her eyes. It's been creeping in since I picked her up from the station, it's not just anxiety, it's something more. It's like it's eating at her, like she's trying to hide it from me, but it's not working anymore.

"Izzy?" I step closer, reaching up, running my thumb over her cheek. "What's wrong?"

She shakes her head, biting her lower lip as her eyes get all watery and her breathing gets irregular.

"Hey..." My voice gets rough just looking at her being upset, my heart heavy. Then I step closer and wrap my arms around her. I don't know what's going on, but it's bad.

Izzy wraps her arms around me too, pulling me tight as she hides her face against my shoulder. Her breathing shudders and her hands scrunch up my shirt. Definitely not good.

"Let's get you upstairs," I whisper in her hair before I slowly
238

walk up the stairs with her, trying to keep her close. Maybe getting her to a more comfortable place will help, somewhere safer.

When we get to my room, I close the door behind us and just keep holding her. I don't know what else to do, the only thing I can do is to be there for her until she opens up to me. However long that takes.

When she finally pulls back, she eyes my shirt, and the wet stains on my shoulder from her tears. "Sorry." Her voice is croaky. "Sorry for..."

I hold her hands, squeezing them a little. "It's okay." I let her sit down on my bed, but as I try to sit on my computer chair, to give her some space, Izzy pulls me next to her.

"I'll be okay in a moment." She nods resolutely. Though I'm not sure if she's talking to me or to herself.

"It's okay if you're not okay." I squeeze Izzy's hand again. "It happens sometimes." I turn on the bed, pulling her down with me, spooning her as I hold her in my arms tightly. I'd do anything to make her feel better again. "You fit against me so well like this," I say the words, even though I don't know why. Just blurting them out, trying to fill the silence.

Izzy's breathing is choppy, and she tightens her grip on my arms. "Elliot..." Why does she sound so sad?

She's breaking my heart with just one word. "Yeah?"

"I don't know if I can do this. I don't know."

"Don't know what?" This is the first time in weeks that I can actually hold her, and I'm getting severely confused. I thought that we both wanted this? To be together? To be able to spend time together?

"All of this." She sits up, and as she looks down at me, her eyes are all red from crying, tears still sliding down her cheeks, and her lower lip wobbles. "I don't know. I don't know how to do *this*. I don't know how to be... I don't know." She shakes her head, looking so lost.

"Which part?"

"All of it." Her whole body shakes with each breath. "Maybe I shouldn't have come here. Maybe this was a bad idea." She stands up, going over to the window overlooking the fields behind the house.

My heart hurts, and I don't know what to say anymore. This is... I thought we were on the same page. I thought we both wanted this relationship to work. But maybe I was the only one? I don't know what to say, what to tell her. I'm too stunned.

Is this going to be the end? Is this the end for us?

After we had such fun at the con and at her place, is this where things will end?

My head whoozes and I close my eyes, grabbing the covers tightly, needing something to hold onto.

Now what?

"Izzy. Just..." I quickly cover my mouth with my hand as a sob escapes me. *Don't do this, please. Don't let this be the end.*

Izzy's footsteps come closer, and when I open my eyes again, she's standing in front of the bed, tears in her eyes. She kneels down, reaching out but not touching me yet. She opens her mouth a few times, before she lets out a frustrated sigh. "I love you." Her voice is barely audible. She squeezes her eyes shut, biting her lip hard. "I'm scared because I love you."

What?

How did we get there? My heart starts beating fast, my brain not having caught up yet. "I love you too." I reach out and pull her back on the bed with me, pull her against me tightly.

"I'm scared. I don't know how to do this. I don't know

240

anything. And... I don't want to hurt you." Now her words are coming out, they're spilling out of her.

I play my fingers through her hair, trying to comfort her, trying to make sense of this. Somewhere in the last while, her mind made a jump, and I'm not entirely sure where. "You're not hurting me. You're doing fine." I run my other hand over her back, up and down, more to make sure this is real and to keep moving, get this nervous energy out, than anything else.

"I know. I *think* I know. But..." She shakes her head, pushing her face into my chest. "I *don't* know."

"What's going on in your head? What's going wrong?"

"Everything. Not seeing you. Bad grades. Wanting to be with you all the time, and not being able to. Everything is going wrong. Everything. And it's only getting worse..."

"It's okay. Things are going to be fine. I'm sure." I want to make them right, but I know that it's not going to be that easy. Slowly it's starting to dawn on me what's going on in Izzy's head, why she looks so upset. "I really do love you." We've not said it before. Today is the first time we've spoken the words, even though I think we've both felt them for a while now.

"Why?" She looks up at me, her eyes so vulnerable and broken. This isn't just about us being apart. This isn't just her struggling with her classes. The look in her eyes, the look I saw when she came here, the way she's been changing, even a little, in the last weeks. I recognise it now for what it is, depression.

"Because you're amazing. You're strong, and you know what you want. And you'll get what you want."

"I'm scared. It will all fall apart."

"No, it won't." I shake my head, then I kiss her on her forehead, remembering things she told me before, about her past. Things that are starting to make more and more sense now. "Your brain is fighting against you. Your brain is distorting how you feel. You know this."

She closes her eyes, relaxing just a fraction before she lets out a shuddering breath. "Maybe. I don't know."

"I think it is. And I think you know. I think you're scared, but not of the world around you but of the things going through your head." I play my fingers over her neck, sliding up and down until I slide them all the way up to her chin, before giving her a soft kiss.

"How do you..." She's about to cry again, but somehow not in the same way as before. This almost seems like relief.

"You told me so yourself. Sometimes depression sneaks up on you. It takes away all the joy and good in your life. I don't know everything about it, but it does sound the same this time, doesn't it? Things aren't that bad, they're actually pretty good, but your brain won't let you see that, it's just darkness."

Izzy nods, sitting up, taking deep breaths. "It doesn't mean it's over though. It doesn't mean that it's going away now. It doesn't mean anything. Knowing doesn't fix it." She still looks defeated, not ready for a fight.

"No, it doesn't. But if we know, at least we can figure out how to deal with it, what we can do so that you can pull out of it." I also sit up, taking her in my arms.

My heart hurts even as relief is flooding me. I was so scared that this would be the end of us. But even knowing that we love each other, knowing what's going on with Izzy, this isn't going to get easier soon. This is going to take a long time to get better.

"I guess I'm going to have to make another appointment

242

with the psych. I thought I was doing so well." She leans against me, relaxing.

"Things messing up in your brain don't care about you doing well or not." That, at least, is something I understand. "It just does it, it just happens."

"Yeah..." She lets out a sigh. Then she looks up at me. "Thanks."

I smile a little. "Nah, it's okay. Better to know this now than five months down the line, or three years."

"Three years?" She eyes me, her eyes growing comically. "You're thinking that far ahead?"

"Why not?" I give her a quick kiss. "We've got most of the worst behind us. At least, when it comes to things that most people don't seem to be able to understand about each other."

She finally smiles a little. "I guess you're right. I'm trans and sometimes struggle with depression. You... I don't even know what your 'relationship struggle/fight' is supposed to be." Her smile spreads more. "You're pretty much perfect."

I snort, shaking my head as I also smile, taking a deep breath. "It's just because you don't want to see the bad things. I like dressing up in dresses."

"They look good on you." Izzy shrugs.

"And I apparently have a soft spot for witty girls." I tap the tip of her nose with my finger.

"You love me for it." She grins, more like herself by the moment. Although the haunting look in her eyes isn't gone, she still looks more relaxed now.

I push her back on the bed, and she lets out a small squeak. Then I straddle her hips, my hands on either side of her before

I lean in for a kiss. "That, I definitely do."

I put my lips to hers as her arms snake around me, pulling me closer. I slowly deepen the kiss, teasing my tongue against her lips and she lets me in, her arms tightening for a moment.

She feels so good, and I'm so glad that this weekend seems to get to a better place than where it started out at.

Now to try and keep it that way…

27
Izzy

Depression = Mental health problem where someone feels low for extended periods of time. Many people deal with depression at some point in their lives, and this is generally caused by a traumatic or other stressful situation. But some people's brains will go into depressive episodes even when there doesn't seem to be a specific traumatic cause for it, in these cases depression seems to be part not just of mental health, but also neurological differences. Sometimes it's combined with other neurological differences, while other times, it appears to be just on its own. For me, I've lived with depressive episodes my whole life. And even though I know this, I still sometimes ignore it, hoping a crappy mood will just go away on its own, even when it's been around for weeks…

I don't exactly know how I can feel so relieved to have Elliot at my side and that he seemed to understand what was going on in my head without me really having to explain it to him. At some level, sure, I knew what was going on, even if I didn't want to admit it, but to have him accept it so easily... I almost feel too relieved about it.

His kisses get my head all spinning, making me almost forget about the bad feeling in my chest, in my head. Making me feel just him, making me feel like this will be alright, just as long as I don't fall back into the dark pit.

When we came into the house, I don't know why, but just being here overwhelmed me. It scared me so much. Meeting Elliot's family, being in his space. It made me doubt that I could ever be who he thinks I am, who I could be in his eyes. It shut down my brain, it made me lose focus of everything. It made me lose focus of why I was here, who I was with, it clouded everything. It was really scary, it made me so scared.

Me confessing my love to him... It was my brain's final attempt to mess everything up even more, hoping to scare Elliot a little with a sudden confession. It was the dark side of my brain trying to prove to me that the bad thoughts were the real truth, that what was going on wasn't real, that that was all fake. That what I thought I had with Elliot wasn't real, that it was all in my head.

And then everything just twisted and turned, changed right there. When Elliot told me he loved me too, I could barely believe it, no matter how much I wanted to believe it. Of course, I wanted to believe it, I clamped onto it really tight.

And now he's holding me, kissing me.

Like nothing changed, and everything has changed at the same time.

I let out a gasp as his hand slides down my neck and dips a little under the collar of my shirt for a moment.

Elliot leans back, looking down at me, smiling. "Do you think it's time to get something to drink now?" It's an easy smile, one that calms my heart but makes my stomach do a little flip.

I nod. Yeah, having something to drink would be a good idea now, but that means facing his parents, probably. "How do I look?" I've been crying for I don't know how long, I've lost all sense of time, and my face feels like it's all puffy.

"The same as mine, I think." He touches my cheek, a soft look in his eyes. "I don't know what to do about it. But, if my mum asks anything, we've been watching a sad movie." He winks.

I snort. Yeah, like that excuse ever works.

He stands up and pulls me up from the bed too, wrapping his arms around me and pulling me close. "I love you." His whispered words make my stomach flip again. "If anything, please, hold on to that. I know that it doesn't make much of a difference, probably, but maybe it helps, just a little."

"I love you too. Even if my brain messes up." Talking about it, openly, it's scary, but not as scary as what happens when I don't talk about it and get lost in my head. And I don't want that to happen again. Been there, done that, scared everyone, including myself, not looking forward to repeating it.

"I'm here for you. Whatever you need. I promise." He gives me a quick kiss and then steps back, pulling his shirt over his head.

I swallow hard and I can't help but look at him. He looks good, and it makes my body come to life. It sets a tightness in my belly, spreads a warmth through my body, makes everything tingly and tight at the same time.

Then he opens his closet and bends down to grab a shirt, giving me an even better view of his behind.

Okay, maybe I've just found a new part of my sexuality, I really like his butt...

Elliot pulls on his shirt and then turns around to me, raising his eyebrows as he sees my now bright red face. "Were you checking me out?" His voice dips, shooting electric sparks through my body.

"Maybe." I try to shrug, but my face goes even hotter.

"You were." He steps closer, his eyes shining and he's letting out a laugh which almost sounds relieved. "When you... When I tried on the dress at your place. When I was without a shirt, and you pushed the dress at me. Was that because you were checking me out too?"

I don't know how to respond to that. I've never done this before, this teasing, but more sexually, and I don't know how I should respond. "I guess." My voice is barely there. "I was trying to not take things where they could get awkward. Where..." I shrug, looking away. Where I may freak out or put him in a position where we'd have to break things off because they were getting too heated. I was scared of the way seeing him partially naked made me feel.

Elliot softly takes my hand. "It's okay." He slides my hand under his shirt, putting it flat on his stomach. "It's okay. You can touch. You can feel. Just, please don't tickle." He grins. "I'm not going to push your boundaries or anything just because we're touching. Or just because you're checking me out. That's all part of this. That's all part of me being your boyfriend. It's a pretty sweet deal, if I say so myself." He winks.

Then there are footsteps on the stairs and a knock on the door. "Elliot? Izzy? Do you want to come down for something to drink and maybe a snack?" It's a woman's voice.

I quickly pull my hand back and step away from him, almost scared to be caught even though the door is still closed.

Elliot rolls his eyes. "Yes, Mum. We're down in a moment."

248

"Okay. See you in a moment." And the footsteps retreat again.

Elliot bursts out laughing and then looks at me. "I guess we really have to do this now. Don't we?"

I nod. Yes. We can't stay up here the whole time, and it seems that we've been found out anyway.

Meeting his parents, or at least his mum. Yeah, not something I've ever done before... Meeting my boyfriend or girlfriend's parents, mostly because I've not had someone before.

W A S D

Elliot's mum is very friendly, though I can also see the ways that she's trying to figure out how Elliot and I fit together. He said something about his parents not really understanding his crossdressing, and I guess I can see that. She keeps shooting me these curious glances, especially when we were talking about the dress I gave Elliot. But she doesn't ask about our red eyes, or why we went upstairs immediately as we came here, which is a definite bonus. Although, there is always the chance that she thinks that we went to do some sexual things right as we came here… Which puts a nervousness in my stomach, but I guess that assumption isn't too strange, we probably would have, if it weren't for the situation we're in.

Elliot keeps touching my hand, keeps holding it under the table whenever he can, and it keeps giving me butterflies in my stomach. It keeps giving me these feelings and sensations. And it keeps distracting me.

"So." Elliot's mum looks us over. "Are you going to do anything fun tonight? A party or something?"

I glance at Elliot. I have no idea, and it's not like I know many places around here. I just know how to get to my friends' houses, but that's about it, even when we all meet up, it tends to be to game or to go to the city centre and visit gaming stores…

"Maybe, maybe not." Elliot shrugs. "We'll have to see. Maybe we're just going to watch a movie or something, play some videogames."

"Videogames?" Elliot's mum frowns, then she glances at me. "Are you into those too?"

Am I? I can't help grinning, but before I can say anything, Elliot's already talking.

"She's way better than me at them. Most of them anyway." He grins my way, but I still see the slightly disappointed look in his mum's eyes. She would have liked it if I wasn't into them, because I probably would have gotten him out of the house or something, at least, that's what she thinks.

Then Elliot's phone buzzes, a message. He picks it up, and his face falls, then he glances my way before he replies to it.

"What's wrong?" That doesn't look good.

"Mya and Kevin just broke up." He frowns, sending another message, which results in more buzzing from his phone.

What? No way.

I check my own phone, but I don't have a message from anyone about it. Then I send Kevin a message. 'I just heard about you and Mya. What happened?' My heart speeds up, and not in a good way.

"Mya and her new boyfriend?" Elliot's mum frowns. "They've been together since that same weekend you met, right?"

That's one way to look at it… "Kevin is a friend of mine." Which makes me feel like crap right now. They met because of Elliot and me, and now they're no longer together.

250

Elliot stands up, looking at me. "Want to go over to her place? Maybe we can cheer her up, keep her company?"

"Yeah." I stand up too. "If that's okay... You know." With me being friends with Kevin and all...

"I think it's fine. She just sounds bummed, not angry." He shrugs. "We can just go to get her mind off it."

"Sure." Sounds like an okay plan.

Elliot's mum looks at us both. "I guess that means that you're not eating here today?"

"Probably not, sorry." Elliot strolls out of the kitchen, and I follow him back up the stairs.

There, we quickly put our shoes back on, and I grab my bag with my wallet and things, then I turn to Elliot. For this to happen today, right as we...

He sighs as he looks at me, his eyes sad. "Bad timing, I agree." He nods. Then he takes my hands. "For a moment, earlier, I thought that we would be like that. That I'd be the one messaging her tonight."

"Me too." My voice barely leaves me, still too scared to think about it. For a moment, I thought the same thing, that this would be our end.

"But we didn't." He checks his phone again. "Let's go. It's not that far to Mya's place."

I nod, following him out the house. Let's see if we can get Mya's mind off things for the evening.

W A S D

Elliot was right, it's only a fifteen minute walk to Mya's house, and when Elliot rings the bell, she opens the door, looking mostly frustrated and a little pissed off at him.

"I brought back up." Elliot positions me in front of him,

and Mya smiles a little before she pulls me into the house.

When she's dragged me to her room, she lets me go, turning around to the both of us. "Elliot is just being overprotective. It's not that big of a deal." She huffs as she flops down in front of her computer, typing a message to someone, not particularly quietly. She looks upset, even if she tries to hide it.

Not a big deal. *Right.*

We wait until she turns back to us, calmer now. She pulls a face and sighs. "It was just a summer fling thing. Kevin and I were great in bed, just..." She shrugs. "We weren't that good at all the other couple-y things. He's a good guy, though. Just not... not for me."

I go over to her, carefully giving her a hug, and she tightens her arms around me too.

"You two make it seem so easy. Even with the *things* that would put a strain on any relationship." Mya sighs.

I eye Elliot, who looks a little uncomfortable right now.

"Yeah... About that." He sits down on Mya's bed.

Mya jerks, glancing at me and then at Elliot. "Don't tell me you've broken up. Is that why Izzy's eyes look so puffy?"

"No." I quickly shake my head. "We didn't."

Mya looks at me more carefully, her eyes sad. "Almost, though. Right?"

I nod. Not wanting to think back to this afternoon. "Yes."

Mya stands up, giving me a quick hug and then she's putting on her shoes. "I think I know the perfect remedy for that. We need to raid a liquor store. I think today deserves to be drowned in liquid sorrow."

"And we recover with a hangover together tomorrow." Elliot smiles, also standing up.

"Nothing brings people together like a hangover." Mya

252

grins at him, and this is obviously a thing between them.

Then they both grab my hands and pull me back out of the room.

These two... They're definitely something else.

I don't know what to think about it all. It's been a strange day, and even though the darkness in my head hasn't gone away, being at Elliot's side, it seems to lessen it a bit, it makes me feel just a little bit better. I know that I'll also have to do a lot of other things to really pull back out of it. But I also know that I won't be alone.

And that makes me feel a lot lighter, that knowledge makes everything seem doable, not as big a task.

28
Elliot

Moe = Something which is adorable with the intention to be cute and easy to love. This tends to be split into the *feeling of* moe, finding something really cute, and something *designed to be* moe, designed to be adorable and lovable. Everyone has their own take on what they find moe, but within anime there are series like K-On! which has the sole purpose of being moe, all the characters being lovable in their own way.

As Izzy is taking a quick bathroom break, after just a few ciders and a couple of glasses of water, Mya leans closer to me, looking as seriously as she can, while also being tipsy.

"What happened today?" She may not look so serious, but her voice definitely is serious.

I try to shrug, but that's no use with her. "A few things. Mostly to do with brains messing up." I sigh, tapping my head. If anyone knows what that's like, it's Mya, I've been with her through a few depressive episodes, and I wish I'd seen it in Izzy sooner. "Brains being confusing. And then saying that we love each other." I can't help my smile now, my stomach fluttering now everything has calmed down, and we've had some booze in us.

"You, *what?*" Mya stares at me, her mouth open.

"She said it first." Like that's any excuse or explanation.

"But you said it *too*. Right?" She stares at me.

"Yes." I look away. I know that this isn't usual for me, telling someone that I love them, at least... not as easily as this. At least... Yeah. I don't tend to say to girls that I love them, mostly because, well… I don't have those feelings, often.

"Elliot's growing up. I never thought I'd see the day." Mya grins. "You're serious too, aren't you?"

I nod.

"I envy you a little. She's great. Don't let go of her."

"I won't."

"Because, if you do... I may go after her myself instead." Mya grins.

"After who?" Izzy steps back into Mya's bedroom, dropping herself behind us a little clumsily. "What are you two talking about?"

Mya's eyes shine with mischief. "That if he dumps you, I'll be right there to comfort you."

"Well, you'd be welcome to." Izzy grins, lazily shrugging. "You give great hugs."

We all burst out laughing at that. *Riiiight.* Obviously, there has been enough booze in some people by now.

I pull Izzy into my lap, my arms around her slim waist, holding her tightly, and she lets out a soft sound as she leans into me more.

"Hey, no sticky-sticky near me. Think of poor just-got-dumped-today me."

I raise my eyebrow at Mya.

"Unless I can join in." She wiggles her eyebrows, smirking.

"Nope." Not happening, I'm not sharing Izzy.

Mya holds up her hands. "Fine. But you may want to get her into a bed for now." She eyes Izzy, and when I look at her, I catch how Izzy's fighting to keep her eyes open.

Izzy is falling asleep right here in my arms. Not exactly how I imagined tonight happening.

"You can crash here, if you want to." Mya nods to the mattresses under her bed. "Probably a better idea than dragging her home now."

"Yeah." I sigh, crawling from under Izzy, and going over to the mattresses, pulling them out.

Then I go back over to Izzy. "Izzy, let's get you in bed."

She opens her eyes blearily. "I don't want to go home. I want to stay here."

"You can stay here. We're just moving over a little, it's more comfortable over there." I'm not sure if it's the booze or if she really was just that tired, Izzy's barely waking up, I'm not even sure she really heard me…

"Okay." She sits up and lets me help her to the bed. She's so defenceless right now. It's sweet, but also a totally different side to her. A side I hadn't expected to see. Then she curls up under the covers, keeping wriggling until she can put her head in my lap, like I'm her personal pillow.

Mya laughs as she looks at us. "Yeah, or *that* happens. If that's all that happens when she's drunk, I don't mind her. Sleepy-drunk Izzy isn't too bad, I'm just glad she's not a loud or destructive drunk."

I shrug. It's not bad, and it's kind of cute. Izzy's so vulnerable and looking younger than normal, in a sweet, not a

256

creepy way. If she was an anime character, she would totally be moe right now.

After everything that happened today, I'm not surprised that she's exhausted, especially combined with the last weeks. If I can just be there for her like this, taking care of her, I'll do it. I play with my fingers in Izzy's hair as I look at Mya. "Did you ever think about what things could have been like, if you hadn't caught me in my room that afternoon?" I lean back against Mya's bed, looking up at the ceiling.

I'd been crossdressing for a while when Mya found me as I was trying to get out of a dress really fast, not expecting anyone to come up the stairs. It was awkward, so awkward. But it also meant that I couldn't hide this from her anymore, and she actually was really supportive about me doing this and helped me with trying on dresses and finding my own style.

"Sometimes." She smiles. "But mostly because I have no idea what you'd be trying to wear if you were still figuring things out on your own. Or trying to follow the makeup tutorials." Her eyes are filled with mischief. "But other than that? Nah. You're you, you've always been you. That doesn't change."

I smile too, letting out a quick breath. "Going to AmAnime and crossdressing there. It changed everything, and without you, I would have never dared to do it. Thanks."

"You're thanking me? You did this yourself. And we've had some great months since, haven't we?"

"Yeah." I nod. A lot of great, and sometimes kind of odd, months. But I don't think I would want it any other way.

I look down at Izzy, at her calm face. "If I hadn't gone crossdressing at AmAnime, I wouldn't have met Izzy. And without your encouragement, I would have never gone crossdressing in the first place."

"Well, I guess it's been a very busy and productive summer."
Mya shrugs, smiling.

"Yes, I guess it has been." A very busy and exciting summer.

⌨ W A S D

The next morning, I wake up with my arms around Izzy. It feels good. I tighten my grip around her, holding her a little closer. I could definitely wake up like this every morning.

Then Izzy stirs. "Good morning." Her voice sounds groggy, still waking up.

"Good morning." I nuzzle her neck. "How did you sleep?"

"Pretty good? Although, I've had some strange dreams. But, I think that may have been the alcohol." She turns to her back, glancing at me. "How did you sleep?"

"I slept pretty well too." I run my fingers over her arm, entwining our hands. "How are you feeling today?"

Izzy's eyes go over to me for a moment, before she looks back up, her gaze darkening a little. "Not as panicky as before, but it's not over yet." She lets out a sigh. "I know, that's not really…"

"I don't care if it's what I want to hear. I care about how you feel, nothing else." I sit up, looking around. Mya isn't here anymore, I think she may have gone downstairs to get breakfast or something. "What do you think? What do you want to do today?"

"I don't know. We could go into the city?" Izzy also sits up, pulling on her shirt which slides it down a little bit too far and I can see the top of her bra, it's pink and lacy. She glances up at me before she pulls a shirt up a little again. "Oops?" Her cheeks flash almost as pink as her bra.

"If that's an oops, I don't mind more oopses." I grin, and

Izzy smacks my knee, pulling an annoyed face for a moment but she's also laughing.

"That's not what we're doing here right now. This is not the right place." She grins.

"So there *is* a right place for these things?" I raise my eyebrow at her.

Izzy's grin widens, and she shakes her head. "Maybe. But not right now or right here."

"Fine." At least she seems comfortable enough to tease me again.

Then I hear footsteps on the stairs, and Mya puts her head around the corner of the door. "So you two have finally woken up?"

"Yes." I look up, catching the way Mya's eyes go over the both of us before she smiles.

"Good. Breakfast is downstairs. Any plans for today?" She comes into the bedroom and sits down on the bed. "I don't know if you've got any plans that do or do not involve me, but the weather is great, and I don't know how well Izzy knows the city?"

Izzy laughs. "That was my plan too. I've been here a few times, but cities always change, and it's been a long time since I've last been here and could go into the city to explore." She shrugs a little. "I could... I could also ask some of my friends to come join us if you're okay with that." She looks up at me, a little uncertain.

I reach out to her, touching her cheek. "Gaming or cosplay friends?"

"Both?" She grins. "Mostly gaming, though. They are from the guild."

I look at Izzy and then at Mya. "That doesn't sound like a

bad idea. What do you think?"

"Sounds like a great plan." Mya shrugs. "I hope there aren't too many cute people though. We know how that ended last time with me." She also grins.

"Oh, they're cute, definitely." Izzy's eyes sparkle. "I guess cute people hang out together a lot, so you're out of luck, cutie." She sticks her tongue out to Mya and Mya does the same back.

I stand up. "I guess that we could actually go home to my place for breakfast, change into clean clothes, and then come pick you up when we go into town?" I look around, trying to find the things we took with us here.

Mya nods. "That may be a good idea too."

Izzy also stands up, straightening out her clothes. "Yeah, that's probably the best idea. I could really use clean clothes." She leans to Mya, giving her a quick hug. "We'll see you later, and we'll have a great day today."

The way those words make Mya smile, it fills my heart. Forget having a best friend and a girlfriend who don't get along, or who only tolerate each other, it's much better if they actually get along and are actual friends. It makes everything so much easier.

W A S D

It seems that Izzy has a lot more friends in Groningen than I originally thought. She was talking about some friends, I hadn't expected four of them to show up. Apparently, they're all gamers, they're from the same guild, and they've known each other for years. There is Cerise, she's my age, and studies computer science in Zwolle. Then there is Troy, he's a year younger, and he's still in secondary school. And then there are Fleur and Alex, they are together, that is, together together, they apparently met in a videogame and they've been dating since early this summer. And I have to agree with Izzy, they're really cute together.

Izzy pulls me along. "I want to check out the gaming store. I know they've got a really good second-hand games store around here."

I'm pretty sure I know which store she's talking about, even though I haven't been there in a long time. "If I'd known you wanted to go there, I would have taken my list with me." I should have anyway, probably.

"List?" She raises an eyebrow at me. "What list?"

"My list with games I still want to find second-hand."

"Oh! Well, we can always try again another time, right?" Her hand in mine is so comfortable, like it's never been any different.

"You don't have it on your phone or anything?" Troy eyes me as he walks next to us. "What kind of old-school gamer are you?" He laughs.

"Well, I haven't had the time to make a digital list. It's just been on paper for now. I made it during class." I shrug. I was bored, bored happens.

"Ah. Yes, that makes sense." Troy keeps up with us easily, although the others are lagging behind little.

I look behind me, and Mya is in a deep conversation with Cerise, Fleur and Alex. For meeting people she's never met before, Mya looks pretty comfortable around them. Although, I do have to admit, all three girls are definitely the type of girl that Mya would like.

Maybe Izzy is right, maybe today will actually be a good day. For all of us.

29
Izzy

Bishie = Short for *bishounen* = Means beautiful boy or young man in Japanese. Generally, in anime, manga and other Japanese media it's used to describe young men who are very attractive and sexy, although they don't have to be very masculine. Bishies are often androgynous in their looks, and flamboyant in their character. They are very common in shoujo anime as love interests, especially in the case of reverse harems (one girl, many boys). I actually think, and maybe I'm biased, that Elliot also fits this description.

I keep looking through the old GameCube games they have in the store. There are so many to choose from, and even though I know that this place isn't the cheapest, they do have a really good range of games and they tend to be pretty clean and still work, unlike games from some other second-hand stores. And they also all tend to have their booklets and everything in them too, which is worth the extra price.

Next to me, Cerise is also looking through them, I'm pretty sure she's looking for a copy of Phantasy Star Online 2, because she's been looking for a copy of it for a long time, though never really seriously.

Then she bumps her shoulder into mine. "So?" Cerise raises her eyebrow as I look her way. "Tell me?"

"Tell you what?" I try to not glance at Elliot, but I still feel my cheeks heat up. I'm pretty sure I know what she's talking about.

"You and cute guy. Are you a *thing*? Are you together?" She leans closer, whispering like we shouldn't be overheard. Although, with the music in the store, it's pretty hard to hear the whispering anyway.

I nod, my cheeks heating up more. "Yeah. We are."

"Cute." She grins. "I knew you'd find someone." She keeps glancing in Elliot's direction, who is animatedly talking to Alex about something. "So, everything is working out? He really is as cute as he looks?" Her voice is still light, but her eyes are a little more serious.

"Yeah, he is." I let out a breath. "He's okay with all of me and everything."

"Good." She winks. "Or I would have had to have a very serious *conversation* with him..." Then she taps me on my shoulder. "Also, I think we should probably go outside, we're kind of clogging up the store like this."

I look around. True, this is only a small store, and we're not a very small group...

"Yeah, let's go." I sigh. There weren't any games I really wanted anyway... I go over to Elliot, sliding my hand into his. "Let's go. I'm pretty sure there are other places we can visit."

Elliot grins, leans close, and then gives me a quick kiss on my cheek.

I watch as Alex' grin gets wider, and then she shakes her

head. "Honestly, and *you* complained that I was being all gooey with Fleur all the time at the party."

"Well, you were." I grin back at her. "And this is me we're talking about. I don't do gooey, I just do cute."

"Right." Alex rolls her eyes. "What was that word again? Oh, yes. *Ego.*"

"What was that word again? Oh, yes. *Grumpy.*" I wink at her as we leave the store. "You can be gooey with Fleur all you want, I don't mind."

"*Now* you don't, no." Alex smiles as Fleur comes over to her. "We could go and get something to eat? It's around noon. What would everyone like?"

I shrug. I have no idea, and I don't mind. I'm surrounded by friends, I'm with Elliot, and I've got the whole weekend to do fun things.

I really don't mind what we're going to do, as long as I get to spend it with these people.

W A S D

The rest of the weekend goes by fast. Between hanging out with friends, playing games with Elliot and just watching a movie or anime. It all went by so fast. My mood is a little better, although, I know that that's probably not going to stay like that for very long, things get harder when you're on your own.

I hold Elliot's hands as we're standing at the train station, waiting for the train to arrive, squeezing a little. "I'll call you as soon as I get home."

"Good." Then he comes closer, leaning in. "If there's anything wrong, please tell me. I want to know about those things. Even if I can't really help you, I still want to know about them, even if all I can do is listen to you and give you a long-distance hug.”

“I know.” I shrug. “It’s just, it feels a little weird.”

Elliot softly kisses my cheek. “I know. It’s strange for us both. We’re not used to this. That can make things a little scary. But, I still want to know. Yes?”

I nod. “I’ll tell you, next time.” I look at him, at the soft look in his eyes. He really cares. He doesn’t just say this because he wants to interfere or be annoying, he cares. My throat closes up, a heavy feeling in my chest. “I’ll try. I can’t promise anything.”

“That’s all I can ask for. That’s all I do ask of you, to try.” He slides his hands up, wrapping his arms around me. “I just want you to know that I’m here for you. I’m always here for you.”

“Thank you.” I lean my head on his shoulder. “And the same goes for you. I’m always here for you too.”

“I know,” he whispers, his breath tickling my neck, giving me shivers.

I tighten my grip around him, holding him as close as I can. I’ve always been scared, I’ve always been scared that I would have to change myself to find someone to love me. I’ve always been scared that people wouldn’t accept me. At least, that people wouldn’t accept the way I am and still love me.

And I know that I’m lucky.

I’m lucky that my parents accepted me early on. I’m lucky that they’ve done everything they could to support me.

I’m lucky that I found Jason. I’m lucky that I found Jason when I did and that we became such great friends, that he not only supported me and cared for me but that he was always there to get us both into trouble, and I had to get us back out of it.

I’m lucky that I have great friends, gamers and cosplayers alike. And that nobody even bats an eye at my sometimes crazy antics.

And I'm lucky to have found Elliot. I'm lucky to have found someone who doesn't care, in the best way possible. He cares about me, he cares about who I am, he cares about what I'm like. He cares about me being a trans girl but only in the ways that he looks out for me, only in the ways that he takes care to not to harm or hurt, only in the ways that he loves me.

He loves me.

It starts and it ends there. Everything starts and ends there.

He loves me, and I love him.

"Izzy?" Elliot slowly takes a step back, his eyes on mine steady. "I love you."

My cheeks heat up, aflame, feeling caught, like he was just reading my mind. "I love you too."

Elliot grins. "Now, I'm pretty sure your train is arriving soon, and I'll see you in a couple of days. I've got a long weekend coming up, and we're going to spend it at your place." His eyes shine and are filled with excitement.

I nod. "Yeah, I'll be seeing you again soon."

It won't be a long time that we're apart, I'll see him again soon. So, why does it hurt so much? Why is it so hard to let him go?

He steps closer, putting one hand under my chin, and angling my face up just a little. "Everything will be fine. I promise. We're going to get through this, and we're going to make this work." Then he puts his lips to mine, slow kisses. Slow and careful kisses. Kisses that make my head spin, my body ache, kisses that make me wish that next weekend was already here.

Kisses that make me want to do things that we really shouldn't be doing in public.

"Elliot…" I shake my head before I shoot him a glare. We're in my room, and we're working on new cosplays. There is an event coming up in a while, a gaming convention. So, I'm going as FrIzzyBang and Elliot is going as his brand-new Destruction of Elysium character, AlleyRiot.

"Yes?" Elliot grins at me from the other end of the table. "You were saying something?"

I sigh. "I'm not doing that. I'm not going to do a sexy striptease in my FrIzzyBang cosplay for the competition."

Elliot pouts playfully. "Why not? I'll do it in *my* cosplay."

That stops me for a moment, my body tightening, not sure how to respond to that. "You would?"

Elliot's pout turns into an evil grin. "So, you're interested if I do it, but not when you do it?"

I'm caught! "Ehh…"

He stands up, slowly walking to my side of the table, trailing his fingers over the surface of the table. "You are…" When he's near me, I can see the way his eyes have darkened just a little.

"Maybe?" My stomach does a little flip, heat pooling heavy between my legs. Imagining him in the cosplay of his Destruction of Elysium character, which is a female rogue air spirit, the leather straps, the high boots, the exposed stomach… That's sexy. And the idea of him slowly taking that off… Yeah, I'd like to see that.

He kneels down in front of me, his hands on my knees, his eyes on me, on my face. "You would like for me to do a striptease for you?"

I hold my breath as I nod, my cheeks aflame even more.

"I think we can do something about that." He slides his

hands up a little. "But I'll only do it for you."

My heart beats really fast. I can't even think straight right now.

How am I supposed to react to that? How am I supposed to react to that idea? He's mean. He knows I'm not that good at these things.

Then he stands up, stepping behind me, wrapping his arms around my shoulders, his lips on my neck. "The only reason I will look good in this outfit is because you're making it for me."

I swallow hard, shaking my head a little. "No." My voice is slightly rough. "It's because you always look good."

He gives me soft kisses in my neck, sending shivers down my spine. "Thank you, but you know that's not true. You know that you're great at these things. And I'm very lucky for having you with me." Then his lips move up my neck to my jaw, and he nips at the side of my lip. "And just looking at you working so seriously, it makes me hot."

I reach up, covering his arms with my hands, holding him tightly. "Well then, I guess I should keep working?" I can't help my grin, or the way my heart is beating so fast. Doing this together, doing this side by side, it's special. It's special and amazing in ways that I never thought could happen.

It's not so much the working side by side as it is the working together. We work together so well, there is no confusion or getting in each other's way, we're doing our own thing and also working together when needed. It comes so natural to us, and that makes everything better.

For the convention, I need to remake the FrIzzyBang cosplay from last year, since I no longer fit into it, plus they've changed the gear for the higher levels in the game, so this is a great excuse to update myself to some of the most recent end-game gear. And for Elliot, we're making some old end-game gear, which isn't as fancy, but it's also in a sexier style that may be interesting to try out instead of the super fancy current end-game gear. That was his choice, not mine, not that I disagreed with it. It seems his confidence has grown a lot and I love seeing that, to watch him experiment more.

Elliot lets out a low laugh. "Well, maybe we can keep going for a while longer, but I don't want to keep working too long today."

"Why not?" I try to look at him, but as I do, his lips are on my jaw again, nibbling. "Elliot?"

"Well..." He hums a little. "I've got some other plans for the two of us too, plans that don't include sewing machines."

"Like?" There is something in his voice that makes me interested.

"Well, I've got something in my bag that we can watch together." I can hear the grin in his voice.

"Watch together?" I'm getting curious and confused now.

"Yep. Watch together." He kisses my neck before he lets me go. "I got my hands on the old Cardcaptor Sakura movie on DVD."

"What?!" That's so hard to get! "Are you serious?"

"I may be, I may not me. You'll have to find out." His eyes glitter with mischief as he goes back to his side of the table, sitting down behind the sewing machine with the 'pants', more like hotpants, parts of his cosplay.

"No way!" I stare at him. Not really believing that he'd find something like that. "Meanie!" How can he make me wait when he springs such a surprise on me? I can't believe it.

And I also can, because that's what he's like, always coming up with fun and interesting ideas, and teasing me with them.

I let out a deep sigh as I get back to the top of my outfit, making sure I don't get the seams wrong or I'll have to take it all out again, boobs and chest sizing are so annoying. But worth it if you get it right.

Now I really need to focus, so I don't do anything wrong...

Focus!

30
Elliot

I pull on the top of my cosplay, trying to get it down just a little bit, just a tad lower over my ribs, feeling a slightly too exposed right now. Rogue armour is cool in a game, but walking around like this in public is a totally different matter.

Izzy swats my hand away as she tugs on the bottom of the fabric and applies some sort of sticky stuff to the inside seam before pushing it back against my skin. "That should keep it in place. Now, stop fiddling with it, or it will come loose again." She's smiling, having way too much fun. Although, maybe she's just enjoying being here together.

"Why did you let me talk you into thinking this was a good idea for my cosplay?" Because I'm not so sure anymore, of my cosplay or my sanity. At AmAnime, I knew that I wouldn't run into many people who would recognise me, but not here... This time, some of the guys I usually go to cons with are also attending, and they don't know about me crossplaying or crossdressing yet. And somehow, I thought that going as a sexy female air spirit would be a good idea? What *was* I thinking?

I know what I was thinking... But that was my ego talking, not my sensible self.

"Because it's cool?" Izzy shrugs and steps back, looking me over, her eyes more serious, looking at me like I'm some doll wearing her clothes... Not that I'm not, in some ways. "Looks right. You'll just have to put on the boots and the arm braces, and you'll be ready to go."

I turn to the mirror on the side of the closet. I have to admit, I *can* pull this look off, but that doesn't mean that I'll be entirely comfortable wearing it.

Izzy goes over to her suitcase. "I made you something to finish it all off." She pulls out a plastic bag and hands it to me. "Should make you more comfortable, or at least less cold." She grins, her eyes shining.

"What is it?" I open the bag, looking inside. Inside the bag is a whole bunch of fabric, and as I pull it out, I burst out laughing.

Izzy has made me a cloak to go with the cosplay. Something that will keep me warm, or partially covered up, but wouldn't stand out as odd if I was wearing it.

She shrugs as she looks at me. "I thought you were going to get a little unsure when we were here, and probably a bit cold,

272

walking around like that."

I cover the distance between us, taking her in my arms. "Thank you. Thank you so much." I hadn't thought of this myself, but of course, Izzy already had.

"No problem." Her voice is soft and warm, and when she wraps her arms around me, I feel her fingers play over my back, over the exposed skin there. Honestly, I'm mostly wearing a leather bra-ish top and hotpants/short skirt, to combine with thigh high boots… So both my stomach and my back are totally bare. "You look really good like this." Her nails trail down the exposed skin, sending shivers through me.

"Izzy…" My voice is barely over a moan. My body responds to her so strongly, and we don't have the time to play around, not now.

"Yeah?" Her voice drops too, sexily.

"You're great at torturing me, you know that, right?" I put my lips to her neck, nibbling just a little, which I know she enjoys, and right on cue, she lets out a soft gasp.

"Same goes for you." She pulls me tighter, fitting our bodies together. The corset she's wearing not only makes her waist smaller, but also pushes up her boobs more, and I trail kisses from her neck to her cleavage. "Elliot…" She gasps, her fingers on me tightening.

I grin. What she can do, I can do too. This is not just a one person thing. We know each other well enough to know what turns the other on by now, and it's fun to play…

Someone behind us lets out a cough, and we step apart, my heart beating fast as I look around.

Jason is standing in the doorway, raising his eyebrows at us. "I was going to come pick you two up, but I'm not so sure I should have bothered." He grins, shaking his head slowly.

Even though Izzy and I are here together getting changed, we're both sleeping in different rooms. Izzy still shares with Jason while I share with Mya. We're just getting dressed in Izzy's room right now because she had most of our cosplay in her bags. And getting caught like this by a roommate is probably one of the most embarrassing things ever.

"Hi, Jason." Izzy eyes him. "We're... almost ready to leave? Just a few minutes?" She tries to give him an innocent smile, but it's not really working, not with the flush all over her neck and chest...

"Yeah, and if I'd come here a few minutes later, you would have needed even more time to get ready." He grins and lets out a deep sigh. "Just finish up getting ready, the others are waiting."

"We will." I go over to the final pieces of my cosplay, my boots and arm braces. And I hear Izzy do the same, putting on the final layer of skirts and other details for her outfit.

If I'm going to be standing next to anyone, someone who accepts me and encourages me to be who I want to be. I'm going to be standing next to Izzy. I'm going to be standing next to the most amazing girl in the world. Because no matter what I'm afraid of, she makes sure that I know that I can do anything.

And that, in itself, is a magic I didn't know existed before.

W A S D

I'm really nervous as we're all sitting in one of the food courts, having a quick snack. Some of my other friends are at this con too, and they've never seen me like this, dressed in a crossplay outfit... And it's making me even more nervous than I thought it would.

We've just come from a presentation of a new J-RPG that's hopefully coming out next year with some of Izzy's friends, but my friends were at some other exposition, of some city builder science fiction mix game, and we're about to meet up here before going to the next panel together.

I first spot Mya, who is grinning and excited as she almost bounces over to me. I stand up and catch her in a hug. "Oh, you really should have come with us. You're going to love it when it comes out! The graphics are amazing, and you're going to love the building element in the game! And the aliens!"

Then the other guys also come up to us, and my stomach drops as they look us all over, confusion on their faces.

I step from behind Mya, though I feel how she's taking my hand, giving me courage. "Hey, guys." I give them a small wave.

"Elliot?" Benji, who I've known for years, frowns as he looks me over. "Is that you?" He frowns more, and I don't know what to say, but next to me, Izzy stands up. I can feel how she's trying to figure the situation out, wanting to protect me, as she's done before.

"Yeah. That's me." I nod, still nervous, my heart beating loudly. "And this is my girlfriend, Izzy." I take her hand, hoping to hide the way my hand is shaking. "Izzy, these are my friends, Benji, James and Eli. I normally go to conventions with them, *when* they're going." I level a look at them, trying to keep my voice normal, to not show my nerves.

Izzy grins a little. "Welcome! Well, it seems we've got some more people to add. We'll need to make the circle bigger." She turns to Jason and Troy. Jason is in crossplay too, a cute lolita-style outfit from an obscure J-RPG I'd never heard of, so I didn't ask more. But Troy is just in his t-shirt and jeans, looking a lot more 'normal', although, the logo on his shirt is their DoE guild logo, in rainbow colours, so 'normal' depends on what you compare it to. "Can you guys get us some more chairs?" Izzy moves her hands for everyone to make more space for the guys, taking away some of the nervous energy going around. Everyone was aware of me not having told the guys about my crossplaying yet, so they were all a little nervous for me.

Then Izzy pushes me in her chair and makes herself comfortable in my lap as Mya sits in the chair I just vacated.

"Wait! I recognise you." James stares at Izzy. "You won the cosplay contest at AmAnime! Last year. Same character as you're doing now, but different gear. Right?" His eyes almost pop out of his head. He may have had a little crush on her back then, I think most of us had…

"She won this year too, in the group contest," Mya smugly adds and I shoot her a look.

"Of course! Sakura! I should have seen the similarities." James smiles, then he looks over the group. "You were with a girl cosplaying Aoi. Who was that? Anyone here?" There is a spark in his eyes that tells me that he's pretty interested in finding out, that same spark he had over Izzy.

Both Izzy and Mya point at me. *Thanks, girls.* Like that couldn't have been brought up more tactically?

"*You* were Aoi?" James now really stares at me, blinking a little like he's confused. "Wow. Really? Are you serious?" I'm not sure if he's disappointed or not.

I nod, not sure how to read his reaction. "Yeah, really."

"So…" He looks a little awkward, his eyes darting around. "This is something you've been doing for a while, then? Crossplay?"

I nod again.

"Cool." He lets out a breath. "It looked really cool. On stage, I mean. I didn't realise it was you, it looked really good. Cool." He nods, his head moving in jerks. I can see him think,

276

trying to make sense of things.

"Yeah, I've been..." I shrug a little, still keeping my arms around Izzy, hiding my nerves. "Yeah. Been doing this for a while."

He nods again and then looks me over. "I guess you look cool, it suits you. I'm just trying to..." He moves his hand in my direction. "Figure this out. Just, you, and you."

"Not much to figure out. I sometimes wear dresses or do crossplay." I try to keep my voice steady. "I also still do regular cosplay, so, it's not that different. I'm not different from before." Maybe if I say it out loud, he'll understand. "Well, apart from one thing. I now have a girlfriend who I've been with the longest I've ever been with anyone yet." I let out an awkward laugh and James also laughs, easier now. My inability to keep girlfriends has been a running joke with them…

James slowly starts to grin. "I know. A really cute and talented girlfriend too, from what I've seen."

Izzy moves a little, and when I look up at her, her face is turning slightly pink. "Girlfriend in question is sitting right here, you know." She sounds a little annoyed, but when I meet her eyes, she's grinning, her eyes shining at me.

"Her beautiful behind parked right on my lap." I tighten my arms around her waist, putting my head to her back for a moment. This went okay. Somewhat. I think things will be okay. And having Izzy here, and Mya, and the others, it all makes it so much easier, makes me feel calmer.

"Well, *you* would know about that, having had hands-on experience with it and all." Izzy doesn't miss a beat, and I nearly cough in surprise.

Sometimes, this girl... "Izzy..." I groan, and next to me James and Mya burst out laughing.

"Not the right time for those jokes?" She's teasing me now, trying to sound all innocent, and I take a deep breath.

"Oh, no. It's a great time for jokes, but not when I'm not allowed to test your 'good behind' theory right now." I smile, sliding one of my hands down and pretending to grab her butt, and she lets out a high pitched squeal.

Then she turns to me and gives me a quick kiss. "Later. Not here."

"Oh. Is that a promise?" I wink.

"Too much gooey!" Alex calls out from the other end of the group, and I look past Izzy, shooting her a glare.

"I didn't say anything when you were all over Fleur during the presentation. Did I?" I raise my eyebrow at her, and Alex grins back, all smug.

"That was in the dark, this is out in the open." She takes Fleur's hand as she stares back at me, daring me to say more.

"Fine." I wrap my arms back around Izzy and keep them in *mostly* decent places. "Better?"

"Better." Fleur now grins our way.

I had no idea how some of my friends would respond to my crossdressing or crossplaying when I'd tell them. And I suspected that, like my parents, they may need some time to get used to the idea. But this seems to be going pretty well. I guess I was more nervous than I really needed to be.

Just over half a year ago, I was crossdressing in private, always making sure nobody saw me. Then Mya found out, and she was so accepting and calm about it all. That gave me the courage to keep doing it, and to finally start crossdressing at conventions too.

And then I met Izzy, who was not only accepting of what I did, but also encouraged me to keep exploring, to keep doing

278

what I wanted to do. Having her at my side has been so amazing.

And, of course, Izzy understands things about bodies and brains and gender expressions in ways that so many other people don't get. And she also plainly accepts me just liking to dress up, never wondering if I'd want more, never insinuating that there may be more going on. Just accepting me as I am, and challenging me to do what I want, what I want to do, to go for my dreams.

It has all given me so much more confidence and courage, so much more strength to keep exploring things, to keep fighting for my dreams, or even just small wishes.

With Izzy at my side, with Izzy and our friends at my side, I feel like I can do anything.

Well, almost anything. I think. Probably...

Izzy leans to me, her lips close to my ear. "I love you." The words are only spoken softly, but they're filled with so much warmth.

I tighten my arms around her. "I love you too."

These last months have shown me one thing. Together, we can do anything. Anything we want to do, we can do.

And that all started with a dress... Or two, three, four... Many of them, before and after we met.

It all started with a dress, and my first step of courage to finally put it on and try it out, see if I would enjoy it as much as I thought I would.

It all started with wearing a dress, and has gotten me here, with so many new friends.

I'd never expected any of this to happen. And I'm still a little stunned, but it's still real and right here.

It's all real.

After
Izzy

Dress = Outer piece of clothing consisting of a skirt and a top, generally considered to be just for women in Western cultures. Dresses have always been a big part of my life, I started wearing and loving them at a young age, and I never grew tired of them. But for many people, dresses are also the source of much confusion and pain. People not wanting to wear them when they have to or people not being allowed to wear them when they do want to… But, to me, dresses are about expression of who we are, of who I am, and I think that's super important. Being able to show your personality is really important.

TWO YEARS LATER

"Tell me again, how did we get roped into this?" I glance at Elliot as he's going through the cards with notes he's holding in his hands.

He looks up at me, grinning. "Well, I got roped into it by Annabelle, since I was apparently standing a little too close when they were discussing the panellists for this year's AmAnime. And then I got you dragged into it too." He looks so smug.

"Right." I sigh. Somehow, we're part of the cosplay designing and creation panel. Partially, because we've both won the cosplay contest a couple of times, and probably also a little because of the cosplays we're wearing this year...

It's been two years since the AmAnime convention where Elliot and I met. Where we went as Sakura and Aoi from Magical Princess Club! and everything kind of happened from there. This year, we're going as Sakura and Aoi again, but in outfits from Magical Princess Club Go!! which is the second season of the anime. Of course, as soon as we saw the announcements of the new anime, we knew that we had to go as them again this year. That was kind of mandatory in our case, I think.

But everything has been going so fast these last couple of weeks, I've been so busy, and I have no idea if I can actually do a panel on making cosplay or whatever right now, if I can even think clearly for long enough to answer questions. I'm just so worn down from all the work.

I look in the mirror of the wardrobe and move parts of the skirt around so it fans out better, so it looks poofier.

Then Elliot appears behind me, sliding his arms around my waist and smiling as he meets my eyes in the mirror. "We'll be fine, you'll be fine. You know that. There is no reason for anything to go wrong at the panel." He gives me a quick kiss on my neck, making me shiver in his arms.

I sigh. "I know... It's just..." I shrug. "Do you think this is going to be good enough? I have no idea." I feel like I've not spent as much time on this outfit as I should have.

Elliot finished his degree before the school year ended, but I'm still not done. I have to retake a couple of modules next year.

Trying to combine my webshop and making custom orders for people and staying on top of my classes all at the same time, apparently didn't work as well as I thought it would. So I'm still not finished. And now Elliot's got a job offer in Utrecht, and he's looking for a place to live, we're kind of looking for a place to live together...

So, yeah, lots of changes and stress. And instead of working on our cosplays, we've spent most of our time together trying to find a place to live, and it's not been going too well. Living on your own is expensive as hell...

Elliot tightens his arms around me and then lifts me up, spinning me around. "Stop worrying so much. You're not the person who has to keep the whole panel together. That's my job." He lets me go and then picks up his cards. "We should probably go and meet the others. And I need to check in with the organisation to let them know that I'm there and ready, and stuff like that." He sighs deeply, but his eyes are shining with excitement.

I take his hand, stepping closer. "Well, you know, if *you're* taking care of all that. We should be fine, right?" I give him a quick kiss on his cheek. "With the power of the princesses, we'll all be fine. Chu!" I try to match my voice to Sakura's as well as I can, even if I'm speaking in English and not Japanese.

Elliot grins, shaking his head a little, his eyes soft, then he gives me a kiss. "Chu!"

How his smile and eyes still make my stomach all fluttery, even two years on... I have no idea. But it keeps happening, and to see him grow into himself like this, it's making everything feel so much easier. It's made being myself so much easier too.

Someone in the audience puts up their hand, and Elliot points at them. The boy stands up. "I have a question for those who crossplay..." He looks at Elliot, and then his eyes flit to the guy on the other end of the panel, Angel, who is known for crossplaying too, but hasn't done it today. "I know that when you do really big fake boobs in cosplays, you need to fill and make them look right and everything, but how do you do it when it's a more... moderately chested character?"

Angel looks at Elliot, who's grinning. Aoi is definitely on the 'moderately chested' side of things.

Elliot shrugs. "Actually, Izzy can probably answer that better. She helped me with my crossplays and some of her friends' too, like Ruby's or Jason's." He points to the back of the room, where Ruby and Jason put two thumbs up to us, a huge smile on their faces.

Now all the eyes in the room are on me... We knew that this question would likely come up, but I hadn't expected to be the one answering it. "Ehmm..." My cheeks heat up. "The first thing to consider is if the cosplay can be done flat chested or by creating the illusion of boobs. Magical Princess Club! cosplays are a good example of this. Aoi doesn't need cleavage, and she's almost flat chested anyway. You can get away with either using a little bit of filling or ignore it entirely." I grin at Elliot, that's how he originally did the character, flat chested, though we did fill up the top a little this time.

"And for just a bit larger characters than that?" The guy looks at me again, curious.

"Fillings, or stuffing a real bra in the breast size you want to have, and then trying to hide a lack of actual cleavage with for example a high neckline top. Or if that's not as easily done, use makeup to create the illusion of cleavage after using a different technique for the breasts. It's also how some girls will cosplay characters with a larger chest size than they have without stuffing their bras too much. Makeup can 'make up' for a lot." I grin, the joke so bad that I can't even help it.

"I agree with Izzy." Angel nods. "Try to keep things simple. So if you can ignore something like that, it's going to be easier. Izzy talked about makeup being a great way to hide or enhance things, but sometimes it's also useful to consider the type of crossplay you're going to attempt. For example, Izzy and Elliot had multiple choices in outfits that would have been recognisable as Sakura and Aoi, but they chose ones that are not exactly easy to make, but they fit with their body types and would mean as few mods while making them as possible. Try to match the crossplay to your body type."

Elliot also nods. "One thing I've found cosplaying female characters was that a lack of cleavage can be easily hidden. For example with a top that has ruffles or with something a little bit flowy or poofy around the chest area, but which still pulls in at the waist, so it makes it look like you're not entirely flat."

Now everyone is looking at me again. "What these guys said. That goes for crossplaying and crossdressing. It's often easier to try and sort of use the body you already have to make it seem like you have a different shape than trying to force something totally different. Alluding to boobs is easier than putting boobs into a dress and making sure that they look right and that they stay looking right all day."

"Cool. Thanks." The guy nods. "That was useful." He sits down again.

Then a girl stands up, looking straight at me. "Are you going to crossplay too, like Elliot does? You'd probably look really good as a prince or something." There is laughing from the room, and I glance Elliot's way.

Then I smile, facing the girl. "I think I'm much cuter as a princess. But never say never." I wink at her, and behind her I see Jason grin at me broadly.

Oh, how far I've come. How far we've all come.

A few years back, even thinking of 'dressing as a boy' would get me into all sorts of panicky feelings, but these days... I'm much better. In normal life, I am who I want to be, I am who I feel I am. This is me, I'm me. People see me as I see myself.

Are there things I would like to change about myself? Sure, but doesn't almost anyone? A different hair colour, a bigger or a smaller bra size, differently shaped lips, more freckles, fewer freckles... I think most people have something about themselves that they want to change. But it's no longer anything big for me, it's now all in the small things, the 'regular' things, things everyone seems to worry about.

I'm Izzy. This is me.

Everything started with those simple questions I started asking myself those years ago. Those simple 'what if I didn't' questions.

And most important of all, 'what if I didn't wear that beautiful dress?'

I wouldn't have met any of my amazing friends.

I wouldn't have grown into the woman I am now.

And if Elliot hadn't asked himself that same question, I also wouldn't have ever met him.

What if I did wear that beautiful dress?

What if I did stand up for who I am?

Would life become easier? Maybe, but it also became a lot harder in other ways. It didn't stop me though, those questions and complications. Because by pushing through with it, I would be me, I would be my true self, and that was more important than anything else.

I glance up as Elliot's hand touches my shoulder. The panel is over.

"Are you coming with me?" He leans down, his lips close to my ear. "I think we can sneak away for a few moments."

My heart beats faster at the dip in his voice, butterflies in my stomach, and I nod.

If I'd never taken that first step, keeping my head up high, not letting others decide who I should be, I would never have gotten here.

And *here* is exactly where I want to be.

Emmy Engberts has been writing for years, she writes under different pen names, depending on the topic and type of story. As Rosa Swann, she was involved in the surge of the mpreg sub-genre in gay romance, and most of her work under that pen name are still gay romance. As Skylar Heart she publishes straight romance with characters who deal with difficult subjects, but still end up finding someone to love.

As Emmy, she writes Young Adult fiction with diverse characters who won't apologise for being different and who celebrate their differences.

She is Dutch and has lived in the Netherlands for almost all her life apart from when she studied English and Creative Writing at the University of Chichester in England. This really inspired her to make writing her career and has been working towards that goal ever since.

Emmy currently lives in Groningen with her partner and two cats, and if she's not writing, you can find her playing videogames or working on one of her many creative projects.

www.emmyengberts.com